MAN OF MY DREAMS

Johanna Lindsey

MAN OF MY DREAMS

AVON BOOKS ◆ NEW YORK

MAN OF MY DREAMS is an original publication of Avon Books. This work has never before appeared in book form. This work is a novel. Any similarity to actual persons or events is purely coincidental.

AVON BOOKS
A division of
The Hearst Corporation
1350 Avenue of the Americas
New York, New York 10019

For Lee Ann and Harry
When true love happens, it endures

Chapter 1

England, 1878

"Just *what* do you think you're staring at, Tyler Whately?"

Megan Penworthy's tone was unduly sharp, but then she had meant it to be. It was also, along with the look she turned on him, filled with haughty disdain, as if she couldn't abide the fellow. That wasn't true at all. She actually liked the Honorable Tyler Whately.

He was pleasantly handsome, with light blond hair that needed only a minimum of Macassar oil to control it, a trim mustache, and whiskers that weren't so long that they hid the strength of his jaw. His dark green eyes were rather nice, too. And he was not excessively tall, so that a poor girl had to crane her neck to look up at him. Nor was his body intimidating in its slimness, which was not to say he lacked strength. At twenty-seven, he was a young man with excellent prospects, not to mention a rather sizable estate inherited from his mother's side of the family.

Megan had no doubt whatsoever that Tyler would make a fine husband. She might even have set her own cap for him if her best friend, Tiffany Roberts, hadn't confessed soon after they'd met him, that *she* wanted him.

Those had been Tiffany's exact words. "I want hĭm, Meg." The two girls had always spoken bluntly, at least to each other, and when no one else was around to be shocked by it. But Tiffany had been too excited that day to care if anyone else heard her. "This is truly *the* one. I've never felt so—so—when he smiled at me, well, the feeling was—damn, I can't describe it, but I swear I was going to faint."

"Probably your corset is laced up too tight again," Megan had replied with a teasing grin. "You know you need at least a little room to breathe—"

"Oh, stop." Tiffany had laughed. "I'm perfectly serious. What do I do to win him, Meg?"

Just because Megan was the older by five months, she was supposed to have all the answers, but she knew next to nothing about that particular subject, though she was loath to admit it. After all, men fell all over themselves trying to get her attention. It was embarrassing, especially since she never did anything to attract them. But after two years of having every eligible male in the neighborhood come calling, she had finally concluded it was simply her looks, even though she had the most unfashionable hair color in the kingdom, an atrocious, gaudy, bright rusty-copper color, the one and only thing she had inherited from her father.

So Megan had drawn on common sense that day and said to her best friend, "Just smile and be yourself, and he won't have a chance."

And he didn't. Within two months of meeting her, the Right Honorable Tyler had been moved to propose to Tiffany. They were to be married on her eighteenth birthday, in a little less than three months. And no simple ceremony for this viscount's son. They would be doing it up grand right at the height of the London Season.

Considering how pleased Megan was for her friend, and what a fine fellow she thought Tyler to be, her churlish question to him should have surprised the affianced couple, whom she was chaperoning on the way to church this bright summer Sunday. It did, in fact, surprise Tyler, for her attitude toward him never ceased first to baffle him, then to irritate him, since he never did anything to cause it. It didn't surprise Tiffany in the least, but then she knew the reason for Megan's behavior.

Tiffany had appreciated it at first, when Megan had set out to make Tyler think she was the veriest bitch, for any young man Tiffany had ever been the least bit interested in had understandably fallen in love with Megan instead. It wasn't that Tiffany wasn't pretty. She was quite pretty; her blond curls and deep blue eyes were in the height of fashion. But pretty didn't stand a chance next to the kind of mesmerizing beauty that Megan had been blessed with. So Megan had set out at the start to make sure that Tyler's interest didn't roam elsewhere, most especially in her direction.

But Megan's rather unorthodox strategy had been going on long enough, that Tyler no longer just flushed and stammered apologies for whatever it was the outspoken Megan had taken offense at. He now fought back, and he was getting rather good at it.

As he flipped the reins sharply at the high-stepping bay that was pulling the open carriage away from Tiffany's home, where he had picked up both girls, he remarked without looking at Megan again, "Why, I was staring at nothing at all, Miss Penworthy. Absolutely *nothing.*"

Tiffany stiffened. Tyler had never been quite that cruel in a comeback before. Megan, she saw, took his reply to heart, blushing furiously and turning away so he wouldn't see that his barb had hurt.

Tiffany couldn't blame Tyler. There was just so much nastiness a man could take without getting nasty in return. No, it was Tiffany's fault for not putting a stop to Megan's scheme long before now. The reason she hadn't was that small kernel of doubt she still harbored that if Tyler ever saw Megan as she really was, he would become just as smitten as all the other men who were treated to one of her smiles.

But enough was enough. She *was* sure that Tyler loved her. And if she couldn't hold him by now, then she didn't deserve him, or more to the point, he didn't deserve her. She would speak to Megan right after the vicar's sermon—or maybe before, at least before the hurt wore off and Megan got mad instead. That thought worried Tiffany, because when Megan got angry, which fortunately wasn't often, she could be utterly unpredictable.

Tiffany found her chance when they arrived at the parish church on the edge of Teadale Village. Tyler moved ahead of them to pay his respects to Lady Ophelia and her three daughters. As Countess of Wedgwood, Ophelia Thackeray was in possession of the most lofty title in the neighborhood, and she lorded that over the lesser gentry. Even Megan was not immune to Ophelia's consequence. She never missed an opportunity to put herself before the lady's notice, because the countess was the reigning hostess in the parish and her invitations were highly coveted. Megan would do just about anything to get one.

Tiffany had to pull Megan back from plowing after Tyler to greet the countess, so she could have a few words with her. Megan's impatient look didn't promise she'd be attentive to those words, however, and she was quick to try to forestall them.

"I hope you're not going to mention what happened in the carriage, Tiffany."

"I most certainly am," Tiffany replied, undaunted. "I know what you're doing, Megan, and I love you for it. I'm sure it even helped in the beginning. But I'd like to think I can hold Tyler on my own now, that the sight of those cavernous dimples of yours won't have him fainting at your feet."

Megan blinked, then gave a spontaneous, unladylike hoot of laughter before she hugged her friend. "You're right, I know. I think it's just become a habit, my picking on the dear man."

"So break the habit this very day."

Megan grinned. "Very well, but you don't suppose he'll think something is wrong with me, do you, if I start being nice to him?"

"I think he'll quit subtly suggesting that I stop seeing you."

Megan's midnight-blue eyes flared, then narrowed. "The devil he did! When?"

"More than once, but can you blame him when you only show him your very worst? It baffles him why we're such good friends, since it appears to him that we are so very different in temperament."

"Fat lot he knows," Megan snapped. "We're cut from the same cloth, right down to the ragged hem." But then she bit her lip, unable to hide her concern. "He wouldn't insist, would he, after you're married?"

"You know he's not the least bit high-handed," Tiffany said reassuringly. "And even if he did insist, it wouldn't make a jot of difference. I'm afraid you're stuck with this friend for life, Miss Penworthy."

Megan smiled the smile that released both dimples and gave her a different kind of beauty, a look that was warm, open—approachable. It even gave Tiffany pause, though she was gifted by that special smile quite often. It still made her feel privileged each time it was bestowed on her, and quite certain there wasn't anything in the world she wouldn't do for this dearest friend. It also made the gentlemen in the churchyard who had been covertly watching Megan stop their conversations in mid-sentence to stare openly. Several even took hope from it and determined to try their hand again at courting the incomparable beauty of the parish.

Having said her piece, Tiffany put her arm through Megan's and led her to the church door, where Tyler was still talking with the four Thackerays. She whispered aside with a grin, "I feel lucky today, Meg. That long-awaited invite is going to be ours at last, I just know it. And you look smashing in that new blue poplin. Old hatchet-face will most definitely be impressed."

"Do you really think so?" Megan asked hopefully.

Tiffany wished that damn invite wasn't so important to her friend, but it was. And it wasn't just that the countess seemed to know everyone in the whole of Devonshire, that people came from miles away to her parties, always guaranteeing new and interesting people to meet. That was only part of it, though a big part for a young girl with the same hopes as every other young girl, to find the man of her romantic dreams, since she hadn't found him in the gentlemen of her own acquaintance.

That still wasn't the main reason, for Megan would be having her London Season in a few months and would meet all the eligible men she could hope for then. No, the Countess of Wedgwood had worked hard over the years to make it an *achievement* to be invited to her home. To never end up on the guest list implied you weren't quite up to scratch, or worse, that there was actually something wrong with you, a family scandal perhaps, that just hadn't made the rounds yet. Then again, every other family of note in the parish had received its invite, even if only once, even Tiffany's family. Her parents had gone, but she had begged off with an illness out of loyalty to Megan, though that was one secret she had never told her friend, for it would only have made her more desperate for that invite, and she was already desperate enough.

They had been so sure, the two of them, that the countess was merely waiting until Megan turned eighteen. But two months had passed since then, and the squire and his daughter were still being ignored.

Tiffany squeezed Megan's arm in answer to her inquiry, praying she wasn't just getting her friend's hopes up, only to have them dashed again. But this was the first time in over a month that they would have the opportunity to speak with the countess, thanks to Tyler. Perhaps all Lady Ophelia needed was to be reminded that Megan Penworthy was her neighbor . . .

"Next Saturday, then, Mr. Whately," Lady Ophelia was saying when the two girls joined them. "Just a small gathering of forty or so. And do bring your lovely fiancée."

The countess smiled at Tiffany, stared at Megan for a moment, then turned and entered the church.

It was a direct cut, a deliberate cut. Alice Thackeray, the youngest daughter at seventeen, even giggled before she hurried after her mother. The other two girls, Agnes and Anne, merely looked spitefully pleased.

Tiffany was appalled for only a moment before she got angry. How dare they? Everyone knew that Megan and Tiffany were best friends, and that Megan accompanied Tiffany and Tyler almost everywhere because she was their chaperon. It was as if the Thackerays had planned this slight, timed it perfectly for the greatest effect, this subtle telling that Megan's coveted invitation wasn't going to be forthcoming, ever. Tiffany was afraid she knew why. Megan was just too lovely to have around when one had three less-than-pretty daughters to marry off.

Tyler cleared his throat, recalling them to the fact that they were just standing there. Tiffany finally glanced at Megan to see how badly she was taking the Thackerays' snubbing. Worse than Tiffany expected. Megan's face was as pale as the white ribbons on her bonnet, her large blue eyes awash with tears that were going to spill at any moment, though she was trying to hold them back. Tiffany's heart ached for her, and it made her even angrier that there wasn't anything she could do to help other than to offer her support.

She squeezed her friend's hand, drawing those bewildered blue eyes to her. "Why?" Megan whispered.

Tiffany was angry enough to be blunt. "You're too pretty, damn it. She's got those plain chicks of hers to marry off, but no man will even look at them if you're around."

"But that's so—so—"

"Selfish? Petty? Absolutely, Meg, but—"

"It's all right, Tiff, really—but I need to be alone right—"

She didn't finish, walking abruptly away. "Megan, wait," Tiffany called out, but she didn't. She was even running before she left the churchyard, because she could no longer hold back the tears. Mr. Pocock held out a handkerchief to her as she passed him, but she probably didn't even see him. He stared after her, too, watching her hurry down the lane, away from the church.

"I s'pose we'll have to hie after her, since it's over a mile to Sutton Manor," Tyler remarked.

"That's not why we're going after her," Tiffany replied absently, her attention still on Megan as she stumbled, stopped, dug into her reticule for a handkerchief, then went on without using it. "She and I have walked that distance before." But Tiffany finally glanced at him, and his expression had her hackles rising again. "Don't you dare look smug over this, Tyler Whately. She didn't deserve what that horrid woman did."

"Allow me to disagree—"

"No, I will not. You're going to notice a difference in her after today anyway, so I might as well tell you. The only reason she's treated you abominably was so you wouldn't like her. It was done for love of me, because she knows how much I—I want you, and she didn't want to see me hurt if your interest went to her instead."

"But I can barely tolerate the girl," he protested.

"You didn't feel that way when you first met her, did you?" Tiffany shot back.

"Well, no, but—d'you mean to say it was all *deliberate?*"

"Yes, and if you want to get angry about it, then get angry at me, because I could have stopped her before today, but I—I guess I was still a little worried about your finding out that she's really a very warm, caring person—"

"And spoiled, and willful—"

"Only a little spoiled, but that's to be expected with a father as kind and generous as the squire is. And I happen to be just as willful, Tyler."

"Yes, but in you I find it rather endearing."

"Thank you—I think. But can you understand Megan's dilemma? She *knows* how men see her, Tyler. The attitude she took with you is the only defense she has to keep men from falling hopelessly in love with her."

"But I wouldn't want a wife who looks like her, darling. Good God, no!" And he really did seem appalled at the notion. "That girl needs a man with a strong constitution, with little to no temper, and who doesn't even know the meaning of jealousy. I couldn't abide having every one of my acquaintances in love with my wife—one or two I might tolerate," he added with a smile.

"But all of them, why, it would drive me to despondency."

"You make it sound hopeless for her. What man wouldn't get a little jealous where his wife is concerned?"

"Well, actually, the man's jealousy won't matter all that much, I suppose, if he's assured of her affections. But she'll have to make a constant effort to keep him assured."

Tiffany wasn't sure she liked the sound of that one-sided scenario. "What if she ends up getting jealous for one reason or another—will he have to do some assuring of his own?"

" 'Course not. He married her, didn't he?"

"Not yet he didn't," Tiffany grouched.

Tyler blinked as she whipped the train of her skirt out of the way to march stiffly toward the carriage. He almost leaped to catch up with her.

"I say, we didn't just switch subjects there, did we?" he asked uneasily.

"You tell me, Tyler. Did we?"

"Certainly not," he insisted. "Your friend's case is unique, Tiffany, because *she* is unique—which is not to say I don't find you unique as well, but you see what I mean. There is simply no comparison to ourselves."

"All right, Tyler, I forgive you."

"Thank you—I think."

Chapter 2

"You're eating *again?*" Tiffany asked as she sailed into the dining room unannounced.

The Penworthy butler, Krebs, appeared behind her merely to close the doors, a disgruntled look on his face. He never was quick enough to beat Tiffany to a door, a point he should have resigned himself to a long time ago, but he never had, despite the fact that protocol had been dispensed with where Tiffany was concerned soon after she and Megan had first met.

Surprising Krebs by always using a different entrance to the house when she arrived was a game to Tiffany, one she still enjoyed. If Krebs was lucky enough to see her arrive—and even in that she frequently circled the manor to come around directly to the stable behind it so he wouldn't—he might dash for the kitchen entrance, but she'd choose the French doors off the drawing room. If he waited in the drawing room, he'd soon hear her teasing call, "Anyone home?" as she came from the back of the house to head right up the stairs. Once, when he knew she was expected, he'd left all three doors wide open and waited in the downstairs hall, where Tiffany would have to pass no matter which door she used. She'd come in through the dining room window that day. Krebs didn't speak to her for two weeks after that defeat.

Megan had hoped the Robertses' butler would accommodate her in the same game. But he was a sweet old dear who just smiled at her and wished her a good day when she would appear suddenly in his domain, which took the fun out of it.

She covered a yawn now with her napkin before tossing it onto the table. "This is my first meal of the day, actually, though I've had enough of it."

"Well, do finish your tea," Tiffany said as she sat down next to her. "I could use another cup myself, so I'll share it with you." And then nonchalantly, as if she hadn't been surprised by Megan's remark, she added, "Your first meal, you say? Do you know what time it is?"

Megan shrugged, adding tea to her cup and passing it to Tiffany, who proceeded to add nearly an equal amount of sugar to it. There was no question of sharing after that, since Megan took her tea without sugar, but then they both knew that. There wasn't much of anything that they didn't know about each other after eleven years of friendship. But Krebs was able to anticipate *some* things, and had gone to the kitchen to have Cora deliver another cup.

Cora was the cook's daughter, a pretty girl who had trouble containing her voluptuous curves in the formfitting current fashions, so consequently she was always out of breath because of a too tight corset. Her maid's uniform was simplicity itself, even if it still sported the bustle and long train that had been the standard ever since the crinoline had gone out of style so many years ago. It was the bane of some ladies that their servants wore the same styles as they did, though of a much cheaper quality. Even charwomen went to work with their skirts trailing, but they had ingenious little ties that got the trains out of the way until they finished their jobs, releasing the trains again when they left work.

Megan waited until Cora had bobbed her curtsy and left the room before she confessed, "I overslept."

That *was* a confession, since Megan never overslept and they both knew it. "What is that, the second time in your life? I can understand the first time, after we waited half the night for Lord Beacon's ghost to appear in that ruined manor house he's supposed to haunt. What a disappointment—" She broke off before she got carried away reminiscing, and asked sympathetically, "A bad night?"

"An understatement," Megan admitted.

"Damn, I knew I should have stayed over last night. But I thought you were good and mad enough that you wouldn't start brooding again."

Megan grinned. "You think anger is conducive to a good night's sleep?"

"Well, better than brooding."

"I'm in a position to disagree, Tiffany, believe me," Megan replied.

"Oh, well, then," Tiffany said matter-of-factly. "I guess it got worse after I left?"

"A trifle."

Megan's tears had dried up by the time Tiffany had hopped out of the carriage yesterday to walk beside her along the country lane, leaving Tyler to follow discreetly at a distance so they could speak privately. Tiffany hadn't realized yet that Megan had already put her self-pity aside and was stewing with a healthy fury. To cheer her, Tiffany had suggested she go back and sock Lady O in the nose. Megan had actually considered it, then dismissed the idea as not a good enough retaliation. Since Tiffany hadn't been serious to begin with, she agreed that the countess wasn't worth the scandal that would follow that particular brand of revenge.

But she was pleased that Megan wasn't feeling sorry for herself, and was good and furious over what had happened instead. It was much more healthy. Only Megan was mostly angry at herself for all the time and energy she'd wasted on what had been a hopeless endeavor from the start. She felt like an utter fool. Tiffany felt like one, too, for not having seen it coming sooner. But old hatchet-face hadn't had to be so bloody spiteful in delivering the blow. That was uncalled-for.

"I *knew* I shouldn't have listened to you!" Tiffany exclaimed now. " 'Go home,' you said. 'I'm just fine,' you said. 'It's not as if I haven't been snubbed before,' you said."

Megan chuckled. "Well, that's true enough."

"I don't know how you can laugh about it."

To this day it still made Tiffany furious that the other friends they'd had when they were younger had stopped coming 'round, one by one, when Megan started to turn into a beauty. Quite simply, the other girls felt plain and unattractive next to Megan, and they couldn't abide that. But some of them had actually snubbed her later in public, and that was taking their pettiness too far. You'd think Megan's looks were something she had developed to spite them.

Megan wasn't sure how she could laugh about it either, when having friends turn on you was a kind of hurt that never really went away completely; it just lay beneath the surface waiting for a similar instance to bring it all back. And what the Countess of Wedgwood had done yesterday certainly brought it all back.

"Better to laugh than to cry again, don't you think?" Megan said as she stared at the leftover sausage she was using to make circles in a dollop of jam on her plate.

Tiffany started. "Good God, yes! Absolutely! Do you want to talk about it?"

They both knew the subject had switched to those past hurts now, not the present one. "No—except, when I think of all the fun we've had over the years, I almost feel sorry for those girls that they weren't around to share it."

"Now that you mention it, I guess I do, too. After all, they turned into such boring creatures after they deserted us. On second thought, I don't feel at all sorry for them."

Megan peeked up with a grin. "Neither do I, but it sounded like a nice thing to say."

They both laughed, when it was honestly a dreary subject. Tiffany was quick to change it. "I suppose this late meal means you haven't had your morning ride and are going to be in a rotten mood all day because of it."

Megan usually breakfasted bright and early with the squire, then spent half the morning riding her horse, Sir Ambrose, and the other half grooming it. No stableboy—though they only had one since they owned a mere four horses—was ever allowed near her pride and joy, other than to feed Sir Ambrose, and even that Megan liked to do. For anyone who knew about her tendency to haunt the stables, it wasn't hard to guess that Megan absolutely loved horses.

"Actually, I did have my ride." Staring again at her sausage, Megan added, "Last night."

"You didn't."

"Around two in the morning."

"You *didn't!*"

Megan glanced up to explain earnestly, "I had to, Tiffany, I swear I did. I was near to going crazy."

"Did you take one of the footmen with you?"

"I didn't have the heart to wake them."

"Megan!"

"Well, no one saw me," Megan said, defensive now, realizing belatedly how scandalous it was for a young lady to go out in the middle of the night by herself. "I stayed to the road for Sir Ambrose's sake, since it was so dark last night. And it worked. I went right to sleep when I got back." Tiffany just stared, so Megan added, "That ride did more than just let me get to sleep. On the third trip to the village and back—"

"Third?"

"I ran the route five times—well, I only had the bloody road to stick to, and Sir Ambrose was as game as I for a full-out gallop."

Tiffany rolled her eyes.

"*As* I was saying." Megan got back to the subject. "On the third run it came to me exactly what I could do to set Ophelia Thackeray on her ear in the grandest way possible, and that's exactly what I'm going to do."

Tiffany's expression turned instantly wary. "You didn't reconsider socking her, did you?"

"No," Megan said with a grin, then triumphantly added, "I'm going to build a mansion twice the size of hers and become the new reigning hostess of the area. *That* will show her."

"Uh, how do you propose to do that?"

"Very simply. I'm going to marry a duke."

"Oh, well, that will do it. Which duke did you have in mind?"

"Wrothston, of course," Megan announced. "He's the only one we know."

Tiffany sat up, because putting a name to this duke took the whimsy out of Megan's idea, enough to make Tiffany worry that she might actually be serious. "We don't *know* him a'tall. If you'll recall, he wasn't at Sherring Cross when we took tea with his grandmother. The only reason we even got on his estate was that your father had some obscure acquaintance with the dowager duchess and took the chance of writing her for advice when he was looking for a horse to buy you for your twelfth birthday."

"And it was fate that she invited us to come choose one from the duke's stables."

"Fate? They had hundreds of horses. She was delighted to get rid of one."

Megan leaned forward to whisper that word ladies weren't supposed to know anything about. "They *breed* them at Sherring Cross, so of course she was glad to sell one." Then she sat back to add, "We already have something in common—horses."

"We? As in you and the duke? Good God, Meg, you aren't *really* serious about this, are you?"

"Absolutely." Megan grinned excitedly. "Just imagine, Tiff, a magnificent coach pulling up to the church, with the ducal arms of Wrothston emblazoned on it, while the countess with her still unmarried daughters is standing there agog. Then yours truly steps out of the coach, assisted by the most handsome man imaginable. I will, of course, be magnanimous and bid the countess a good day, and even introduce my husband, the duke. And I will kindly not notice that her mouth is hanging open in shock."

"And it would be, too." Tiffany laughed, caught up in the pleasant fantasy for a moment. "Oh, that would be the perfect comeuppance." Then she sighed dramatically. "If only it *were* possible."

"But it is," Megan replied quietly. "And I mean to see it happen."

Tiffany was appalled to see Megan's stubborn look appear. "Now, wait a minute. Let's at least be realistic about this. If you want to marry for a title, we'll find you a nice viscount. Maybe even an earl wouldn't be impossible. Yes, an earl, which will make you Lady O's equal—don't shake your head at me, damn it!"

"Tiffany, if I'm going to stoop to marrying for a title, it might as well be the big one."

"Then don't stoop."

"I've already decided to stoop. And the more I think about it, the more I like the idea of being a duchess."

Tiffany groaned. "Why do *I* have to be the bad guy here? All right, listen to the facts, Megan. You may have an earl somewhere in your background—"

"Four generations back, plus a baron or two."

"Whatever, you're still just a simple country squire's daughter. Dukes can marry royalty if they want. They do *not* marry squires' daughters."

"Wrothston will, and why not?" Megan replied tenaciously. "He's already rich beyond imagining. He's already got all the consequence he can manage, so he doesn't need to marry a title himself. He can marry for love if he wants, and a duke can bloody well do whatever he wants. My background *does* happen to make me acceptable. Certainly he can do better than a squire's daughter, but he's not going to care a jot for that because he's going to be in love with me, hopelessly in love, mind you. And you know why, don't you? Because of this cursed face of mine. It's given me nothing but grief till now, but now it's going to make up for that and win me a duke."

There was a lot of bitterness and hurt in those words, which made Tiffany cautious in asking her next question. "What about you?"

"What about me?"

"What if you don't love him?"

"Of course I will."

"What if you can't, Meg? What if he's horrible and mean and not lovable at all?"

"He wouldn't dare be. He's a duke."

Tiffany almost smiled at that ridiculous certainty. "But what if when you meet him you just know, deep down, that he won't do a'tall, that he'd only make you miserable? Would you still want him?"

After a long pause Megan said, "No."

Thank God for that, Tiffany said to herself with a sigh. She felt on firmer ground now and so plowed on. "He could be ugly, you know."

"Are you forgetting that parlormaid who whispered to us how handsome he was?"

"She was trying to impress us."

"We were already overawed. We didn't need to be impressed anymore that day."

"That's another matter. You can't *really* want to live in a place like that."

"Are you joking?" Megan gasped. "Sherring Cross is the most magnificent home imaginable."

"It's not a home, it's a bloody mausoleum spread out over a good six acres. The stable alone was bigger than this house, and this is no small house you have here."

"I know. It was all so grand," Megan said dreamily.

"Grand? People probably get lost in that house every day and die."

Their eyes met on that remark and they both suddenly burst into laughter.

"Die, Tiff?"

"Well, worry about it, at any rate." They laughed again; then Tiffany finally conceded the point. "All right, I guess it isn't beyond impossible to win a duke, not for someone who looks like you. Are you absolutely sure, Meg?"

"Yes. Ambrose St. James can start counting his bachelor days good-bye."

"Good God," Tiffany gasped. "I forgot you named your horse after him."

Megan blinked. "So did I."

Again they burst into laughter, but were interrupted this time as Krebs opened the doors to announce the Honorable Tyler Whately's arrival. Megan gave him a brilliant smile with the greeting, "Good morning, Tyler. My, don't you look dashing today. If you'll just give me a moment to run up and get my bonnet, we can leave."

She sailed past him without receiving a word of greeting from him, but the man was still dumbstruck by the smile she'd bestowed on him. Tiffany hid her own smile behind her teacup, pleasantly surprised that she wasn't the least bit jealous over his reaction to her dear friend.

She remarked blandly, "You'll have to do better than that, Tyler, if you don't want her to revert to being nasty to you again."

He snapped his mouth shut, shoved his hands in his pockets, and scowled. "God, I don't envy the man who wins her hand, indeed I don't."

"He's already been chosen, so let's hope he wins her heart along with her hand."

Tyler's brow rose questioningly. "Did I miss something between yesterday and today?"

"Nothing much—but did you ever think you would feel sorry for a duke?"

Chapter 3

"This is taking precaution too bloody far, Mr. Browne. Walking, by God. Freddy would laugh his arse off if he could see it."

Mortimer Browne gave the tall man at his side another disgusted look. All he'd heard were complaints of one kind or another since they'd left Kent. But he'd been warned to expect them.

"You wouldn't be walking if you'd brought another horse along as I suggested."

"D'you hear how he insults you, Caesar?" Devlin said to the horse of that name.

Mortimer gave the stallion Devlin was leading a killing look for snorting in agreement, but he pressed on with the bare facts. "Traveling at night as we been doing is one thing, *Mr.* Jefferys, but during the day, you see a lot more and get seen a lot more, and it'd only make folks wonder what a bloke like you is doing riding a horse like that, wouldn't it, now? You're here to disappear, not to draw extra attention to yourself."

"And you're here to badger me to death, I suppose," Devlin replied. "But in case you haven't noticed, the village is no longer in sight, and there isn't another bloody soul on this road."

"There wasn't, but there is now, or are you blind as well as pigheaded?"

Devlin ignored the carriage that had just come over a rise. Instead he stopped short to give Mortimer one of his more intimidating looks. From that six-foot-three, well-filled-out frame, it most definitely did some intimidating. But Mortimer hadn't been chosen to accompany this young man because he was known to buckle under. Just the opposite. And besides, he had his orders straight from the one and only person Devlin wasn't quite up to defying, and that gave Mortimer the upper hand—some of the time.

"We was told the squire's holdings ain't that far down the road," Mortimer explained reasonably. "When we reach it will be soon enough for you to get back on that fine beast. Till then, kindly remember you're no more than a stableboy now—"

"Breeder, Mr. Browne," Devlin cut in succinctly. "A breeder of fine horse-flesh *and* trainer of same. Yes, a trainer, too. That has a nice ring—"

"But you don't know the first thing—"

"That's what you're along for, to see I don't make a fool of myself."

"That's not why—"

"That's why *I* agreed to your obnoxious company. If I have to live in a stable, I'll bloody well have top say in that stable, or this harebrained idea ends right now."

Mortimer opened his mouth to argue, but he could see on *this* point it wouldn't do him a bit of good. So he nodded curtly, but went back to giving orders that had a better chance of being heeded.

"Since that *is* a carriage coming our way, and most likely carrying some of the local gentry, pull your hat down to conceal—"

"Oh, give over, Browne," Devlin bit out, obviously at the limit of his patience. "We're at the bloody end of the world here. If those country bumpkins recognize me, I'll eat these atrocious boots you dredged up for me to wear."

"Could you at least slouch a little?"

"No." And that "No" had a definite ring of finality to it. "I'm walking, *walking,* for God's sake, with a moth-eaten jacket dangling from my shoulder, scruffed boots unworthy of a charity box, and I'm sweating, Mr. Browne. *Sweating!* Not another bloody concession am I inclined to make. Not another one."

"Sweating in a bloody white lawn shirt," Mortimer mumbled beneath his breath. "The very mark of a gentle—"

"What was that?"

"Nothing, Mr. Jefferys, nothing at all," Mortimer said. "But if we fail in this endeavor, we know whose fault it will be, don't we?"

"Indeed we do."

That wasn't reassuring in the least.

It wasn't unusual to see folks walking along the road from Teadale, even leading horses behind them instead of riding them. What was unusual today was the quality of the horseflesh on that road.

Megan noticed the black Thoroughbred long before Tyler was moved to remark, "By God, did you ever see such a fine-looking stud?"

Tiffany and Megan exchanged an amused look. The word "stud" wouldn't have slipped out if Tyler weren't so impressed that he could even forget there were ladies present. But they were closer, and the black stallion's elegant lines were unmistakable now. Indeed, none of them had ever seen such a magnificent animal.

With her love of horses, Megan was as impressed as Tyler, if not more so. She had prided herself on having the finest horse in the parish, in all of Devonshire for that matter, but this Thoroughbred put Sir Ambrose to shame, and she couldn't even begrudge him that. He was just too beautiful. She could imagine the ride he would give, the speed a skillful rider could get out of him. It wasn't fair that stallions were considered unsuitable mounts for ladies, for this was one horse Megan would dearly love to own. She wildly considered asking her father to buy him. He always gave her anything she wanted— within reason. But then she had to dismiss the idea, certain that the owner of that animal wouldn't part with him for any price. *She* certainly wouldn't if he were hers.

It barely registered on her that Tyler had stopped the carriage, except that the stallion was right there in front of her now for her to admire, and she couldn't take her eyes off him. She started to stand up, with every intention of getting even closer, but Tiffany's laugh and whispered "Behave" recalled her to the fact that a lady didn't just walk up and examine someone else's horse, not without the owner's permission, at any rate. She turned now to get that permission from the man who held the stallion's reins—and promptly forgot about the horse.

He stood there, sweaty and dusty, and she thought him the most handsome man she'd ever seen. Without considering the impropriety of it, she cast her eyes over him with the same avid intensity she had given the stallion. Tall, broad, divinely put together, and clean-shaven, revealing every arrogant line of those stunning, sun-gilded features. She even found beautiful the hand that rose so slowly to remove his hat, and even the wildly unkempt hair that was as black as pitch. And then she ran into the most amazing turquoise eyes— and suddenly realized they were staring right back at her.

The jolt she received from those eyes caused her to become aware of what she was doing, and she immediately looked away, grateful for the wide brim of her own hat that would conceal from all concerned the hot color of her mortification. She simply could not credit what she had just done. The only excuse she could think of was that she had been avidly admiring the stallion, then to see an even more magnificent specimen, though of a different breed . . . that *was* no excuse for the way she had stared at a complete stranger. She had never stared at men she did know the way she had looked at this man.

And then the picture of him, still branded in her mind, pointed out the poor quality of his attire, the slowness of his manners, as if he weren't used to them, the lack of even a neckcloth, which no gentleman would be without. He wasn't gentry, then, and thank God for that; at least she hoped he wasn't, so her unspeakable behavior wouldn't make the rounds of her acquaintances. It might be mentioned in a few taverns, but she could live with that—no, she couldn't. God, *what* had possessed her?

But Tiffany hadn't noticed, thankfully, and Tyler was still utterly engrossed in the stallion and hearing about its bloodlines, in answer to the question he'd just asked. What else had been said, Megan couldn't imagine. She wanted to be away from there. She never wanted to lay eyes on that fellow again with his secret knowledge of her wretched behavior.

" . . . as if I had the blunt to own him," that deep voice was saying in something of a churlish tone.

"Then who does?" Tyler wanted to know.

"Squire Penworthy's the proud new owner."

Megan's head whipped around, but again she was struck first by the handsomeness of the fellow, so much so, with his eyes meeting hers head on, that she almost, to her horror, forgot his incredible statement.

As it was, it took five long seconds for her to remember and let the words tumble out. "I don't believe it. My father would have said something to me."

"And who is your father that he would know anything about it?"

"Squire Penworthy, of course."

It was his turn to pause overlong, but then his full lower lip curled up the slightest bit. "Ah, well, I don't see that his decision to start up a stud farm would be any business of yours, now would it?"

That was perfectly true—in most cases. Not in hers, however, when her father knew she would take a keen interest in the acquisition of new horseflesh, for whatever the reason. He would just have found a more delicate way to mention it. Not like this fellow, who seemed to take an undue amount of pleasure in saying the word "stud" as he did, which was saying it rudely. Even Tyler moved uncomfortably upon hearing that "forbidden" word, forgetting he had said it himself only moments ago.

Those turquoise eyes were still on Megan, flustering her with their directness, and now that he had her attention again, they moved over her in the same slow manner that hers had done to him—deliberately, she didn't doubt, an exact tit for tat. And there wasn't anything she could say about it without his announcing to the world—or to their small group—that he was merely repaying the compliment. But what he was doing was no compliment. It was an insult of the worse kind, something no gentleman would do no matter the provocation, but then he was proving he wasn't of that stamp with every passing moment—unless he thought she welcomed his personal attention. Good God, he might think just that after what she'd done.

"Then you're only delivering the stallion?" Megan blurted out. "You'll be gone afterward?"

The hopeful note in her tone had Tiffany looking askance at her. The man on the ground didn't miss it either. He seemed confused for the briefest moment; then he smiled, a downright nasty-looking smile that made Megan brace herself, and with reason.

"I'm a horse breeder, miss, and I come with this one, 'cause no one else can handle him but me. You don't think his previous owner would let a horse like this go without assuring he has the proper care, do you? Not bloody likely. But I'm also a horse trainer, so I'm a right valuable chap to have around. I have a knack for it, you see, 'cause I treat them all like women— with a gentle hand for the most part, a firm one when needed, and a good slap to the hindquarters when they get too feisty."

Now why the devil had he said that, Devlin wondered. Just to see if her cheeks could get as bright as that god-awful titian hair? Redheads did not blush becomingly. This one did, damn her.

The gent was starting to sputter indignantly, however. Devlin would have been surprised if he didn't. But he gave the blond chap a look of innocent inquiry, and got a look back that said, What could one expect of a horse breeder but ill-bred manners?

But the squire's daughter was good and furious now and not trying to hide it. "Drive on, Tyler. I'll have him dismissed before he's settled in, I guarantee it."

Devlin heard the young man's answer as the reins snapped and the carriage pulled away. "I'm sure he didn't mean that as it sounded, or at least, not as an insult."

"The devil he didn't."

"She's right," Mortimer said beside Devlin as they both stared after the departing carriage.

"Found your tongue again, did you?"

Mortimer's cheeks exploded with color. "So I lost it. I ain't never seen anything the likes of her before, but what's your excuse? You didn't lose your tongue, you lost your bloody wits. That was *the* squire's daughter, the same said squire that don't even know yet that we're going to be guests in his stable, *or* that he's bought himself a prime piece of horseflesh. What if she had had that bloke take her right home instead to complain to her father?"

Devlin scowled because that hadn't occurred to him, when it should have. But he dismissed it by saying, "So we would have had a little race to see who would get to the squire first. Need you wonder who would win?"

"Oh, that's a fine solution, guaranteed to get the little miss in a worse snit. Why'd you have to go and insult her in the first place?"

"I thought I was being crudely in character."

"Whose character, a breeder of fine horseflesh who by his very trade associates with the gentry enough to know better, or a guttersnipe who don't?"

Devlin suddenly laughed. "I think I will be safer if I assume the guttersnipe's manners, at least around that little gem."

"Safer?"

"Without question," Devlin replied. But since that hadn't answered Mortimer's confusion, he added, "I do believe you were right, Mr. Browne. My wits went a-begging, and they haven't come back yet."

"She *was* something to look at, wasn't she?"

"If you like brassy redheads."

Mortimer snorted. "And you don't, I suppose?"

"No, thank God. If I did, I'd prob'ly have been laid to waste. But you know, Mr. Browne, I'm inclined to think now that I just might enjoy our sojourn in this tail end of the world."

"I hope that doesn't mean you intend to amuse yourself with that little miss."

"Amuse? Certainly, or didn't you notice she and I just declared war?"

Chapter 4

Arnold Penworthy glanced up from the letter in his hand to give Devlin another long look, his third since he'd opened the letter, but then he went back to reading. He had warm, friendly brown eyes. Even disturbed as he was now about what he was being asked to do, his eyes were still friendly.

She was nothing like her father. Devlin had felt like a bloody giant when the squire had stood up from behind his desk to accept the letter Devlin had handed over. The squire was definitely on the short side, might even be an inch or two shorter than his daughter. And rotund as a stout barrel of ale, whereas Devlin knew corsets, from as many as he'd had the pleasure of removing, and would hazard a guess that Miss Penworthy's hadn't been cinched in all that tight to give her that slim, hourglass waistline.

Miss? He didn't know. She could be married. She certainly looked old enough to be married. That could even have been her husband with her today. Devlin wasn't going to ask.

"It doesn't say here why he wants me to hide you in my stable," the squire suddenly pointed out.

Devlin considered his answer carefully, but finally opted for bluntness in saying, "A friend of mine wants to blow my head off."

A bushy red brow shot up. "A friend, you say?"

Devlin nodded. "My best friend, actually. It's a misunderstanding that he's too hotheaded to try straightening out just yet. So it was thought best for all concerned if I disappeared for a while."

"I see," the squire said. He didn't, but he went back to reading.

Their hair was perhaps the only thing they had in common, father and daughter, though the squire's wasn't that bright copper-red that hers was, but was faded with age and liberally laced with gray. And he had freckles, a whole slew of them across his nose and cheeks. You'd think he might sport whiskers to hide some of them, but he didn't.

Devlin wondered if there were freckles anywhere on her body. There'd been none on those ivory, soft cheeks.

What the devil was her first name?

He wasn't going to ask.

The squire had to be reading the letter a second time through, it was taking him so long. Devlin couldn't care less, for his mind was back on that dusty road, trying to come up with an excuse for his asinine behavior.

He might not have pulled his hat down at the approach of that carriage, as Mortimer had told him to do, but he'd kept his eyes downcast, a most humble bearing to assume, he'd thought, rather pleased with himself for thinking of it. But now he had to admit it would have been infinitely preferable to have seen her from a distance first, rather than to just look up and have her right there before his eyes. One needed time to adjust to such radiance so that one did not make a bloody fool of oneself. At least she hadn't noticed his slack-jawed astonishment, nor had her companions. All three of them had been staring at Caesar, long enough for Devlin to get his mouth shut, though that first question asked of him had needed to be repeated once before he'd actually heard it.

Caesar usually did create something of a sensation, but then so did Devlin. It was the first time he'd been ignored *entirely* in favor of his horse, however, at least by females. And to actually feel annoyed by it, for God's sake. Only then she'd given him *too* much attention, looked him over as if he were the prime stud, with the same thoroughness that Caesar had gotten from her. On the one hand, he'd bloody well felt insulted to be examined like that, as if he were on an auction block with the bidding about to begin. On the other hand, he'd been hit with a jolt of pure lust.

That in itself was a rather rare experience for Devlin. A man of strong appetites he might be, but he saw to them with such ridiculous ease, on such a regular basis, that he was usually too well sated to get aroused to the point of lust. But then women young and old had been thrusting themselves beneath his notice for as long as he could remember. It spoiled a man, indeed it did, to be the object of so much prurient interest.

But the redhead's interest didn't strike him as being prurient, which didn't explain his reaction to it. He had been offended and aroused by it. Whatever she had intended, however, such behavior was beyond unseemly, and so he'd thought to teach her a lesson by giving her back the same bold perusal. But instead the sight of her well-shaped breasts and cinched-in waist had increased the heat in his loins and probably fried his wits along with it.

Was she spoken for?

Devlin was having some difficulty sitting still in the chair he'd been offered. Every noise he heard beyond the study door made him wonder if it was her returning. Would she just burst in on her father to demand Devlin's dismissal as she'd threatened? With that red hair, he imagined she did do things spontaneously, thoughtlessly, passionately . . .

Devlin stifled a groan. He could not stay here. One of the reasons he had agreed to rusticate in the country had been the fact that he needed a break in his routine, and he could look on this sojourn as a sort of vacation, a time to put worries and cares aside for simple peace and relaxation. But he could not envision any peace with someone like her around, and at the moment, he was a bundle of nerves just waiting for her to walk in, which was utterly absurd. He would simply have to find somewhere else to bury himself—and let her think she had run him off? Not bloody likely.

Those friendly brown eyes came back to Devlin again. Hers had been the darkest blue of midnight. And not the least bit friendly.

"This horse he mentions as an excuse for your being here sounds frightfully expensive. Do I actually have to buy it?" the squire asked.

Devlin sighed, grateful to have something else to think about. "No, sir, Caesar isn't for sale. You only have to say you bought him, for anyone who asks."

Penworthy frowned worriedly. "I'm not very good at that sort of thing. Tongue gets tripped up over the littlest falsehood."

Would that we all had that problem, Devlin thought with a touch of amusement. "There is no reason for you to be uncomfortable with this arrangement. I will merely grant you temporary ownership of Caesar in return for your hospitality, said ownership to be relinquished upon my departure. A gentleman's agreement. Is that satisfactory?"

"Then I would actually own the animal? I wouldn't be lying if I said so?"

"You would be speaking the absolute truth, sir."

The squire smiled in relief. "My, won't Megan be surprised."

Devlin pounced. "Megan?"

"M'daughter," the squire replied. "She has an uncommon appreciation for fine horseflesh—uncommon for a girl, that is. Her own horse—"

"I feel I should warn you, sir, that I've already had a run-in with your daughter, and she took an instant dislike to me, though I can't for the life of me figure why. I don't usually have that effect on the ladies."

The squire chuckled as he took in Devlin's features again. "No, I don't imagine you do."

"It might be necessary to point out to her that I come with Caesar and so can't be dismissed."

"Took that much of a dislike to you, did she?"

"That was my impression."

"Well, since you do come with the horse, and I've just bought the animal, there's no question of dismissal—not that I could dismiss you, mind, since you don't actually work for me." The squire frowned then, not quite sure he had that right. Then he digressed. "I've spoiled her, you know. First to admit it. Just can't seem to say no to her. But I'll be firm in this case. It's not every day I get asked a favor by the likes of *him*," he ended, nodding at the letter.

There had never been any doubt of the answer, but Devlin asked out of courtesy, "Then the arrangement is acceptable to you, sir?"

"Absolutely, Mr. Jefferys." The squire smiled. "Most happy to oblige."

"And I needn't point out that this must be kept in strictest confidence? Not even your family is to know my true reason for being here."

"No need to worry about that. There's just m'self and Megan."

"Then she isn't married?" Devlin could have sworn he wasn't going to ask that question. "What I mean is, do you have a son-in-law who might question you about suddenly starting up a stud farm?"

"No, not yet I don't, though I expect it won't be long now—stud farm, you say? Does that mean I'll be buying more animals?"

"A few mares—what do you mean, it won't be long now? Is she engaged?"

"Who?"

"Your daughter."

The squire's brow knit, showing his difficulty in keeping up with the double subjects. "M'daughter ain't, last I heard—no, no, I'm sure she ain't. She'd tell me if she was, don't you think?"

Devlin *hoped* they were speaking of the same thing. "Yes, certainly."

"But you met her. Can't help but notice she's a pretty girl, can you? And she's having her come-out in London shortly. No, I expect it won't be long after that."

Megan Penworthy in London? Devlin's brows were knit now, though he didn't know it.

"The mares, sir," Devlin said somewhat curtly. "They will be yours for the duration of my stay here, just like Caesar. But you needn't concern yourself with the operation. It takes a while for a stud farm to get started, after all, much longer than I intend to be here. We will merely go through the motions for appearances, you understand. It may not even be necessary to do any actual breeding, but having the mares here will lend credence to the operation."

"A stud farm," the squire mused, shaking his head with a chuckle. "Never even considered one, you know. Megan will certainly be surprised."

She'd already been surprised, Devlin recalled. She hadn't believed it, in fact, which was what seemed to have got her animosity up to begin with, though he had to admit he'd helped on that score at the end. Not that a stud farm, real or not, was any of her business. He'd told her that, too. So there was no reason for the squire's daughter to cross paths with the squire's new horse breeder again. And Devlin would go out of his way to make sure of that.

He stood up. "If you have no further questions, I will take my leave."

"You're welcome to stay in the main house."

"Appreciate it, sir, but that would defeat the purpose of my being here. I'm to keep out of the way, and I can't do that as a guest. That's just what my friend will expect and be looking for."

"Well, if you need anything, just tell Mr. Krebs. He's m'butler and will see to it—"

"Father, I—"

She didn't burst in as Devlin had imagined she would, but she did come in quietly without any warning. Obviously, she hadn't expected Devlin to still be there, for her mouth snapped shut when she noticed him, her body stiffened perceptibly, and the look she gave him was just short of withering. Devlin, to his horror, realized that the way she had looked him over before didn't have much to do with the lust he had experienced, for his body was reacting to her again without the least bit of encouragement on her part.

"You're back early, m'dear," the squire remarked. "I believe you have met Devlin Jefferys?"

"Yes—I did." The word "unfortunately" hung unspoken in the air. "I'm sorry to interrupt, Father, but I need to speak with you—privately."

"Certainly," the squire allowed. "Mr. Jefferys was just leaving."

"Leaving?" She glanced at Devlin. "As in back to where you came from?"

That hopeful note was in her voice again, and it rankled just as easily as it had before. "Not quite that far, Miss Penworthy. I was just going to get settled in."

"Then you might want to wait in the hall," she replied stiffly as she held the door open for him. "Because I am quite sure my father will wish to speak to you again in just a few minutes."

"I will?" the squire said.

Devlin gave her a slow smile as he walked toward her. "By all means." And then when he reached her, he said softly, so only she could hear, "I'll wait so you can show me the way to the stable yourself."

Her look said she'd show him the front door or nothing. Devlin would have laughed if the study door hadn't closed so quickly behind him. He was left in the not-quite-empty hall staring at the Penworthys' butler across the way, who stared back inquiringly.

"I'm to wait," Devlin announced, at which point the helpful servant indicated one of the two benches on either side of the front door at the end of the hall. But Devlin smiled confidently to himself. "No need, Mr. Krebs. I guarantee it won't be that long a wait." And he wasn't about to move and miss hearing any possibly raised voices on the other side of the study door if he could help it.

Chapter 5

Megan whirled around the second the door closed and leaned across her father's desk to demand, "A horse-breeding farm?"

"You don't like the idea?"

"It's a splendid idea, Father, but why didn't you mention it sooner?"

"A surprise?"

Megan missed the question in his answer. "It was a surprise, all right. I made a bloody fool of myself, it was such a surprise."

The squire never took Megan to task for her less-than-ladylike vocabulary, since she was careful not to use such colorful words in mixed company—and she had got them from him in the first place. It amazed him sometimes that this was his daughter. He wished his dear wife had lived long enough to see what an extraordinary girl they had produced, but she'd died not long after Megan's third year.

"And that stallion must have cost a fortune!" Megan continued, but recalling Caesar, she got sidetracked. "Is he really yours?"

"He is now."

"And you're really going to breed him?"

"That's what I got him for. But these things take time," he cautioned.

"Yes, I know, and you can't breed a stallion like that to just any old mare. We'll have to buy the very best—"

"Already got some. They'll be delivered soon, and believe me, I got them at a bargain price."

"Well, good for you. We'll also have to enlarge the stable, of course, but you've probably already made plans for that."

"Enlarge the stable?" the squire repeated weakly.

"And the horses will have to be exercised. I can help with that, especially with the stallion. Oh, I can't wait to ride him!"

"Now, Megan—"

"Now, Father," she cut off his admonishment. "You know you don't have to worry. I'll be careful, and I won't ride him where anyone will see me do it."

She went on with more assurances, while outside the door, Devlin was grinding his teeth. Ride Caesar? Her? Not bloody likely. And when was she going to get around to demanding his dismissal?

Inside the study, the squire finally interrupted his daughter to say, "You'll have to ask Jefferys."

"What?!"

"He knows the animal, knows his temperament. He may not be ridable. And that's not what I got him for, after all."

There was a long silence while Megan just stared at her father. Then she burst out, "Damn! Not ridable? But I wouldn't ask *him* anyway, and speaking of him, he's not the least bit suitable for such an important position, Father. You'll simply have to find another—"

"He said you took a dislike to him. Can't imagine why. Damned fine-looking fellow, if you ask me."

"Damned rude fellow is what he is."

"But he comes highly recommended, m'dear, *very* highly recommended."

"I don't care if the queen recommended him—"

"Damned close," the squire mumbled.

"—his arrogant manner is offensive. I want him dismissed."

"Can't do it."

"Of course you can. Just send him back where he came from. How difficult can it be to find a replacement? I'll see to it myself, if you'd rather not."

"You'll do no such thing, m'girl. And I won't dismiss the man, so leave it go."

"Father?" She used the cajoling tone that usually got her her way.

"Now, now, none of that. Mr. Jefferys comes with the horse, a condition of the sale. If he goes, so does the stallion."

"But that's absurd!"

The squire shrugged. "Can't be helped. The seller wanted to be certain the stallion would have the best care possible. He trusts Mr. Jefferys to see to it."

"Good God, no wonder he's so bloody arrogant. He *knows* he can't be dismissed."

"I found him most likable m'self. He knows horses, knows everything to know about horse breeding." But then the squire's tone turned concerned. "I wouldn't want to dismiss him, Megan, but if he's done something that is totally unacceptable—"

"No, no, it was nothing specific," she quickly assured him. "I just—took a dislike to him, as he said."

"He's not a guest," her father pointed out. "It's not as if you have to entertain the fellow in your parlor. You prob'ly won't see much of him a'tall."

"I suppose that's something of a consolation, since we're obviously stuck with him."

She came around the desk and kissed her father's cheek to show him she wasn't too disappointed. But she was. The very thought of having Devlin Jefferys around agitated her as much as he himself had earlier. *Why* did he have to be the condition to having that magnificent stallion? If the horse weren't such a prize . . .

Megan ran right into the man as she turned from closing the door to the study. She'd had him on her mind, but she had completely forgotten that she'd told him to wait in the hall.

Her hands came up automatically to brace against the soft white lawn of his shirt. She felt muscles leap under her fingers, and her cheeks scalded with the impropriety of touching him, however accidentally. She jumped back, only she did it too quickly, right onto the train of her skirt, which pulled the bustle down and nearly made her lose her balance completely. By the time she got her shoes untangled from her skirt, Devlin Jefferys was laughing.

"Women do occasionally fall prostrate at my feet, but not trying to escape me."

"No doubt they swoon from your vulgar insinuations," Megan retorted before she looked up at him.

She wished she hadn't. He was still too close for comfort, and still so handsome he stole her breath. And those eyes, good God, they were lovely, such a perfect blending of blue-green, and such a wicked combination with that jet-black hair.

Nearly a half minute passed before they both realized, at the same time, that they were simply staring at each other. Megan looked away first, her face hotter than ever, so she didn't see the flush that also came to Devlin's cheeks.

"They have been known to swoon, though not from vulgar insinuations, which I rarely make. I'm much more direct, Miss Penworthy, in getting right to the heart of the matter. Shall I demonstrate?"

"No!"

"Too bad. You do look so nice in pink."

He was referring to her blushes, the lout, which he took such a delight in causing. She dared to look up at him again, just to give him a fulsome glare. His expression was smug, if not downright triumphant, and when she realized why, she gave him another blush to gloat over.

"Ah, I see your lagging memory returns finally," he almost purred. "You lost. It's time now to pay up."

"Pay up?"

"Take me out and show me your stable. That's what I waited here for."

He made it sound somehow unsavory, sexually unsavory, as if he weren't talking about a building, but part of her anatomy. "Our stable isn't hidden out in the woods somewhere, it's behind the house. A fool could find it, so I suppose you can."

"I should have known you'd be a spoilsport."

"I wasn't aware we'd placed a wager," she replied stiffly.

"Weren't you? You would have been quick enough to show me the door if you had got your way. You threw down the challenge, I accepted—and won."

"In that case, I'd say you cheated with unfair knowledge of a certain ridiculous condition."

"And I'd say, since you're *obviously stuck with me,* you ought to accept defeat graciously."

Those words sounded suspiciously familiar, making Megan gasp. "You were listening at the door?"

He gave her a mocking bow. "Wouldn't have missed it for the world."

She hissed through her teeth, "Only what one can expect of someone with the manners of a pig!"

His brows shot up in surprise, which she didn't doubt was feigned since his lips were just short of actual grinning. "I'm trying to step down, but I don't believe I'm aspiring to that level."

She didn't try to make sense out of that remark. What she tried to do was walk past him, but he moved, and still filled the immediate path to escape.

"So a demonstration is in order after all?" he said, and his arms suddenly came up to brace against the wall at her back, caging her to the spot so she couldn't miss his husky whisper. "We're alone now. Would you like to examine me with your hands as thoroughly as you did with your eyes?"

She made a sound of screeching outrage that wasn't all that loud, just damned indicative of her feelings on the subject. Then she ducked beneath his right arm and ran toward the stairs at the end of the hall.

But she could hear his laughter behind her, and the taunt, "Now *there* were the manners of a pig, Meg-O-m'dear. Did you notice the difference?"

She halted, feeling safe now with some distance between them, and turned to hiss, "Between this vulgarity and your earlier crudity? No difference a'tall."

"Well, then, speaking of manners, you may as well look as touch, Miss Penworthy. It has the same effect on a man—coming from you."

"Bastard!"

"Spoiled brat," he shot back, then dipped his head mockingly and sauntered out the front door.

And the man was whistling, as if he were supremely confident he had won that round, while Megan was so furious she felt like running after him to do physical violence. She barely restrained herself. But if he ever spoke to her again . . .

Chapter 6

"I want to ride you, you can't imagine how much. Will you let me?"

Devlin's eyes snapped open at the sound of those softly uttered words coming through the partially open door. The door had no lock, wouldn't even close properly. But the first order of business yesterday had been a new bed to replace the moldy, lumpy cot in the room he had allocated to himself. Fixing the door hadn't been a priority, not over his comfort. Now he wished it had been.

Just what he needed to wake up to, the sound of lovers trysting in *his* stable, especially when he had gone to sleep fantasizing a tryst of his own, more than a tryst actually, with the hot-tempered Miss Penworthy. Of course, in his fantasy she wasn't hot-tempered, just—hot. She didn't speak at all, didn't even open her mouth, except for his kisses, and to make use of a velvety soft tongue . . .

Devlin groaned as heat filled his loins again, just as it had last night when he'd imagined that redhead adoring his body. He was definitely going to have to avoid such thoughts, at least until he found a willing female in the area to see to the raging need they aroused.

He made a quick review of his current options. There had been that pretty little innkeeper's daughter the other night who had flirted with Mortimer after Devlin had shown no interest. Mortimer had in fact gone back to spend another night at the inn last night. Devlin wondered if he'd staked a claim there. Common courtesy required that he ask first.

Then there'd been the housemaid who'd come with the clean bedding yesterday. What was her name? He couldn't remember, but her overly generous attributes had reminded him of his last mistress, and she'd fairly drooled as she looked Devlin over. An easy tumble, that. Could have had her yesterday without the least effort on his part. Should have. But he'd just as soon avoid any dalliance with the squire's house staff. Servants tended to gossip outrageously, and he preferred to keep his liaisons discreet.

He had little doubt he'd find someone suitable to his taste and needs who would be agreeable to a brief affair, only the present condition of his body demanded he do so rather quickly, preferably today. Damn Megan Penworthy. And those lovers on the other side of his door weren't helping one bloody bit. Servants from the manor, no doubt, who hadn't yet heard that the stable was now occupied by more than horses. And they were up damn early. A glance at the one small window in the room showed it was barely dawn.

"Sir Ambrose just might be jealous, but I don't care. I can ride you both."

A husky laugh accompanied those words drifting through his door. Devlin stifled another groan. He tried to remember what was outside the door in this back section of the stable. Two stalls, wasn't it? And with Caesar in one of them, he was surprised the stallion wasn't snorting in disapproval at the disturbance.

Devlin felt like doing more than snorting. In fact, he was getting damned angry that his sleep had been interrupted by the feminine voice that was beginning to sound familiar, though he couldn't quite place it. He was even more angry at the effect it was having on him, because it *did* sound so familiar.

"That tickles." A giggle. "So you like that, do you? I thought you might. Sir Ambrose loves it."

Devlin shot out of his bed, in the grip of an inexplicable rage now that a face had finally come to him to go with that softly purring voice. He yanked the already open door wide, but abruptly halted at that point. No lovers cavorting in the one empty stall. No man to beat to a bloody pulp. Just Megan, standing in a pool of lantern light, with Caesar nibbling sugar out of her cupped palm. She was dressed in a jade-green riding habit, her bright copper hair in a thick braid lying like a flame down the center of her back. She hadn't heard Devlin, her full attention lavished on the animal she'd been seducing with her soft words and edible enticements.

Even with her innocence before him, the rage didn't leave Devlin completely. It couldn't. It had been too hot to begin with. He wasn't even aware of its cause, since jealousy wasn't in his sphere of normal emotions. But he'd classed this female as virginal, which put her off limits for himself— and accounted for a good deal of his previous irritation with her. So that brief, damning conclusion he'd drawn when he finally recognized her voice, that she wasn't virginal after all, was in fact sharing her exquisite little body not just with the lucky fellow she was presently with, but also with the soon-to-be-jealous Sir Ambrose—that had sent him over the edge, especially since he'd been lying there with a full arousal caused by thoughts of the same female.

He realized that he'd made a mistake—a ridiculous one, to be truthful—but that didn't help to calm him either. He decided he'd had good reason to be annoyed—a mild word for what he'd felt—after he'd denied himself the pleasure of seducing her himself, only to think she was actually quite free with her favors. But she wasn't, he'd still have to deny himself, and, perversely, *that* was what was keeping his emotions on an upper level.

"What are you doing here, brat?" His sour tone matched his mood.

Megan didn't turn around, but her back straightened stiffly, telling him she recognized his voice. Her hand dropped slowly to carelessly wipe the remaining white crystals on her skirt. Caesar didn't appreciate that, his head coming completely out of the stall in search of more sugar.

"I will thank you to address me properly—"

"So don't thank me."

"—or not at all, preferably the latter."

She whirled around then, about to say more, but no words came out other than a silent "Oh" as her eyes took in the sight of Devlin wearing no more than his trousers, and those had been half unfastened for comfort, revealing a considerable amount of skin below his navel. Helplessly, curiously, almost compulsively, her eyes moved over all that bare, golden skin, skimming the wide shoulders, the long, muscle-defined arms, the broad width of chest that narrowed down in his hard leanness to a flat stomach, then hips that flared out only minimally from his waist. Black hair lay thickly over his upper chest, with only a few strands swirling about his nipples, none at all on his smooth middle, but just below the navel it grew again in a straight line that disappeared into his trousers. And below that—a thick bulge straining at the bit of material still fastened on his trousers.

Her eyes went no farther, stayed fixed with a bemused intensity on that most private area of his anatomy, and Devlin watched her breathlessly, felt his tumescence grow even more under her stimulating regard, and couldn't believe she was doing this to him again. He'd slept in his trousers for modesty's sake because the door wouldn't close. He'd be standing there bare-assed naked if he hadn't, for he'd had no thought whatsoever about clothes or lack of them when he'd bounded out of his bed to demolish her lover. Would she still be staring like that if he *was* completely naked? He had a feeling she would.

"If my door would've closed properly, you'd have more to see right now, since I usually sleep in the buff. I can still rectify that. Would you like me to take them off?"

Her eyes had snapped up to his with his first word, but they rounded now as his meaning sunk in, and before the hot color could come flooding into her cheeks, Megan bolted. But not quickly enough. The rage that had been simmering in Devlin was now joined by the passion she'd just stirred to life, unleashing a primitive impulse in him that wouldn't let her escape this time. He leaped after her, his long legs closing the distance in seconds, and before she could even think to scream, he swung her around, gathered her close, and kissed her.

She felt nothing but shock in those first moments, then fear, because of what he'd just said. Her feet weren't touching the ground, her braid was gripped at its base so she couldn't avoid the ravenous onslaught of his mouth, and her body was crushed to his, but she began to struggle anyway, pounding at his shoulders and arms, unable to reach his chest because she was pressed too hard to it.

She didn't like what he was doing to her. His mouth was hurting hers. The arm holding her up was going to crack one of her ribs, she was certain. She was losing a good many hairs at her nape because of her own struggles and his grip that wouldn't loosen the tiniest bit. And she couldn't breathe, had actual visions of expiring of suffocation. Fortunately, self-preservation forced air through her nose right when she was starting to see dots before her eyes, but that only solved one of her discomforts. So she continued to punch, to push, to yank at his hair, but he ignored all her efforts and continued to grind his mouth down on hers.

It took Devlin a long while to realize that the woman in his arms was actually fighting him, seriously fighting him, without the least bit of pretense about it. It was such a unique experience, but then so was his complete loss of control, which had kept him from even noticing that his unbridled passion wasn't being reciprocated. But he *had* noticed finally, and his head came up so he could look down at the object of his madness. No tears, but something more than wariness in those big blue eyes, more like fear.

"You hurt me," she said in a small, accusing voice.

Good God, had he really? What the bloody hell was this woman doing to him, that he could behave in a manner so alien to his own nature?

"I'm sorry." And he was, sincerely, at least for hurting her. "But I went to bed with you on my mind, woke up hearing your voice, and I'm afraid having you caress me with those lovely eyes of yours again destroyed my common sense."

That sounded like a complaint to her ears instead of an apology, and one that put her at fault for what he'd just done to her. But it took care of her fear, swiftly replacing it with rising fury.

She was about to blast him with that new emotion when he added, "How did I hurt you?"

Angry that he didn't know, her eyes flared but she was quick to enlighten him, especially since his hold on her still hadn't slackened. "You're breaking my back. You've probably pulled out most of my hair. And if my lips haven't been shredded on my own teeth, I'd be surprised."

To his own ears, those sounded suspiciously like the petty complaints of a sulking young miss who didn't know the first thing about passion. But a slap would have been preferable to a man known for his finesse in the bedroom. He was insulted. He was reminded of why he'd always avoided virgins like the plague. He was also reminded that she *was* an innocent young miss, but one begging to have that fact changed by her very brazen behavior. All told, he absolved himself of guilt as well as amends-making, which he no longer felt she deserved. He wished he could rid himself of his lust as easily, but it was still running rampant, and was partly responsible for the pique that wouldn't let him apologize again.

"Incidentals, certainly," he replied to her charges, though he did set her on her feet to adjust his hold on her, which he had no thought of relinquishing just yet. "This is what you get for eating me with your eyes."

"I didn't!" she gasped.

"You did. And it's what you'll get the next time you do it, and the next. If you keep it up, you might eventually learn how to kiss a man properly."

He wanted to hurt her at that point, because he was hurting so badly with wanting her. And he'd come to his senses already, so he knew he'd go on hurting, that he couldn't, *wouldn't*, do anything more than kiss her. The warning was also designed to make her stay the hell away from him, because he had no doubt whatsoever that he wouldn't be able to withstand a steady dose of Miss Penworthy's unusual brand of enticement.

Her response was a heated "I hate you!" which actually made Devlin grin.

"I'd be wounded, devastated," he told her, the grin still on his lips putting the lie to those words, "except you haven't asked me to let you go yet, have you, which you should have done—if you really hate me."

"Let me!—"

"Too late."

And his mouth came down on hers again, only there was a wealth of difference in this kiss. Cognizant of her innocence this time, keeping it firmly in mind, he brought his own experience to bear, coaxing, gently persuading, enticing her mouth to open, and, when it finally did, swooping in to claim the prize. Good God, she was exquisitely sweet.

He received only two more punches before her hands were clinging to his arms instead. Her stiffness relaxed, letting her soft curves melt into his hardness, a response he was more accustomed to. But it made him want to thrust his tongue deep, to tap her passion, only he was afraid it would have the opposite effect on a virgin—how should he know?—so he kept a tight rein on the urge, continually cautioning himself to go slowly, carefully. He was also ready for a quick retreat if she thought to clamp her teeth down on him, but that didn't occur to her, innocent that she was.

She wasn't even participating in the kiss, was just accepting what he was doing to her, but that was perfectly fine with Devlin, for the hold he had on his passion was so tenuous, he didn't think he could bear it if she tried to kiss him back—if she even knew how. He didn't care about that either; her inexperience was all he could handle now. Her lips were soft, only slightly swollen from his previous assault, her breath sweet, her bemused acquiescence sweeter still, and her warm, pliant body . . . *God, God, give me strength.*

But Devlin's had run out, the urge simply too great to be inside her, and he couldn't stop himself from grasping her hips and pressing her against the full magnitude of his need. Her gasp told him she'd never felt the like. His own body told him he was about to carry her to his bed. He needed her anger back and quickly. He needed his bloody face slapped.

He released her lips, standing there trembling, in an agony of lust, fighting to get his breath back, and his sanity. "Now you know," he said to get what he needed before he took what he really needed. "Let me know if you ever want to feel it without these clothes between us."

After a long moment of stunned silence, he got the slap he'd asked for, but it didn't have the desired effect. Instead it made him want to grab her back and kiss her again. So he switched tactics to a more direct insult.

"The proper thing for you to have done in the first place would have been to close your eyes immediately against my semi-nakedness and turn around so you wouldn't be further offended by it. But then you're not quite proper, are you, Miss Penworthy?"

Another slap, deserved or not, for he'd just spoken the bare-faced truth. And then she disappeared around the corner that would take her to the front of the stable.

Chapter 7

Megan ran all the way to the house and straight up to her room. She stood panting against her closed door, her eyes squeezed shut, her body still trembling in reaction. Finally she let out a low groan.

He'd been right, so right. She'd behaved with the utmost impropriety *again*. She should have closed her eyes the very second she realized he wasn't fully dressed. Instead she'd let that splendid male body mesmerize her into doing the unthinkable again, staring at him, "eating him with her eyes," as he'd so crudely put it. But that was just what she'd done, without thought, without a care that he was watching her do it.

It was no wonder he'd offered to take his trousers off for her. How could she blame him after she'd stared the longest at *that* part of him? All he'd done was read her mind, because she *had* wanted to see what was under those trousers.

His appendage of procreation had seemed so huge, and she'd felt it later, actually felt it right through the thickness of her skirt, pressed hard at the juncture of her thighs. The feeling it had caused at the touch of it there, fear, yes, but also the most exhilarating sensation, starting at the point he was touching and spreading, rushing, tingling to the far extremities of her body. That was something she wished she hadn't discovered, that, and that other feeling that had come in her belly the second time he kissed her.

Megan groaned again and pushed herself away from the door to pace the floor in her agitation. None of it should have happened. All she'd wanted to do was make friends with the stallion so she could eventually ride him. She'd had no desire to come across Devlin Jefferys, just the opposite, which was why she'd gone to the stable so early, hours before her usual time, because no one would be up to see her.

It had been a good plan, foiled only by a damned door latch that wouldn't close—and a light sleeper. She'd been whispering to the horse, for God's sake. That shouldn't have awakened Devlin, even with his door open. But he'd said the sound of her voice woke him. He'd also said he'd gone to bed thinking of her. Had he really? Likely not. He said so many outrageous things, after all, that half of them had to be lies just meant to shock her, for that man dearly loved to shock her.

She stopped pacing, drawn against her will to the window that overlooked the side yard—and the stable. It was set far back behind the house, but still to the side of it, so she could see the entrance clearly and anyone arriving or leaving. She heard a horse now, and expected to see Timmy, the stableboy, arriving on the old nag he rode to work each day. Instead the black stallion burst out of the stable with Devlin on his back.

She wished he were leaving for good, but knew he wasn't. The stallion wasn't even saddled, and Devlin wasn't wearing his boots. He had put on no more than a white shirt like the one he'd worn yesterday. She wished next that he would lose his perch, but she didn't get that wish either. Man and horse rode as if they were made for each other. In moments they were gone from sight, but not from her mind.

Damn him, if he weren't so devilishly handsome, she wouldn't keep making such a fool of herself. But she'd never known anyone who looked like him, who could make her so forget herself.

She *had* been unforgivably rude by staring at him again. But he'd been ruder still with that crack about dropping his trousers. He'd had no call to say that. He hadn't had to be vulgar every time he opened his mouth, either, but he had. And he certainly hadn't had to attack her. She was *not* going to take the blame for that, too. But maybe she ought to.

Hadn't he told her that staring at him like that was just like touching him? No! Megan wouldn't believe that she had provoked him. Nor would she believe his threat about kissing her again if he caught her staring at him like that. He wouldn't dare—would he? A low, despicable rogue like that? Of course he would. She never would have believed he'd have the audacity to do it in the first place, but he had. And *why* couldn't she stop thinking about it?

If only he hadn't kissed her that second time, which had been so different from the first, and so incredibly nice. She'd felt so dizzy, her stomach such a swirl of sensation. To her shame, she hadn't wanted him to stop. But he had, and no wonder. He'd told her right out that she didn't know how to kiss.

She frowned, remembering that. It was true that she had no experience in that area. The one kiss she'd had previously had been stolen by one of her local suitors, a mere peck on the lips, so brief that it was over and done with before she could decide if she liked it or not.

But she was going to be married soon. Shouldn't she know a little more about it before she did any kissing with her duke? She didn't want him to find her as lacking as Devlin did. Only now that she knew whom she was going to marry, it wouldn't be fair to encourage any other suitors who might try to kiss her, so she'd lost the opportunity to learn how to go about it. And she hadn't even paid attention when Devlin was kissing her, too caught up in what she was feeling for the first time to take note of what he was doing to make her feel that way. Nor was she about to let *him* kiss her again. That was out of the question. A horse breeder! That he had dared . . .

She was still standing there at the window when he returned shortly thereafter, his hair wet, his shirt now clinging to his damp chest. He'd gone for a swim, then? Not to *her* pond, she hoped. The very thought of him in her own private swimming hole infuriated her. It was bad enough that he was living in her stable.

Bristling anew over the man's audacity, she realized a moment later that he'd noticed her. He had stopped the stallion far short of the stable, right below her window, in fact, and was staring up at her. She stared back despite his warning, deliberately, defiantly, knowing that in her room she was safe from him and his threats. She even smiled smugly to herself.

But he continued to stare also. Even as he dismounted and moved to stand at the front of the stallion, he didn't take his eyes off her window. She began to think he was going to make a damn contest out of it, until he suddenly reached down and pulled his shirt off.

Megan gasped and yanked her draperies closed, but she could hear his husky male laughter, which was worse than his whistle yesterday—telling her he'd won another round. This was utterly intolerable. *He* was utterly intolerable. She would have to speak to her father about him. The man had to be put in his place.

Chapter 8

Megan had the opportunity to speak to her father over breakfast later that morning. She even worked out in her mind exactly what she would say, partial truths mostly, but damaging enough to get Devlin Jefferys a blistering setdown without actually warranting a dismissal, which would lose them the stallion. All she had to do was insert her account of Devlin's behavior between talk of her upcoming trip to London and her plans for today. She chickened out. She was afraid, and rightly so considering his insolence, that he would have his own accounting to give, which would paint her as culpable as he was.

She decided instead to warn Devlin of her intention if it became necessary, which she hoped it wouldn't, since she hoped not to have to speak to him again on any matter. After all, he might be under the impression that she wouldn't say anything to her father, because she hadn't said anything when she'd first asked for his dismissal, and Devlin knew that, had been listening at the door. So if he thought she *would* speak out if he wouldn't leave her alone, then he'd bloody well leave her alone.

But despite her confidence in her conclusion, Megan was still nervous when she entered the stable at her usual time after breakfast. She relaxed, however, when she saw that no one was about, not even Timmy, who usually was. She could hear noise in the back of the stable that sounded like hammering, but she wasn't about to investigate. She went straight to Sir Ambrose's stall.

She always gave her horse a quick rubdown before her ride, then a more thorough grooming when they returned. She thought about skipping the rubdown today, however, wanting to be gone as quickly as possible while Devlin still wasn't around.

"G'mornin', Miss Megan."

She started, but only for a second. "Good morning to yourself, Timmy."

"He's somethin', that Caesar, ain't he?" Timmy said as he climbed up on the stall rail to sit next to her saddle draped there.

It was their customary routine, since she didn't require his help, that he'd sit there and keep her company while she saw to her horse. It was soothing, that normalcy, and almost made her decide not to break her own routine.

"You were given a job to do, Timmy. Get to it."

Megan groaned inwardly at the sound of *that* voice. Likely Timmy did, too, for the boy responded instantly to the command in that tone, scrambling down from the stall rail and actually running to the back of the stable.

"You had no business doing that," Megan said, turning to see Devlin filling the front of the stall. "Timmy was merely keeping me company."

"Not when I've given him a job to do. He happens to be under *my* orders now."

She started to disagree about who was Timmy's ultimate employer when she realized she was looking at him. She snapped her mouth shut and turned around.

"What? No argument?"

"Go away," was all Megan said, and that in a mumble.

"Don't think I will," Devlin replied, just to be disagreeable, Megan was sure. "I live here, after all. In fact, you could say this is my house for the time being."

His cheerful tone was irritating in the extreme, but Megan managed to refrain from commenting about him and stables going hand in hand. She wasn't going to say another word to him. She was going to simply ignore him until he went away.

She moved to get her side saddle, but Devlin was suddenly behind her, his chest crowding her back as he reached for it instead. Megan turned to yank the saddle out of his hands. She got it, only because he wasn't expecting her to try to take it, but she'd yanked too hard. Her pull, along with the weight of the saddle, sent her stumbling back, and, unable to catch herself with her hands full, she landed on her backside in a small pile of hay.

She let out a screech of indignation and slapped the hand away that came down to help her up. How many times was she going to make a fool of herself in front of this man? She'd already lost count.

"I was only trying to help," he said, "since I'd sent Timmy off."

She didn't detect any laughter in his tone, but his mouth was probably grinning from ear to ear. She still wouldn't look, but *when* was he going to take the hint?

She got to her feet and dusted the straw from her riding skirt before she reached down for the saddle. Silence greeted her while she prepared Sir Ambrose for riding. She wasn't even sure Devlin was there any longer, but she still wouldn't . . .

"All right, you haven't looked at me but once since I've been standing here." His tone had turned sharp with annoyance. "Have I suddenly grown horns?"

Megan couldn't keep her mouth shut on that one. "I believe you had them already."

"Look at me when you insult me!"

She didn't, but she took a moment to explain to the dense man, "You may have forgotten your warning, Mr. Jefferys, but I haven't. I have no intention of provoking you again by looking at you."

"You're provoking me right now," he growled, then added with slightly less heat, "There's looking, and then there's *looking,* and you know which bloody kind I meant. Besides, I was angry when I said it. Chances are, the next time you stare at me like that, nothing will happen. Care to try it?"

"No."

"Just as well. That bloody pond was colder than I cared for."

She looked at him then, with acerbity. "That 'bloody' pond, Mr. Jefferys, happens to be *my* pond. I'll thank you to stay out of it."

"Then don't get my body so heated that either it's a cold dunking or I carry you off to my bed."

Her face heating, she said in a tight voice, "You can use the pond."

"I thought you might say that."

She led Sir Ambrose out of the stall and over to the mounting block, seething over the smugness in his tone.

"Stubborn brat," she heard mumbled behind her, apparently not for her ears, because he then said loudly, "You were supposed to ask for my help with that saddle."

"Whatever for? I see to my own horse, for both grooming and saddling."

"*Your* horse?"

Her eyes narrowed on his surprised expression. "You find something unusual in that?"

"Only to wonder how you came by a Thoroughbred like that."

"Sir Ambrose was a present for my twelfth birthday."

"*That's* Sir Ambrose?" He started to laugh.

Megan caught herself grinding her teeth together. "What the devil do you find so funny?"

"I hate to be the one to point this out to you, Miss Penworthy, but that horse is a female."

"I'm perfectly aware of that."

He lost his grin. "Then why the devil do you call her Sir Ambrose?"

"I named her after her previous owner, Ambrose St. James."

"Why?" he demanded sharply, frowning at her. "Had you met him? Did he look like a bloody horse?"

Megan was amazed at the sudden anger he was displaying. "No, I haven't met him yet, nor do I know what he looks like. But what difference does that make? And what business is it of yours what I call my horse?"

"None. Certainly," he replied stiffly, actually scowling at her. "Except that's a bloody stupid name to give a horse, particularly a *female* horse."

"If you ask me, Devlin's a stupid name to give a man, conjuring up images of devils and the like. Then again, I guess it suits *you* rather perfectly, doesn't it?"

His answer was to set his hands to her waist and lift her until they were eye to eye. "Do you remember what I told you I do to horses *and* women who get too feisty?" he asked in a softly menacing tone. Megan could only nod, words failing her. "You're due, Miss Penworthy."

She landed on her saddle with a jarring jolt for its being unexpected. The hard landing served to also jolt her out of that brief moment of intimidation he'd made her feel. But Devlin hadn't waited around for her to recover her temper. So Megan merely stared after the odious man as he sauntered back into the stable, his latest threat making her seethe.

He wouldn't dare lay a hand on her hindquarters. He'd better *not* dare. She had a good mind to follow after him and tell him so—only that tone he'd used was still ringing in her ears. Maybe she would tell him another time. Yes, some other time, when she wasn't so . . . mad.

Chapter 9

"Pink?" Devlin said as he stared at the drapery Mortimer had just hung over the single window in his new bedroom. "That was the best you could find? Pink?"

"I was lucky to find anything at all ready-made in a village the size of Teadale. And I don't know what you're complaining about. This room needed a little brightening."

The room needed to be torched, in Devlin's disgruntled opinion. "Did you fix the door latch?"

"Right 'n' tight. Some rugs will be delivered later today."

"No carpeting available?"

"Not in Teadale."

Devlin sighed, feeling extremely put-upon. *It'll do you a world of good,* Duchy had assured him. *Might even teach you some humility, which you're sadly lacking, dear boy.* Duchy hadn't seen the squire's stable, however, which had been uninhabited by human occupants for a goodly number of years. Even Timmy would rather go home each night to his mother's over crowded cottage than sleep in one of the two small rooms that had once been used by stable grooms, but were now used only for storage. Devlin had found it incredible that a man of the squire's consequence had no more than one stableboy, and only four horses.

"Some paint on these bare walls would be appreciated," Devlin said. *"Not pink."*

"You'll have to sleep with the smell," Mortimer warned.

"I'm sleeping in a bloody stable," Devlin replied pointedly.

Mortimer chuckled. "You're right. One more noxious odor won't make much difference."

Devlin saw nothing humorous about it. He had a mind to throw caution to the wind and abide at the inn with Mortimer, but Duchy's warning to stay out of public houses was still prominent in his mind. When the devil was he going to learn how to say no to Duchy?

"I will need more shirts," Devlin said, looking down in disgust at a white sleeve that was already stained. "At least a dozen."

"Didn't I warn you gentleman's white didn't belong in a stable?"

"Just send for them, Mr. Browne, and while you're at it, find out if there are any available women in the area."

"Available for what?" Mortimer asked in all innocence, but at Devlin's pointed stare, he said, "Oh," then, "Now see here, I ain't no—"

"Spare me the dramatics, Mr. Browne, or I'll—"

"Have to suffer along with the rest of us."

Devlin cocked a brow. "Struck out, did you?"

"This is a nice, quiet neighborhood. If a bloke wants a tumble around here, he has to marry to get it."

"Not even a tavern wench?" Devlin asked incredulously.

"Not even a tavern other than the taproom at the inn," Mortimer was delighted to say.

"What do I have to do, ride to London?"

"You don't dare show yourself there unless you're ready for that duel." Devlin merely glowered, so Mortimer offered, keeping the grin from his lips, "I hear tell there's a nice pond near here."

"I'm already acquainted with that bloody pond," Devlin snapped.

But now an image of Megan mounted on her Sir Ambrose came potently to his mind, thanks to the mention of his morning dunking in icy water. Sir *Ambrose*, for God's sake.

His urge had been to ride after her to make sure she didn't get hurt on such a spirited animal, but common sense said if she'd had the animal as long as she'd claimed, then she could ride it well enough. Common sense had little to do with the urge to follow her, however.

"Add a case of brandy to my order," Devlin said now in disgruntlement, then asked, "Not even one fallen dove in the whole area?"

"Not a one."

"Make that two cases of brandy."

Megan almost avoided the high meadow today, considering her bad mood. It was where Tiffany would meet her several mornings a week, to join her for her morning ride. Tiffany wasn't as enthusiastic about riding as Megan was, though she was accomplished enough, and she didn't come out every morning.

The girls had no plans to meet today. Tiffany was spontaneous about when she would show up, so Megan always included, in her daily jaunt the high meadow that lay between their respective homes, just in case.

Tiffany was already there when Megan entered the meadow, which was unusual, since Megan was early herself, her own schedule having been moved up in her haste to vacate the stable.

"It must be cleaning day to get you out of the house this early of a morning," Megan said as she drew up alongside her friend. "Or is your mother in another one of her redecorating moods?"

"Neither. I just have news that I couldn't wait to share, but I'm also dying of curiosity."

"I suppose your curiosity has to come first?"

"Absolutely." Tiffany grinned. "Especially since you didn't even come back with the carriage yesterday, but sent a footman with it. I would have come over later in the day, but my mother had already got my promise to read at her Poets Society meeting, and last night we had Tyler and his parents to dinner."

"How did that go?"

"Very well, considering how nervous I was. Now tell me, did your father *really* buy that incredible horse?"

Megan grinned. "He really did, and some mares, too, though they haven't arrived yet."

"You must be thrilled to pieces. Tyler was, too. He couldn't stop talking about that stallion last evening. Told his father all about him. They've got a wager going that it's likely a retired racer, so I wouldn't be surprised if they both stop over for a closer look sometime this week. Did you ride it yet?"

"You know ladies don't ride stallions."

"That wouldn't stop you," Tiffany replied knowingly. "Then you haven't?"

"Not yet." Megan sighed.

"What about his handsome trainer? Did you get the fellow dismissed?"

"Do you think he's handsome?"

"Divinely handsome. Don't you?"

Megan shrugged. "He has a certain attraction, I suppose, if you can overlook his rudeness, which I can't. But no, I had no luck getting rid of him. When Devlin Jefferys said he comes with the horse, he meant it literally. The damned sales agreement stipulates that he can't be fired."

"How unusual."

"It's preposterous, is what it is," Megan replied, some of her anger returning just thinking about it. "You wouldn't believe the license it gives him— to be arrogant, rude, outrageous in his behavior."

"Did something else happen?"

"Yes, all of the above."

"How strange," Tiffany said thoughtfully. "Men don't usually act that way around you."

Megan stared at her friend for a moment before agreeing. "They don't, do they?"

"It sounds almost like how you behaved toward Tyler."

Megan stared a bit longer before agreeing again. "It does, doesn't it?"

"Well, Mr. Jefferys *is* a bit more handsome than most," Tiffany pointed out. "Do you think he has the same problem you do, of having every woman he meets fall in love with him?"

Megan said, straight-faced, "Not every woman I meet falls in love with me."

Tiffany burst out laughing. "You know what I meant."

"Yes, but the fact remains that Mr. Jefferys isn't the least bit lovable."

"Neither were you to Tyler. Just the opposite."

True, but Megan couldn't see a man making use of the same ruse. Deliberate? All those insults deliberate? Even the kiss no more than a means to another insult?

Reminded of the kiss, Megan said, "I really don't want to discuss that horse breeder. It has occurred to me that I have somewhat of a problem that you might be able to help me with. I don't know the first thing about kissing."

"Kissing?" Tiffany said blankly.

"Yes, how to go about it. I think I should know before I meet my duke, don't you?"

"Not necessarily—now, wait a minute. You don't expect *me* to teach you, do you?"

"Don't be a goose. But you do happen to know more about it than I. Did Tyler teach you? Did it come naturally? Did it take practice?"

"Practice, yes. Tyler didn't know he was teaching me, but he was. And no, I wouldn't say it comes naturally, since I was too nervous to enjoy it the first few times, though now it does seem like I always knew how. But—Meg, we don't do any *serious* kissing, you know, just brief kisses good-bye and hello, and that only when no one is looking, as you well know."

Megan was the one who, as Tiffany and Tyler's chaperon, had turned her head away more than once so no one would be looking, so she was grinning when she asked, "But has he put his tongue in your mouth yet?"

"Megan! However did you learn about that?"

"Quite by accident, I assure you," Megan replied evasively. "Well, has he?"

"No, but Tyler has mentioned it, to warn me, he said, so I wouldn't be alarmed if he ever got carried away and did it. He also said that after we're married, well, that that kind of kissing is part of—"

"That?" Megan whispered.

"Yes, *that*. But it sounds rather disgusting, if you ask me."

"It's not actually."

Tiffany's eyes rounded. "Megan Penworthy, who put his tongue in your mouth?"

"Did I say—?"

"You didn't have to."

"Oh, all right," Megan grumbled. "Devlin Jefferys did, and before you ask why I didn't mention it, it's because I get furious every time I think about it."

"The *horse breeder?*"

"I *told* you his behavior was outrageous. And he blamed it on me because I was staring at him."

"Were you? Staring at him?"

"Let me ask you this first. If a man appeared before you half naked, would you turn around immediately?"

"Are you joking?" Tiffany chuckled. "I'd probably look a bit before I turned around."

"Well, I forgot to turn around at all."

"You saw him naked!?"

"Half naked, and I can see I'm going to have to explain everything." It took a while, but when she'd finished, Megan said, "Maybe you're right, that he's doing it deliberately. Do you think I ought to tell him that he needn't worry, that my heart is soon to be spoken for?"

"I think you ought to tell your father instead."

"If I do, we're going to lose that stallion. Father will dismiss him instantly."

"Well, that's a coil, isn't it?" Tiffany said indignantly. "Damned if you do or don't. There has to be something that we can do to make him mind his manners."

"We?" Megan grinned.

"Well, now that you've told me—"

"You aren't to worry about it. I've decided to ignore him, and if that doesn't work, then I will tell him that I'm going to marry St. James. No one in their right mind would dare tempt the ire of an all-powerful duke, even an unprincipled rogue like Jefferys. For whatever reason they began, the insults will stop immediately with that disclosure, you mark my words."

"You're undoubtedly right. You might even get some groveling out of him in his haste to make amends to the future Duchess of Wrothston."

"Groveling isn't necessary. I'll settle for seeing his shocked expression along with Lady O's the day I return in the ducal coach."

Tiffany suddenly gasped. "I almost forgot my news—which, by the way, is going to get you closer to that day of reckoning. My mother received invites to a pre-Season masked ball from her old friend Elizabeth Leighton. And my father's *Times* that arrived yesterday had a mention of the very same ball because of the notables on the guest list, which includes—"

"Him?" Megan squealed in delight. "And here I've been agonizing on *how* I would manage to meet him. Your mother *is* going to accept, isn't she?"

"I believe she can be persuaded."

"And I can go with you?"

"Would I go without you?"

"There, you see? Fate is pushing me in the right direction. It's almost as if it weren't my decision a'tall, but preordained. Where is it? When?"

"The Leightons live in Hampshire, and the ball is next week—now don't look so horrified, Meg. That's plenty time to prepare—"

"Not for a new gown."

"You've plenty—"

"This one has to be special. I'm catching a duke, Tiff, a *duke.*"

"You're right," Tiffany conceded. "There's no point in taking chances with this preordained stuff. I'll race you to—"

"I'll meet you," Megan called over her shoulder as she took off. "I'm too anxious to hold Sir Am—"

Tiffany couldn't hear the rest, but didn't need to, just as she didn't need to have it clarified that she would find Megan at Miss Whipple's shop, their village seamstress. Mind reading was only one of the benefits of having a very close friend.

Chapter 10

Having found a lovely green poult-de-soie silk along with white tulle to fashion a stunning new ball gown, Megan was in high spirits when she returned home late that afternoon. Understandably, she was loath to ruin her good mood with a trip to the stable, even to return Sir Ambrose. But grooming her horse was a joy to her that she wasn't going to give up either. So for the first time, she sent a servant around to the stable to collect Sir Ambrose's grooming apparatus, and proceeded to tend her horse right there in the front yard in the shade of a hickory tree.

Ten minutes after she began, Devlin Jefferys showed up. "Just what do you think you're doing?" he demanded without preamble.

His appearance wasn't as detrimental to Megan's good mood as she'd thought it would be. His own mood seemed to have soured with her presence, however, or had he been brooding all day? He certainly looked irritated at the moment. The thought brought a half smile to Megan's lips.

"Why, whatever does it look like I'm doing, Mr. Jefferys? Surely it's rather obvious, isn't it?"

Her half-condescending, half-effervescent tone had him gritting his teeth. "Timmy can do that."

"Certainly he can, but I enjoy doing it myself. Didn't I make that clear this morning?"

"Then why aren't you doing it where it should be done, instead of making a spectacle of yourself on your front lawn?"

"Spectacle? Without an audience? Come now, let's not exaggerate. And why I'm not in the stable should also be quite obvious. I was trying to avoid your very unpleasant company. So just what are you doing out here, ruining a perfectly good plan?"

He stared at her for a long moment before he shoved his hands in his pockets and said in a low mumble, "It was not my intention to run you out of your own stable."

That was an outright lie, but Devlin had spent the afternoon bored to tears; the only thing he'd had to look forward to was Megan's return. He hadn't thought she would try to avoid him entirely. He had counted on her entrenching and fighting to the bitter end—as anyone with that red hair would—and he had bloody well been looking forward to it.

But now? "Perhaps I owe you an apology," he said, the words a mere whisper, sour on his tongue.

"More than one, but who's counting?"

Oh, she's asking for it. Give her an inch, and she thinks she can walk all over me.

"Very well, accept my apology in duplicate."

Megan managed to conceal her surprise over this amazing about-face. Of course, he didn't sound the least bit sincere in his apology, sounded more like it was being forced out of him at the point of some gruesome consequence. She took a moment to wonder what he found so loathsome that an apology to her was the lesser evil. And in that case, why even bother?

But on the oft chance that he really was offering her an olive branch and was merely being churlish about it, she said, "I'm not sure a simple apology will suffice for what—" She paused, noting the tensing of his body, the drawing together of his black brows. *This round to me, Mr. Jefferys,* she thought smugly to herself before giving him a bright smile. "But on the other hand, I am presently in much too good a mood to hold grudges, so I accept your apology—in duplicate."

Devlin barely heard her. He was still trying to recover from the staggering effect of the smile she'd just given him. Who would have thought two dimples could be such disarming weapons? He was bemused, his thoughts gone adrift, his tongue tied in knots. He felt as if he'd been knocked on his arse.

That girl ought to have freckles, he thought in pure disgruntlement. Why the devil didn't she? There ought to be *something* to counteract a smile like that, which made a man want to wrap his arms around her and protect her for the rest of his days.

Devlin shook himself mentally. At her expectant expression, he merely nodded, and curtly at that, annoyed now that he wasn't even sure if she'd accepted his apology or not. But he wasn't going to ask her to repeat what she'd said. He moved around her to lean against the tree trunk and watch her. If she'd refused his apology, she'd have more to say, wouldn't she? At the very least, she'd ask him to go away. She didn't. What she did was ignore the fact that he was still there.

The devil. Now that he'd got the temporary cease-fire that he hadn't really wanted—if he had got it—he didn't know what to say to the girl. The normal conversation he'd offer one of her class would sound ridiculous coming from a "horse breeder." Besides, he rather liked being the horse breeder with her. It gave him freedom in his speech that he ordinarily wouldn't have. A rare pleasure, that, not having to guard his tongue or his temper.

"I'm going to a ball this week in Hampshire, a masked ball."

Devlin's brows rose at that unsolicited statement. "Now, why are you telling *me* that?"

Megan shrugged. "I'm just excited about it. I felt like telling you."

"You mean you felt like rubbing my nose in it, since it's not something I'd be invited to."

"That, too." She peeked at him from beneath her lashes. "Is your nose especially sore?"

Devlin just managed to choke down a burst of laughter. "Not especially. I've been to a ball or two."

"What?" she scoffed. "Those public masked balls at Covent Garden?"

"How did you guess?" he replied dryly.

"That's not the same as rubbing shoulders with dukes and earls."

"You have me there, brat—now, don't get your hackles up, Miss Penworthy. That just slipped out."

She didn't comment. She went back to rubbing down the mare with a bit more vigor. Devlin grinned, watching her pointedly ignore him again. She sparkled when she was mad. Her cheeks bloomed, her eyes brightened. He imagined she would look just so in the heat of . . . The tightening in his loins forced him to squelch that thought.

"What's so special about this ball in Hampshire?" Devlin thought to ask. "I'd think you'd be more excited about your Season in London, which is shortly to occur."

Megan turned to give him her full attention. "How did you know I am to have a Season?"

"Doesn't every young girl your age hie herself off to London in search of a husband?"

"Not every one, no. I may not go myself if everything goes well in Hampshire—oh, except for Tiffany's wedding. I'll have to go for that, but—"

"If what goes well in Hampshire?" Devlin asked a bit more harshly than he realized. "Are you anticipating a proposal?"

"Good heavens, no." Megan laughed. "I'll only be meeting him for the first time. My hopes are high, but not *that* high."

"In other words, you've already picked him out, but he doesn't know it. Who is this poor sod you've set your cap for?"

"I'll thank you to keep a respectful tone when you speak of my future husband."

"So don't thank me," Devlin snapped, then: "You aren't joking, are you? You really intend to marry a man you haven't even met?"

"Yes," she replied stiffly. "So you can stop worrying, Mr. Jefferys. My heart will soon be spoken for."

"Oh, you intend to fall in love, too, with this faceless—*do* you know what he looks like?"

"Well, no, but—"

"Aha! You're after a bloody title, aren't you?"

"So what if I am? You think it's never been done before?"

"It's done all the time, but the titled gent usually gets something he wants out of the arrangement. What have you got to offer?"

She was mortified by his sneering tone. "Well, that was a short truce, wasn't it?" She turned away to lead Sir Ambrose to the stable.

Devlin stubbornly fell into step beside her. "I'm sorry. That was uncalled-for."

"What's one more insult to add to all your others? Maybe Tiffany was right and it's a habit with you, to keep women from 'falling at your feet.' But as I said, you needn't worry about me doing any 'falling,' Mr. Jefferys. It was a ridiculous assumption on your part that I would—if you made it. I'm not the least bit attracted to you."

Red flag—bright, bright red. "That statement can be easily disproved. Shall I show you how?"

"Are you thinking of causing a spectacle on my front lawn?"

"We've already reached the side lawn, if you haven't noticed, and yes, I'm bloody well thinking about it," he growled.

"Well, don't. My father, who will be sure to hear about it after I scream my head off, won't like it one bit. Neither will my future husband, and the Duke of Wrothston is no one to trifle—"

"*Who?*"

Megan looked back, because Devlin had stopped in his tracks. She was delighted by his shocked expression. "I thought that might give you pause," she said smugly.

"Did I hear you right?"

"You did. I will be married to Ambrose St. James, the present Duke of Wrothston, before the year is out. And you, Mr. Jefferys, will not be invited to the wedding."

"Why . . . *him?*"

"Why not? I happen to like his stable."

"You like his—"

He ended up sputtering, so Megan shrugged and went on without him. The little man Devlin had arrived with was at the front of the stable as she led Sir Ambrose to his stall.

"Good day to you, Miss," he said respectfully, doffing his hat.

"Good day to yourself, Mr.—Browne, isn't it?"

"Yes, Miss."

"And how is our fine stallion today?"

"Caesar is in fine fettle, just fine."

She turned to Devlin, sensing his presence behind her. She decided to take advantage of the present regret and anxiety she was sure he was experiencing, now that he knew what a powerful man she would soon be married to.

"I want to ride the stallion."

"No."

"Just like that? No?"

"Your hearing is excellent."

So much for her assumption. "You're impossible!" she told him before she stalked out of the stable.

"I'm impossible?" Devlin said, glancing at Mortimer. "She's got her husband all picked out, Mr. Browne. Hasn't met him yet, but she's got her cap set for him. Guess who it is."

"Someone you know?"

"Yes, I know him. I bloody well know him. She thinks she's going to marry the Duke of Wrothston."

"But—" Mortimer's eyes rounded. *"You* are the Duke of Wrothston."

"So I am."

Chapter 11

❧❧❧❧❧   ❧❧❧❧❧

Ambrose Devlin St. James, fourth Duke of Wrothston and a slew of lesser titles, was at the moment immersed in physical labor of the menial sort. He was pitching hay, and doing it with a vengeance, but also with a mindless sort of detachment that made him unaware of the soreness developing in his hands or the sweat soaking into his fine lawn shirt.

He had begun the labor in an effort to keep from smashing his fist through a wall, which was what he'd had the urge to do after his latest encounter with Megan Penworthy—and her most startling revelations. Pitching hay, however, did not take his mind off the encounter as he'd assumed it would. Just the opposite. The exertion seemed to fuel his anger with every pitch.

So she was going to marry him, was she? Over his dead body. The nerve of that girl. The bloody audacity, to set her sights on him before she'd even met him. At least the other women who'd coveted his title, and he'd lost count of their number, had wanted him for himself just as much if not more. He ought to be used to it by now, but damned if he was. Besides, Megan's case was unique. He could be a wastrel or the veriest saint, and she wouldn't care, because it wasn't the man she was after to marry, it was the bloody title. Good God, she'd even admitted it, and without the least embarrassment over owning up to such a cold-blooded aspiration.

He had taken her for spoiled, willful, hot-tempered even, but not for opportunistic. And when he thought of what could have happened if not for Freddy's temper and his need to absent himself because of it . . .

He didn't recall accepting an invitation to a ball in Hampshire, but then he accepted a good many invites that he promptly forgot and needed his secretary to remind him of. So it wasn't unreasonable to assume that if he were home where he should be, instead of playing the coward at Duchy's insistence, he would have gone to that ball in Hampshire, met Megan there under entirely different circumstances, and just might have succumbed to that devastating smile of hers without the least suspicion that she was a conniving little adventuress out to snare his title.

The thought chilled him to the bone—and enraged him. He ought to show up at that damn ball and give Megan just what she deserved, a callous rake, a dissipated rogue, a cad of the first water to scare the very drawers off the girl. But if she thought he'd be there, then a rumor had to be making the rounds that he was expected, which meant Freddy would hear of it. And although Devlin's disappearance would lead Freddy to assume he wouldn't show up at such a public affair, Freddy wouldn't take any chances. He'd be there with his pistols primed just in case. Not enough time had passed for Devlin to hope otherwise.

But how much time *would* be enough? Two months, according to Duchy. "The gel will be desperate by then, if she really has got herself with child. She'll be forced to give up the real father's name, or to accept whomever her brother finds to marry her. Can't see Sabrina Richardson doing *that*, as willful and vain as she is, but Freddy will insist. He won't let the matter go just because you can't be found. He'll have to marry her off, which will leave you with only the one problem, instead of two."

The second had been how to avoid the altar with Freddy's scheming little sister, Sabrina, while the first one remained how to avoid getting his head blown off by his best friend. But two months was a long time to rusticate. Devlin was hoping Freddy would use his head before then and remember that Devlin didn't even like his damn sister, so he certainly wouldn't have seduced the chit and got her with child as she claimed.

The irony suddenly struck him that he was here to avoid marriage with one scheming young miss, only to run smack into another. The one was using lies to get him to the altar, the other would use a devastating smile—or would she? Just how did Megan Penworthy think to win him? How far would she go to get him and his stable? His *stable*, for God's sake. That was the most infuriating and insulting thing of all, that she'd picked him because she liked his damn stable. Oh, and he mustn't forget that he, Devlin Jefferys, wouldn't be invited to the wedding. Well, he'd bloody well like to see her have it without him.

"Is there a purpose to what you're doing?"

Devlin glanced back to see Mortimer leaning against one of the horse stalls, calmly surveying his handiwork. Devlin looked around at the hay scattered everywhere—on the horses, in the water, on himself. But he raised a brow in his most haughty manner, and endeavored to ignore the stinging heat in his hands that he was finally aware of.

"There is always a purpose to what I do, Mr. Browne. This one just escapes me at the moment."

Mortimer gave a hoot of laughter. "She got to you, did she?"

"No, she did not," Devlin denied emphatically. "It's this idleness that is getting to me, if you must know. Something will have to be done, Mr. Browne."

"Like what?" Mortimer asked warily.

"We can begin by enlarging this stable."

"We?"

"Find us a master carpenter, but we will help."

"You didn't do too well with a pitchfork. What makes you think you can do better with a hammer?"

Devlin didn't deign to answer that. "And send word to my secretary to have my correspondence forwarded here. In fact, tell Mr. Pike to come himself. There's no reason I can't conduct my business from—"

"Your grandmother isn't going to like this one bit," Mortimer warned.

"Duchy means well, but she doesn't always know what's best for me. She felt I could use the rest. I agreed at the time, but I've bloody well changed my mind. Resting here is driving me nearly mad."

"It ain't rest that's driving you mad, it's that—"

"Don't contradict me, Mr. Browne. Just carry out my instructions."

"And how do you expect to explain Mr. Pike, who don't know how to be anything but condescending after working for you for so long?"

Mortimer had a point. Devlin's secretary was as toplofty as any lord, and wouldn't know the first thing about dissembling.

"Very well, just the correspondence will do for now—and the carpenter. We'll start on the stable tomorrow."

"Don't you think you ought to get the squire's permission first?"

Devlin sighed. He wasn't used to obtaining permission from anybody for anything. For a moment there, he had forgotten the role he was playing. It had been pleasant to forget.

"I'll speak to the squire, but I don't foresee any problems, since I will be paying for any improvements myself."

"Unnecessary improvements," Mortimer grumbled, "Since you and the extra horses won't be here long enough to enjoy them."

"Incidentals, Mr. Browne. I need the work. I need to keep busy. See to it."

Chapter 12

The study door opened just as Megan reached the bottom of the stairs. She started to call out a greeting to her father, but it was Devlin who stepped out instead. She was on her way to the stable for her morning ride, but she hadn't quite prepared herself for another encounter with this man. And it definitely took some preparation.

Once again he was wearing gentleman's white in his shirt—her father must be paying him too much—tucked into unfashionably snug black trousers—bloody show-off. Didn't he know tight trousers had died with the renowned Beau Brummell? All he needed was the neckcloth to look like a gentleman, too much like a gentleman, for he already had the bearing—and the arrogance.

"Well, good morning, Miss Penworthy."

He was actually going to be civil? *Careful, Megan, don't faint.*

"Good morning to yourself, Mr. Jefferys."

"The mares should be arriving sometime today," he remarked offhandedly.

"I suppose I won't be allowed to ride them either?" she asked, trying to keep her resentment out of her tone, but not succeeding at all.

"I don't see why not."

His answer caught her off guard, taking some of the stiffness out of her stance. "Then why can't I ride Caesar?"

"He's not a lady's mount. If you want to ride him, you'll have to ride double with me."

"That's out of the . . . all right."

Changing her mind in mid-sentence managed to catch Devlin off guard this time. "You surprise me, Megan. You do realize, don't you, that riding double means you'll have to put your arms around me?"

She hadn't thought of that, but she wasn't about to admit it. "Yes, certainly."

"Are you sure you can bear to touch me?"

"You show me what that horse can do, and I won't even notice that I'm touching you."

"Well, I'll bloody well notice."

Megan stiffened at his sudden surliness. "If you can't bear it yourself, why did you make the offer?"

"Because I didn't think you'd accept."

He sounded so little-boy sulky, she couldn't resist grinning, or taunting, "You aren't going to be a spoilsport about this, are you? You made the offer. I accepted the offer. And I'll have that ride now, if you please."

He scowled after her as she sashayed past him and went out to the stable. He didn't please, not one little bit. But he'd give her her ride. He'd let Caesar take the bit and give her the ride of her life. And if he survived it, he'd bloody well keep his mouth shut from now on.

Caesar was in top form, and game to prove it. The countryside sped past, a blur of greens, browns, and the occasional bright splash of wildflowers. And Megan laughed. She laughed in delight and exhilaration, thrilling to the speed and grace of the powerful stallion beneath them.

Devlin had guessed the ride would be pure hell for himself, however, and it was. Her arms wrapped tight about his waist was bad enough, but he had prepared for that and endeavored to ignore it. Her breasts pressed into his back was worse, but he could withstand it, his blood only thrumming in slow pulsebeats that kept him just short of actual arousal. But the laughter was doing him in. Her enjoyment was an incredible aphrodisiac, a husky tremor that vibrated straight to his loins.

By the time he circled back and came to the secluded pond that Megan termed hers, he was in as much discomfort as he had been the previous morning when he had stumbled upon this swimming hole and made quick use of it. He stopped and dismounted now, abruptly moving off without helping Megan to do the same. He needed distance at the moment, and took it by rounding the small pond until he was on the opposite bank. There he shoved his hands in his pockets and stood facing the cluster of white oaks and elms that formed a three-quarter circle around the pond. He closed his eyes, making an effort to forget that he wasn't alone. His companion wouldn't let him.

"You're very brave to leave me sitting on this animal," Megan called out. He didn't mistake her meaning. "That isn't a sidesaddle, Megan."

It annoyed her that he had twice now used her given name without permission, but she let it pass again. It annoyed her also that she was being rudely ignored, and that she didn't let pass.

"A little thing like that wouldn't stop me if I was of a mind to continue this ride without you."

That got him to turn and face her, and she found his scowl quite satisfying, until he said, "I'll wager your father has never laid a disciplinary hand on you, has he?"

She didn't mistake *his* meaning. "You wouldn't dare. You'd be dismissed instantly."

"I believe you know I would dare. Care to put it to the test?"

With the pond between them and the stallion beneath her, Megan raised her chin a notch. But she still wasn't up to calling him on that particular subject.

"Do you make an effort to be unpleasant, Mr. Jefferys, or does it come naturally?"

"The only effort I'm making right now, brat, is to keep my hands off you. So don't push it."

She thought he was referring to the last subject, until she caught the look in his eyes. He wanted her again. The knowledge should have offended her, but it didn't. It gave her a warm, tingling feeling instead, and brought on a boldness that she wasn't quite accustomed to.

"Perhaps you ought to have a swim," she suggested, remembering yesterday morning and the reason he had given for coming here.

"Perhaps I should." After a long pause he asked, "Will you watch?"

"Will you kiss me again if I do?"

"If you're that brazen, I'll do more than kiss you," he promised.

She was getting into the realm of the unknown now. Common sense insisted upon retreat. Yet when he slowly reached out to lift his shirt over his head, she didn't take her eyes off him. Would he really strip down to nothing right there in front of her? The impropriety of it was scandalous. *He* was scandalous—but so beautiful, like a piece of fine art. Were he a statue, she could admire him for hours upon hours. But he was real, and audacious, and Megan knew instinctively that she was playing with fire each time she got near him.

She must have been mad to think she could test her wings and play the coquette with him. A gentleman knew his limitations. Devlin Jefferys had none. But it was so unfair that her curiosity couldn't be appeased this easily, that there had to be an unacceptable consequence for it. She wanted to keep watching Devlin, she really did. To be honest, she wanted to find out what he meant by "more" than a kiss, too. But she didn't dare do either. So when those long fingers of his started unfastening his trousers, Megan promptly turned her back on him.

"Coward," she heard softly whispered.

"Prudent," she countered. "And in the name of decency, put your clothes back on, Mr. Jefferys."

"I'm only taking your suggestion, Miss Prudence," he reminded her.

"I didn't mean for you to swim naked."

"I'm not partial to wet clothes," he retorted.

"Then don't swim."

"Are you suggesting the alternative, Megan? Because after you just caressed me with your eyes again, it's got to be one or the other."

These sexual innuendos were exciting, but far beyond Megan's limited experience. Fortunately, he couldn't see the color that stole into her cheeks, but it was still embarrassing that he could so easily fluster her.

"Swim if you must, then," she conceded, "but do be quick about it."

She heard a splash accompanied by a sharp hiss and smiled to herself. The water was usually icy in the early morning, which was why she never swam until the afternoon, when it had warmed up considerably.

"I could have told you it would be cold," she said.

"Don't sound so smug, brat. Cooling off is what I needed, remember?"

"Must everything you say allude to—to—?"

"The day will come when you're in the same condition as I, and when you are, you won't feel like discussing the weather, believe me."

"I believe I'll have more sense than to get myself in that condition," she said primly.

Devlin gave a hoot of laughter before he realized something. "Were you implying I don't have any sense?"

"Was it so obvious?"

"I've got news for you, Miss Innocence. Desire isn't selective of place, time, or the individual. If you think I *like* being aroused by you, think again. When it happens to you, and it will eventually, you won't have any more control over it than I do. You either make love or suffer with it."

Her curiosity about this subject got the better of her. "Does that mean I'll have to dunk myself in icy water?"

"Actually, I don't know if that would work for a woman. Never thought to ask. Would you like to conduct a little experiment to find out?"

"How?"

"I make you want me, then you find out if this pond can alleviate the problem."

"I'm not allowing you *can* make me want you, but in either case, I have more sense than to swim with you around, so no, thank you."

"Smart girl."

More splashing indicated that he might be leaving the pond. Megan continued to resist looking behind her, but it wasn't easy.

When the splashing ended, she asked, "You were just funning me, weren't you, Mr. Jefferys?"

" 'Fraid not."

She chose not to believe him. Her curiosity was piqued enough. She didn't need even more improper things to wonder about.

After a while she finally demanded impatiently, "Are you dressed yet?"

He said right behind her, "You mean you didn't peek even once?"

She turned to see that he hadn't submerged completely. His clothes were damp only from the waist down. But even in that briefest glance down his long frame, she noted that the bulge in his trousers hadn't diminished very much.

As usual, he caught the direction of her gaze.

"It didn't work." He stated the obvious. "But then how could it when all you could talk about was sex?"

She gasped at that accusation. "Me? *You* were the one. You even admitted it."

"Shows what a bloody fool I am," he said tersely as he mounted again in front of her and set off at an easy gait so she wouldn't have to hold on tight.

Megan didn't know why she had even attempted conversation with this man. They had nothing in common—well, nothing except horses, and that was a safe enough subject.

"Even though you have been typically outrageous, I still thank you for the ride. Caesar is magnificent, the finest, the fastest . . . where does he come from anyway?"

"Sherring Cross."

She stared at his back incredulously. "I should have known. There are no finer stables in the land."

"I grew up in those same stables you've got such praise for."

"You didn't," she scoffed.

"Very well, I didn't."

A full five minutes passed before she broke down to ask, "Do you know him, then?"

"Who?"

"You know very well who," she admonished impatiently. "The duke."

"I thought I did."

"What the devil does that mean?"

"It means the man has changed, Megan. He's become a bounder, a cad, a seducer of innocents."

She leaned away from him, affronted. "You're a liar, Mr. Jefferys. And I'll thank you to keep a respectful tone when you mention the duke."

"So don't thank me."

Chapter 13

That afternoon, Devlin was the only one in the front of the stable when a well-dressed young gentleman walked his horse in and tossed the reins to him.

"New, aren't you?" Devlin was asked.

"To my great misfortune," Devlin mumbled under his breath, but louder he said, "If you're here to see the squire—"

"Miss Penworthy, if it's all the same to you," the chap replied disdainfully on his way out.

Devlin stared at the reins in his hands, wondering if he looked like a bloody stableboy. "Timmy!" he bellowed.

So she was having callers, was she? That was nothing to him—except, what the devil was she doing receiving callers when she'd already decided to marry him—the duke? He had a good mind to go over to the manor and let that chap know that she was almost spoken for . . . at least, in her mind she was.

He was standing at the entrance to the stable, staring up at her empty window when another man rode up. This one was older, heavyset, but decked out in his Sunday best, his hair slicked down with Macassar oil. Again Devlin got tossed the reins to the horse.

"The squire ain't here," he heard himself saying quite churlishly.

"Ain't here to see the squire," was the fellow's amiable reply.

"You still might want to come back another time. Miss Megan already has a caller."

"Not surprised," the man said. "She usually does. But I come in handy. Had to break up a fight once between two of her more jealous suitors. Also had to toss Aldrich Little out when he started bawling after she turned him down. Made quite a spectacle of himself. Upset the poor girl for months."

"If you're still calling, then you haven't proposed to her yourself?"

" 'Course I have. But I'm not easily dissuaded. I come 'round once every month to ask her again. It could be just a matter of mood, don't you know. Catch her at the right time and I might get lucky."

The fellow was too likable to dislike, but that didn't mean Devlin liked the situation one little bit. A matter of mood? Was she playing them all along? Did she thrive on the attention?

When he remembered that incredible, highly inflaming conversation he'd had with her at the pond this morning, he couldn't help wondering if she wasn't as provocative with all her suitors. Was even her innocence a ruse? *I believe I'll have more sense than to get myself in that condition,* she'd said. No, only an innocent could say something that ridiculous. And to be honest, he'd had a devil goading him this morning, because he hadn't affected her the way she had him. She'd merely enjoyed the ride, while he'd suffered acute discomfort from it. So maybe he had instigated the whole improper situation. After all, what other innocent young miss would he have stripped naked in front of, daring her to watch, hoping she would so he'd have an excuse to behave even more improperly?

Good God, had he really done that? He was twenty-nine years old and he'd never in his life behaved so irresponsibly. What was it about that girl that made him forget a lifetime of good breeding and turn into the cad, the bounder, the seducer of innocents that he'd accused himself of being—and to which she'd defended him? Bloody hell, she had actually defended him! 'Course, she had to, didn't she, after she'd claimed she was going to marry him? Matter of principle, that. Nothing personal. How could it be personal, anyway, when she didn't even know him?

"I say, are you there?"

Devlin turned to find another man had come into the stable leading his horse, only this one he recognized as the blond gent who had been with Megan the day he arrived. "Toss me those reins and I may deck you."

Tyler was taken aback, but after a moment he said hesitantly, "Well, then, I suppose I'll keep them. Woolgathering, were you?"

"Was I?"

"You seemed miles away when I came in."

"Not so far as that," Devlin grumbled.

He might have been preoccupied enough not to have noticed the gent's arrival, but that didn't account for his unreasonable anger. He actually still felt like decking the man; would jump on the first excuse to do so. This one Megan didn't just entertain in her parlor, she went *riding* with him. And what else did she do with him, he'd like to know?

"I suppose you're here to see the squire's daughter?"

"I'd just as soon not. See much too much of the girl as it is."

Devlin took a step forward, unaware that his fingers had curled into fists. "Just what does that mean?"

"She's my chaperon." When that remark got only a blank stare from Devlin, Tyler explained. "I'm marrying her best friend, Tiffany Roberts, so Megan accompanies us everywhere—to my great misfortune. But Tiffany's father is old-fashioned and insisted, so what's a chap to do? It was either Megan or Tiffany's mother. Thought I was getting the better bargain, but I would have preferred the mother, believe me, if I'd known what a shrew Megan could be."

"You mean I'm not the only one she's singled out for hostility?"

Tyler chuckled. "You too? Well, don't take it to heart. She put me through hell making me wonder what I'd done to offend her when I hadn't done anything. Could have sworn she despised me. And now to find out it was all deliberate." Tyler shook his head bemusedly.

Devlin held his breath, waiting to hear the rest. "Deliberate?" he finally had to prompt.

"Every bit of it, all the derision and contempt. That girl's got a way of making a man feel about three inches tall. Couldn't understand it, but Tiffany finally confessed that it's a defense Megan uses to keep men from falling in love with her. And they do, you know. I've seen it happen again and again. For myself, she did it for Tiffany's sake, though it wasn't necessary and she's finally figured that out and ended the hostilities. I'm amazed to say she's actually a sweet girl. Damned if I was aware of it before, but she is."

Devlin was damned if he agreed. But he no longer felt like clobbering the man. He did wonder, however, why the fellow had volunteered such personal information.

Tyler was suddenly wondering the same thing as he recalled the fact of just whom he'd been speaking to. The Penworthy horse breeder. And yet there was something about the man that made Tyler feel he was in the presence of an equal rather than a servant. Servants didn't usually threaten a lord, after all, as this one had done the moment Tyler entered the stable. They didn't usually wear fine lawn shirts of a better quality than his own, either. And for someone of the servant class, the fellow wasn't all that respectful, was more in the way of condescending. Strange behavior, to say the least, but possibly accountable for Tyler's nervous chatter.

"The squire ain't home, if he's the one you're here to see," Devlin said.

"Actually, I've come by to have a look at his new stallion."

"Caesar?" Devlin suddenly smiled, clapping Tyler on the back and leading him toward the rear of the stable. "You should have said so. He's right back here."

"He's a racer, isn't he? Or he was?"

"What makes you think so?"

"I've been to the track a time or two, and that stallion seems damned familiar."

"St. James may have raced him a few times."

"The Duke of Wrothston? Good God, he's *that* Caesar? But that horse is famous! Never defeated. How on earth did Penworthy end up with him?"

"A favor owed, I believe."

"Then you used to work for St. James?"

"You could say that."

Tyler decided that explained the man's haughtiness. The more toplofty the lord, the more toplofty the servants.

"Wasn't aware the squire even knew the duke." Devlin just shrugged, but Tyler didn't notice as they came upon Caesar's stall. He whistled in admiration. "Now that's a horse worth stealing. I hope he's well protected."

"I protect what's—" Devlin had started to say "mine," but amended it to "in my charge."

"Glad to hear it, because there just happens to be a thief newly come to the area."

"A horse thief?"

Tyler shook his head. "Highwayman. Two coaches were robbed just the other night—" He broke off to stare curiously at Devlin. "The night you arrived, actually."

Devlin grinned. "Are you implying—"

"Not at all, not at all," Tyler quickly assured him. "It's obviously no more than a coincidence. But speculation will be making the rounds, so you're sure to hear about it again. It's been years since we've had a highwayman in our parish, after all, so he's guaranteed to be the topic at every tea and gathering for a while."

Later, Devlin discussed the possibility of horse thieves with Mortimer. At Sherring Cross it wasn't a problem, since he employed nearly as many grooms as he had horses. But this was country, there were no grooms, and the squire's stable left much to be desired in the way of security. Short of sleeping at Caesar's feet, which he had no inclination to do, Devlin ordered a bolt installed on the stable doors. There was no point in taking chances with a thief in the area.

Bloody hell, it wasn't something he'd ever worried about before, not until Tyler Whately—the fellow had finally got around to introducing himself— had mentioned it. The rest of what Tyler had mentioned, about Megan at least, was worth a good laugh. Imagine that girl being deliberately offensive to keep a man from falling in love with her. She'd even accused him of the same thing—because she was familiar with the ploy? She *had* been antagonistic toward him from the very first. But he didn't think for a moment that she was pretending with him. He'd been too temper-provoking himself for her hostility to be anything but real.

Yet it made him wonder how she'd behave with a man she didn't want to ward off. How, for instance, would she act with a man she'd set her cap for?

Chapter 14

"They say he has a terrible temper."

"*Where* did you hear all this gossip, Tiff?" Megan asked while staring across the ballroom at the man Tiffany had pointed out. "We only just arrived here today."

"Yes, but while you were resting this afternoon, Lady Leighton's daughter was talking my ear off."

"But how do you know who is who?"

"Because Jane dragged me into her bedroom, which overlooks the front of the house, and I swear she had something to say about every single arrival."

"But people are still arriving."

"I didn't say I know something about *everyone*, just the early—"

"Was *he* an early arrival?"

"I'm sorry, Meg, but they're not even sure he's going to come."

Megan stopped her avid perusal of the crowd to give Tiffany her full attention. Even behind the domino mask she was wearing, her distress was obvious.

"But he *has* to come!" Megan insisted with more hope than conviction. "The *Times* said he would, and who can you believe if you can't believe the *Times*?"

"I know, and he did accept the invitation, but . . . apparently your duke is somewhat absentminded when it comes to his social calendar. He'll agree to go to one affair, then promptly forget about it. Then he'll accept another invite for the same day and forget that, too—then accept another. Are you getting the picture?"

"Too many places to go on any given day?"

"Exactly. And so he won't end up offending one hostess in favor of another, he usually just skips every affair and stays home."

"How would Jane know that?"

"Because of all the times her mother has invited him, and they've lost count of how many, he's only shown up twice. She says it's also a joke in the ton, not to count on St. James to make an appearance unless no one else is counting on him to do the same."

"I don't think I like the ton making jokes about my future husband," Megan said.

Tiffany noted the stiffness in that response and quickly said, "Did I say joke? Joke is definitely not the correct word I wanted. It's simply a recognized fact, Meg, and one that even St. James acknowledges with good humor."

"Then he's not coming," Megan replied with acute disappointment.

"Now, how do we know that? This is a pre-Season ball, after all. How many invitations can be floating around?"

"It's all right, Tiffany. You don't have to bolster my spirits."

Tiffany was looking at a girl who might as well be at a funeral for all the joy in her expression. "Don't I?" she said in exasperation. "You aren't going to enjoy yourself now, are you?"

"Sure I will."

"Damn it, you won't. I know you. I'll wager you're already thinking up some excuse to retire, when we haven't even made our appearance yet."

Which was perfectly true. They had come downstairs, but had gone straight to the gallery that overlooked the ballroom, to spend a few moments observing everyone below without being observed in return. But it was still early. The orchestra that had been hired for the evening, and which was situated in the center of the gallery, was just starting its second set. And the room below contained only half the people that would be there later.

Megan smiled ruefully. "You do know me too well, don't you? But I can't help it, Tiff. The disappointment is crushing me."

"But why?" Tiffany asked, genuinely perplexed. "If you don't meet him here, you'll have another chance when you go to London for your Season."

"That's just it," Megan replied. "I was hoping to avoid that altogether."

"Avoid it?" Tiffany repeated incredulously. "You'd been looking forward to it!"

"I'd been looking forward to finding my own Tyler, which we both agreed could only be done in London. I wasn't looking forward to going to London, however."

"But why not?"

"Let's face it, Tiff, we're country girls who aren't the least bit sophisticated. I just know I'm going to make a fool of myself somehow. I've been so nervous about it and, well, I thought that since I'd made my choice, I wouldn't have to go through with that. I would meet Ambrose here and he would then come to Devonshire to court me."

"Of all the unrealistic—where, I ask you, would a man of his consequence stay in our small parish? With our reigning hostess?"

"He wouldn't dare," Megan said unreasonably.

"But that *would* be the only logical place for him," Tiffany said reasonably.

"There's the inn."

"You would put the Duke of Wrothston in Teadale's tiny inn?"

"He's going to be in love," Megan insisted. "He won't care where he stays."

"Don't count on it, Meg. He's used to the very best accommodations. Are you forgetting he lives in a bloody mausoleum? He probably has a bedroom as big as that ballroom down there."

"Don't exaggerate."

"Who's exaggerating?"

"You are. His bedroom is probably only half as big as the ballroom."

"Don't skip the point, Meg. If he does follow you home, he won't want to stay long at the inn, or in Devonshire, for that matter. You can't expect him to suspend the business of his everyday life for a complete courtship. He's got a dukedom to see to, after all. A week maybe, and that's if he comes, and that's not long enough—"

"Sure it is."

"Megan! You can't accept a proposal after only a week's acquaintance!"

"I can, too," Megan replied stubbornly.

"That would cause a bloody scandal, and you know it. Besides, *he* won't be that impetuous. He might fall in love with you instantly. That's a definite possibility. Tonight even. But he'll still take the requisite amount of time to consider marriage. And *that* means that he'll visit you every few weeks to continue the courtship, which is going to take a long time at that rate. Or you can go to London as planned, where he can see you more often and make up his mind the quicker. Either way, you end up going to London."

"Damn," Megan said in disgust. "I'd actually convinced myself it was no longer necessary."

"What exactly has you so nervous?" Tiffany asked hesitantly.

Megan sighed. "More treatment like I had from the Thackerays."

Tiffany frowned. "I should have known your misgivings were only recent. You *were* excited about London before old hatchet-face gave you the snub. But that situation was unique, Meg. It's not going to happen again."

Megan smiled bitterly. "You don't think there will be mamas in London who won't want me at the same parties their marriageable daughters attend?"

"It won't matter once it's learned who's courting you," Tiffany said with complete confidence.

"I don't see what that will have to do with it," Megan replied.

"Don't you? Mark my words, *he'll* make sure you're invited to every place he is, and he's got the power and influence to open any door in London for you. You'll end up invited to places that you wouldn't have been otherwise."

"I don't see why."

"Because your romance with the duke is bound to be the sensation of the Season, that's why. Everyone who is anyone will want a hand in playing Cupid to further it along."

"That's ridiculous."

"That's human nature and it stands to reason. You're going to be the ton's new darling, because you will have attracted the interest of their most eligible bachelor."

"*If* I ever get to meet him."

Tiffany grinned. "Don't be so impatient. If he comes tonight, the romance begins or ends, depending on the impression he makes—and you're not to forget your promise."

"I know, I know. Only if I think I can love him."

"Good. Now, on the other hand, if he doesn't show up, then think of tonight as practice for all the balls you'll have to attend later. This is our first, after all, or had you forgotten that in your preoccupation with *Ambrose*?"

Megan laughed at the silly connotation Tiffany placed on the duke's first name. "I know it's a horrible name for a man, especially after we're used to applying it to a horse. I'm stuck with it, however."

"*He's* stuck with it. You can call him anything you like. 'Your Grace' for starters; 'darling' when the time's right. Feeling better?"

"Absolutely. Now, what were you saying about that fellow with the temper?"

Chapter 15

"Frederick Something-or-other is his name."

"Something-or-other?"

Tiffany made a face, saying defensively, "What do you want from me? I heard too many names to remember them all. This one's a marquis. I remember that only because Jane mentioned that he's a very good friend of—guess who?"

Megan's interest perked up. "No kidding? But that increases the odds on Ambrose showing up."

"Not necessarily. The marquis just happens to have an estate near here that he was visiting, but remember, Kent as well as London is a long way off."

"Ambrose could have an estate near here, too."

"That's true," Tiffany allowed. "But don't count on it. They would have arrived together if they both were in the area, don't you think?"

"Possibly—unless Ambrose was detained for some reason. But I could just end the suspense by going down and asking Lord Frederick if the duke is coming. Our hostess might not know, but he ought to."

"That might not be such a good idea."

"Why not?"

"Well, look at it from the broader picture. He meets you and falls in love."

Megan nodded. "Yes, we already agreed—"

"Frederick does."

"Him? But why should he?"

"For the same reason your duke is likely to. And remember that they're good friends. If the marquis saw you first and confesses to love you, won't his good friend the duke forsake his own feelings to preserve the friendship?"

Megan laughed. "That's getting much too complicated. And besides, I wouldn't give the marquis the least bit of encouragement. So what harm can a little conversation do? And I'd be asking about his friend, showing clearly in what direction my interest lay."

"Now, there's another thing. Are you sure you want St. James to know that you were *clearly* interested in him *before* you met him? Because what are good friends for if not to confide such things? So don't think Lord Frederick wouldn't mention it. And a man doesn't like to know that he's been singled out for pursuit. They like to do that sort of thing themselves, after all."

"I see your point. Asking about Ambrose might give the wrong impression—well, the right impression, but one I'd rather not give. Not that I won't confess all eventually."

"But *after* the wedding."

"Exactly." But then Megan frowned. "Or would that be considered too devious?"

Tiffany's brows shot up before she grinned. "So now you're devious?"

"Well, aren't I? The whole courtship thing is going to be a waste of time just for his benefit. If I were honest, I'd tell him right from the start that I'd like to marry him."

"You can't do that!"

"I *know* that, Tiff. But isn't omitting that the same thing as lying?"

"No, it's just standard romance protocol," Tiffany said with firm conviction. "It'd be nice if we women *could* be that honest, but if we were, we'd scare away half the men we end up married to, the half that insist that the idea of marriage be their idea exclusively. And don't be so hasty in calling your courtship a waste of time either. That's the only time you'll have to get to know your duke and figure out if you can love him or not, because I *hope* you're not thinking it's going to be as quick for you as it probably will be for him."

"You don't think that's possible?"

"Highly impossible, Meg. He's going to fall for your stunning face first, then your sweet self later. But then you're quite conceivably the most beautiful girl in the kingdom. He isn't likely to be the most handsome man, however." Then Tiffany snorted. "That horse breeder in your stable might have that distinction, but your duke won't."

The mere mention of Devlin brought him fully to Megan's mind. She wished he could have seen her in her lovely new ball gown. The green poult-de-soie hugged her figure where the scooped neckline and capped sleeves weren't revealing it. The added white tulle flounces in the underskirt were an extravagance. With her hair artfully coiffed and her mother's heirloom pearls at her throat, she felt she looked sophisticated, even if she wasn't, especially with the matching green domino adding a touch of mystery. Devlin would have been dazzled by such splendor—and for once kept his insults to himself.

"My duke *is* going to be handsome, Tiff."

"Absolutely," Tiffany agreed. "Just don't expect *incredibly* handsome, all right? That's asking for disappointment."

"I suppose." Megan sighed. "Very well, now that we've established that I must give Lord Frederick Something-or-other the cold shoulder, we have to figure out how I'm to recognize Ambrose if he shows up. Did Jane happen to describe him to you when she was doing all her chattering?"

"She did say he's very tall. Of course, she's very short, so tall to her could be anywhere from here to here," Tiffany said, raising her hand from the level of Megan's head to a good foot above it.

"What else?"

"Black hair, or dark brown—she wasn't sure on that. And eyes some shade of blue or green, unusual, she called them. And by the way, *she* thinks he's incredibly handsome. Those were her words. But then she also thinks Lord Fred down there is incredibly handsome, so you have to take her opinion as a bit exaggerated."

Megan glanced down again at Lord Frederick, noting that he was rather tall himself and also had black hair. She couldn't tell much more about him from that distance and with his domino mask in place, but his body was nicely put together, his evening clothes were impeccable, and the younger women who were present seemed to be fawning over him.

"Oh, I don't know." Megan grinned. "I'd say he's probably very handsome."

Tiffany instantly caught the drift of her thoughts. "That's to be expected, since he's the highest-ranked lord here at the moment, and a bachelor."

"Poor man," Megan said dryly. "He must have to put up with that kind of adoration all the time."

"No more than your duke does," Tiffany replied. "Sure you can tolerate that?"

"But it won't be like that after he's married."

"He's a duke, Meg. There will always be women who will want one thing or another from him—even for legitimate business."

"That's not funny."

Tiffany grinned cheekily. "I thought it was. Oh, don't frown. I was only joking—well, not quite. There *will* be women who will try to take him away from you just because of who he is."

"But tell me something. If he loves me, do you really think I ought to worry about it? And be honest instead of down-on-my-duke for a change."

Tiffany chuckled. "All right, I'll concede gracefully. If he loves you, you won't have a thing to worry about. He'll be the one to suffer the talons of jealousy, not you." After a moment she added sheepishly, "Was I really being 'down-on-your-duke'?"

"With every other breath."

"I'm sorry, Meg. I guess it's hard to be positive about a man we haven't even met yet. I can't very well say the Duke of Wrothston is wonderful and perfect for you when we don't know if he is or isn't. All he has in his favor at the moment is his title, which might put him at the top of your list, but doesn't recommend him to me. I just want you to have a man who is absolutely right for you, and I'm afraid that you're going to let this getting-even-with-Lady O thing cloud your judgment and convince you that he's right for you—and he very well might not be."

Megan leaned forward to give her friend a hug. "I love you for caring like that. And it's all right, you can continue to play the skeptic if it makes you happy. Chances are, I might not even be attracted to the man." *Like you are to Devlin?* Now where had that thought come from? "And that will be determined at our first meeting."

"And end it?"

Megan nodded firmly. "That quickly. But on the other hand—"

"I'll be the first one to point out his good qualities—once we know what they are."

"Fair enough."

Chapter 16

"Would it be all right if I spoke with your father about marriage?"

Megan missed a step. Her dancing partner didn't seem to notice.

He was an excellent dancer. There had been a half-dozen previous partners who weren't, so she'd noted that right off. This one had a pleasant face, and right now a very earnest expression on it. She'd guess he was somewhere in his early thirties.

If he were younger she could have laughed and made some silly reply to his question. But she was afraid he was serious. Only she didn't want to be serious herself just now. She'd been having too much fun this evening, just as Tiffany had predicted she would.

Every single dance had been promised, except the two she'd saved for the duke if he'd bothered to show up, which he hadn't. But even that didn't bother her so much now. She realized she'd been letting impatience rule her emotions, when there was plenty of time to meet St. James. And with half the people at the ball from London, she wasn't quite so nervous anymore about her Season there, having found out that these people weren't so intimidating after all.

"Now, this is what London is going to be like," Tiffany had whispered only moments ago, just before Megan's present partner had made his way through her ring of admirers to claim this dance. *"Are you sure you want to settle for a stodgy old duke?"*

Megan *was* still set on her duke, at least until such time as meeting him might change her mind. But in the meantime, she could see no reason not to enjoy her "success," as her popularity tonight could definitely be termed. A serious proposal of marriage from a stranger was not her idea of enjoyment, however. It was absurd, was what it was, and deserved a bit of absurdity in return.

"You may speak to my father, certainly," Megan told her partner—she couldn't remember his name. "But if your subject is marriage, I feel I must warn you that you may be shot."

He missed a step now. Megan noticed.

"I beg your pardon," he said after a moment of incredulity. "Did you say shot?"

"Indeed."

"But—but—"

"Oh, it's not as bad as it sounds, sir, and it's only if marriage is mentioned. He's been plagued too often with proposals of marriage, you see . . . the women just won't leave him alone."

He missed another step. Megan kept from laughing, but it wasn't easy.

"Women? But I meant—"

"And I'm afraid he swore, actually swore, that he if heard that word once more in the next three months—he was rational enough to put a limit on his temper—no matter who mentioned it, he would shoot them. Now, I don't know if he meant he would kill them. He might have just meant a wounding. Yes, that's possible. But in either case, I did feel you ought to be warned."

"Appreciate it, indeed I do."

She thought he just might. And the fellow didn't have much more to say for the rest of the dance. He left her rather abruptly once it was over, and for the first time that evening, Megan had a moment alone. But it was a brief moment.

"I believe the next dance is mine."

The voice gave her a start, coming from directly behind her, and was entirely unwelcome, since she had hoped for a few minutes to herself. She wondered if she could pretend not to have heard and simply walk away. No, that would be too rude, though walking away was still an option as long as it was accompanied with a good excuse, which she had, considering the man's presumption.

So to avoid being drawn into conversation, she turned only slightly so he'd know she was replying to him and said with a degree of curtness, "No, actually, I'm not partnered for the next dance, and I'm going to keep it that way. Excuse me, but I was just going to take some air."

"That was going to be my suggestion, so I'll join you, if you don't mind."

"The air is free for the taking, of course, but I'd prefer to take mine alone."

"How unromantic of you, Miss Penworthy."

She turned then out of simple curiosity. He was tall, very tall, and masked.

"Have we been introduced?"

"I would have remembered that pleasure, so the answer must be no."

"Then how did you—?"

"I asked. But allow me." He bowed ever so slightly. "Ambrose St. James, at your service. Are you sure you won't reconsider?"

Was he kidding? She'd given him up as a no-show, yet here he was, and he was much more than she had been hoping for. What she could see of his face beneath the black domino was definitely handsome, and his body was as finely put together as Devlin's was—*stay out of my thoughts, horse breeder*—though she would certainly never see Devlin arrayed so splendidly in black evening clothes. His eyes were too shadowed by the domino he wore for her to distinguish their color, but his hair was black and slicked back without a single strand out of place. She was attracted, quite definitely attracted. And to think he might have left offended by her initial curtness.

But before she blurted out, "Of course I've changed my mind," she realized how fickle that would sound after her firmness in putting him off. So she gave him a tepid smile, pretending an indifference she was far from feeling.

"You're very persistent, aren't you?"

"When it matters," he replied.

His own smile was quite startling in its sensual appeal. Megan imagined that Devlin would smile like that if he ever bothered to—*you're doing it again.*

"Why should it mat—?"

He interrupted her impatiently. "Let's not chew it to bits until your next dance partner shows up. You've already changed your mind, dear girl, so come along."

How did he know? she wondered as he ushered her, rather quickly, out to the raised terrace. And she didn't care for the sudden abruptness that had come right after his lovely smile, when he'd looked beyond her, almost as if he were trying to avoid someone he'd seen approaching. So as he headed for the steps that led down to the formal gardens, Megan veered toward the terrace railing instead.

"The air is quite satisfactory right here, I believe," she said, tugging her elbow out of his hand.

"No stroll through moonlit gardens? *Very* unromantic, Miss Penworthy."

"Look who's talking," she mumbled.

He grinned engagingly. It was as startling as his smile, and no doubt designed to disarm her now noticeable pique.

"Don't be angry, dear girl. There are several people here that I'd rather not speak with, and one of them was bearing down on us—which means I won't have much time with you. That very thought is devastating me, and is accountable for my appalling lapse in manners."

His excuse was acceptable since she had guessed as much, but that last remark had her forgiving him completely. She even blushed slightly because she could disconcert him that much. The man was *definitely* interested, and wasn't that what she had been hoping for?

She was thrilled with the thought, which brought on a degree of shyness as well as regret as she pointed out, "The next dance is spoken for, so you won't have much time in either case."

"Then I must take advantage of what little time I do have," he said as he swept her into his arms for the current waltz.

Megan was caught off guard by the unexpectedness of it, so it took her a moment to realize she was being held much too closely. When she did, she stiffened slightly, and was promptly treated to the sensation of his warm breath tickling her ear and sending gooseflesh down her neck and arms.

"The urge to hold you in my arms was simply too overwhelming. The urge to kiss you was even more overwhelming, so you see I am trying to behave."

With his arms around her causing exciting remembrances of another bold embrace, and with his seductive words cutting clean through her defenses, it was on the tip of her tongue to say, "Then kiss me," because the urge was there for her, too. But she recalled that she was sadly lacking where kissing was concerned, so she said nothing, wanting this first meeting of theirs to be as memorable for him as it surely was going to be for her.

She was delighted that she would be able to relieve Tiffany's worries, because Megan now had no doubt at all that it would take very little effort to fall in love with Ambrose St. James. She sighed happily and relaxed in his arms, for everything was going just as planned.

He heard her, felt her yielding, and stiffened, for nothing was going as he'd planned. But then he hadn't expected her to be so ravishing tonight, so incredibly lovely, that she'd made him forget what he was doing here. Yet what he'd just told her was perfectly true. There was nothing more he wanted to do just now than kiss her. And he had no doubt she'd let him kiss her, and probably more, because this was not the Megan he knew; this was the scheming little miss out to snare a duke, and by God, she'd think twice about it after tonight.

His intentions recalled, he maneuvered them back to the terrace railing and abruptly ended the dance. But there was definitely a moment of keen regret when he saw her dreamy expression turn to surprise as he let her go. Again all he wanted to do was kiss her. He squelched the urge with the reminder that another man wouldn't have stood a chance against this kind of temptation—*he* wouldn't have if he didn't know her game. She deserved the lesson he was about to give her, the lesson he'd risked a run-in with Freddy to give her. Maybe next time she'd be more careful in her choice of victims.

Megan felt awkward under his pensive stare. She wished she could see his eyes, but they were even more shadowed in the dimmer light on the terrace.

"You don't care for dancing after all, Your Grace?" was all she could think to say for the moment.

"Ah, so you *do* know?" he said in reference to her "Your Grace."

She shrugged, though silently she berated herself for having called him that without a formal introduction. "Doesn't everyone?"

"In London, yes, but not in the country." Then he sighed. "A pity, that. Spoils half my fun."

"Why would it?"

"People tend to behave differently than they ordinarily would when they know who I am. All they can see is the title, not the man who bears it."

Megan detected a large dose of bitterness in those words that made her feel distinctly uncomfortable. She was guilty of just that, seeing only the title—no, that wasn't quite true. The title had been her first consideration, yes, but everything else hinged on the man. If he didn't suit, then it wouldn't matter what title he bore, for she wouldn't have him.

"I'm sorry," she said, and meant it. "That can't be an easy thing to live with."

He shrugged. "One of the little drawbacks of being a duke."

"I hope there are some benefits to compensate."

The comment had him grinning again. "Oh, a few."

Now why did that "few" sound so very wicked? No, it was the grin. That grin was definitely not wholesome.

"One of those things wouldn't be getting away with being a trifle high-handed, would it?"

She meant it teasingly. He answered seriously.

"A trifle? I dragged you out here, dear girl. That was most assuredly high-handed of me."

"Yes, it was, and now that you mention it, I realize you haven't apologized for it."

"Another benefit. I rarely apologize. Who, after all, would dare bring me to account for my actions?"

She didn't like the sound of that. Were Tiffany there, she'd be pointing out that they hadn't come across many good qualities yet, and Megan would have to agree. What the devil had happened to the charming man who had only moments ago confessed to an overwhelming urge to kiss her?

"I believe I would have no difficulty in doing so, Your Grace."

He half sat, half leaned on the railing, crossed his arms, and gave every indication of being amused. "Would you indeed? Your own character is so exemplary, then, that you can cast stones?"

Neither the subdued lighting on the terrace nor the half mask she wore could hide her blush completely. "Absolutely . . . not. I don't claim to be anywhere near perfect, but then I don't represent such an exalted title."

"And if you did, would that make you any less spoiled or willful?"

Megan stiffened. "What, I would like to know, has led you to assume either of those things about me?"

"A good guess?"

Disappointment was welling up again, much worse than what she'd felt when she thought she might not meet the duke tonight. It was nearly choking her, and that made her furious. She didn't know what had gone wrong, but if she didn't leave now, she'd say something to end the possibility of any future encounter—*if* she decided to give him a chance to redeem his appalling behavior.

"I believe I've had too much air. Good evening, Your Grace."

"Not so fast, my dear."

Not only his words detained her. His arm had snaked out as she'd turned to leave, and she now found herself drawn nearly between his legs.

"I've made you angry again?" he ventured with galling good cheer.

Megan decided that he had to be an idiot to ask that question. "Absolutely, and it's increasing by the second. Let me—"

"That wasn't my intention."

She felt a spark of hope. Maybe he just wasn't himself tonight. Maybe he thought her more sophisticated than she was and she'd merely misunderstood his insults. "What *was* your intention?"

"I want to see a lot more of you."

Exactly what she had hoped to hear—before this abrupt change in him. Now she wasn't at all sure if she ever wanted to see him again.

"Why?" she asked boldly.

"I'm becoming bored with my current mistress. I think you might do to replace her."

"Your *mistress*?"

He went on blithely as if she hadn't almost screeched. "Yes, I think you might do nicely. Can't say for certain, though, until I try you out. Shall we find a secluded spot in the garden to—"

The crack of her palm against his cheek cut off his shocking suggestion. Megan pushed away from him. He didn't try to stop her this time. But she didn't leave. She wanted to do more than just slap him. She wanted to rail at him for being exactly what Devlin had said he was, a bounder, a rogue, a seducer of innocents, but she was too angry to get the words out.

She thought about ripping off his domino. After all, she didn't want to mistake this rake if she *did* ever see him again, which she sincerely hoped would never happen. To think she'd actually been disappointed earlier that she might not get to meet him tonight, and even more so only moments ago.

"Ah, there you are, Miss Penworthy. I believe this dance is mine."

She turned with a start, feeling almost guilty for being caught alone with such a wicked man as she now knew Ambrose St. James to be. But it was the duke's friend, Lord Frederick, to whom she had promised the next dance. Two of a kind? Possibly. More than likely, actually, so both were to be avoided henceforth.

"You, sir, keep detestable friends," she told the marquis in her most chilling tone. "That one in particular." And she pointed a stiff finger behind her.

"That one?" Lord Frederick asked.

His bewilderment made her frown, then turn to see why he hadn't understood her perfectly. But the reason was quite clear. The previously occupied perch on the terrace railing was now empty.

The odious Duke of Wrothston was gone, vanished, with not even a bush stirring on the other side of the railing to mark his passage. Too bad he hadn't done so sooner, before she'd met him. No, it was better to know, and now she knew. As far as she was concerned, Ambrose St. James and his title could rot.

Chapter 17

"Why haven't you told me, 'I told you so'?"

They were on the last leg of the journey home, the Robertses' coach jostling along at a steady put-you-to-sleep pace. Tiffany's mother was in fact dozing on the opposite seat, so the girls had had no conversation for a while.

Tiffany had been about to fall asleep herself, but that softly uttered question brought her wide awake. "I thought you weren't brooding about that anymore."

Megan had done nothing else but brood about her colossal foolishness. She'd just kept it to herself after their earlier discussion, when she'd related the entire humiliating encounter with Ambrose St. James.

"Why haven't you?" Megan repeated. "I certainly deserve it."

"No, you don't," Tiffany said loyally. "And I wouldn't do that to you. Besides, it might not have seemed like it, but I was really hoping everything would work out just the way you wanted it to with St. James. So I guess I'm just as disappointed as you are that it didn't."

"I'm not disappointed," Megan assured her. "At least not anymore. What I am is furious with myself for pinning all my hopes on a man we knew absolutely nothing about—which you tried to point out numerous times. I still can't believe how stupid that was. But I'm also furious with him. I can't seem to help it. You'd think a duke would have more integrity than to be a bounder, wouldn't you?"

"Absolutely. The title probably corrupted in his case. It's been known to happen."

"There ought to be a law against it," Megan grumbled.

Tiffany said nothing. She waited. After a moment the expected laughter came.

"I don't believe I said that," Megan said, still softly chuckling.

"I don't either, though I happen to agree."

Megan burst into another round of laughter. "Stop, or I'll wake your mother."

Tiffany got serious again. "It's true, though. Great power and wealth do corrupt, and St. James has both in abundance. A pity. Maybe if he'd been an impoverished duke, he would have been a bit more honorable."

"And desperate for an heiress, which I'm not."

Tiffany sighed. "Well, it's water under the bridge now, so are you ready to do things in their proper order?"

"You mean meet the man first?"

"That, too, but more importantly, fall in love first. That really *is* the way it's being done these days, you know."

"I know," Megan replied. "That just doesn't guarantee me the title."

Tiffany wasn't that surprised to hear this. Megan could be exceedingly stubborn and single-minded at times—most times, actually.

"So you *do* still want the title?"

Megan shrugged, her expression dispirited. "I don't know—no, that's not true. I'd still like to set Lady O on her ear, and I can't very well do that without a titled husband, so I guess I would still prefer it. I'm just not going to count on it."

Tiffany clicked her tongue. "Sounds like you're giving up before the game begins."

"Just being realistic from now on."

"Realistic? You want to talk realistic? Are you forgetting that you actually did what you set out to do—well, at least half of it?"

Megan frowned. "What are you talking about?"

"The first part of your goal was to gain the amorous interest of the Duke of Wrothston. That you did, and then some. It's not *your* fault that he turned out to be a lecherous rake with immoral propositions on his mind, rather than decent ones. You still caught his interest, Meg."

"I did, didn't I?"

"So I wouldn't worry about that title. There will be dozens more for you to choose from when you get to London. But this time you meet them first, *then* you decide which one you're going to fall in love with and let it happen—unless you fall in love first and that decides it for you. There is always that possibility, you know, and frankly, I highly recommend it."

"You would, but then there aren't very many men as wonderful as your Tyler."

"True, but you're forgetting I fell in love with Tyler before I knew he was wonderful, the very day I met him, as it happens. I was just so fortunate that he *is* wonderful, but I don't think it would have mattered very much if he'd had a few bad qualities. We have to take the good with the bad when the heart makes the choice."

"That does *not* sound too encouraging, Tiff. In fact, it only supports my previous contention that I'd do well to choose the man first, then let love take its course."

"Suit yourself, as long as you meet him first to determine that you won't be wasting your time on another bounder—and as long as you're in love before you agree to marry him. You will agree to that at least, won't you?"

"Absolutely—only how long do you think it takes to fall in love my way?"

Tiffany rolled her eyes. "You're asking me, who did it instantly? How should I know?"

Chapter 18

❧❧❀ ❀❧❧

Megan was surprised by how anxious she was to get home. And once she was home, she was frankly amazed that her urge was to go straight to the stable, rather than into the house to greet her father. She supposed she just missed her horse. She *had* missed her morning rides. But that shouldn't account for such a compelling impulse, especially when she'd been away only four days.

And she had been away from home before. There had been that trip to Kent for her twelfth-birthday present—*why* couldn't she have found out back then what an odious man the duke was?—and a few shopping expeditions to towns that offered more than Teadale. Her father had accompanied her those times—maybe that was the difference, but her conscience told her otherwise.

Why don't you be honest? You want to see that horse breeder.

Absolutely not. If anything, he's the last person I want to see.

Sure he is.

You're forgetting his knowledge of St. James. He probably knew exactly what would happen at the ball, or guessed it would happen, while I was arrogantly informing him that I would be marrying the man. How can I face him after that?

With your usual charm . . . and arrogance.

Very funny. But what if he asks what happened? Not what if; he will ask.

You can lie.

And when I don't happen to marry St. James within the year, then what? Devlin will be good at gloating, you know he will. He probably wrote the book on it. I could have taken it from Tiffany, but an I-told-you-so from him—I'd probably shoot the man.

You have to face him eventually, so admit it, you can't wait.

I can't wait to be humiliated? When did I become a glutton for punishment?

When you noticed how handsome that man is.

Very funny.

Somehow, Megan managed to go to bed that first night home without giving in to the urge to see—her horse. But she was up at the first tinges of dawn the next morning, and on her way to the stable before the sun actually made it over the horizon. She was bubbling with anticipation that she refused to acknowledge, so she was incredibly dumbfounded to find the stable doors not just closed for the night, but also locked. Locked? Since when and why?

Megan stood there for several minutes, prodded with impatience, disappointment, and a number of other unwelcome emotions. She wondered how much noise pounding on the doors would make. Too much, especially since only the horses slept in the front of the stable.

She was about to go back to the house to wait for her normal hour for riding when one of her emotions got the better of her, and she marched around to the back of the stable instead. Of the several windows at the back, only one was covered with curtains. She tapped lightly on it, then a bit harder when she got no immediate response. But then the curtains—she felt a moment's amusement upon noting that they were pink—were yanked apart, and the window was opened more than the crack it had been.

She had to be grateful—*or not*, her conscience put in—that it still wasn't light enough for her to see very clearly into his darkened room, because she could just barely discern that Devlin Jefferys was standing in front of his window quite naked. It was lighter where she stood, so he had less difficulty seeing who had disturbed his sleep.

"What the devil are you about, brat, at this ungodly hour?" he demanded with a great deal of sleepy irritation before she could get her mouth open.

Megan bristled at the uncomplimentary name he persisted in calling her, but didn't bring him to task for it. Her eyes were adjusting and getting a clearer image of him by the second, and, cognizant of his previous threats about staring, she felt it was more prudent to find something else to look at. So she turned slightly, facing the bare frame of the extension that was being added to the back of the stable—and suddenly realized there might have been another way in without having had to wake him.

That realization caused a certain amount of embarrassment, prompting her to apologize. "I'm sorry. I found the doors locked, but I've just noticed a back entrance. Go back to sleep, Mr.—"

"What back entrance?"

"Why, where the stable is being enlarged. Surely a door has been cut—"

"Why don't you go have a closer look before you make assumptions, Megan? You'll find that the extension is going up and will be nearly complete before an opening is cut to connect it. What's the point of barring the doors out front if a bloody hole is left in the back?"

She detected the amusement that had slipped into his tone with that explanation, and that got her back to bristling. "Then the stable *is* completely locked?"

"Isn't that what I just said?"

"How dare you lock me out of my own stable? By what right—did my father tell you to lock it?"

"I don't need your father's permission to protect the horses," he said with a degree of condescension. "That happens to be my responsibility."

"Protect them from what?" she scoffed. "Open the doors, Jefferys."

"Go back to bed, Megan. The doors will be opened at a decent hour."

"I don't choose to wait until a decent hour, I choose to go riding now. Open the bloody doors."

"You insist?"

"Isn't that what I just said?" She tossed his own words back at him.

"Very well, you asked for it."

She glanced cautiously up at the window to find him gone. She bit her lip, frowning. He wouldn't do what that "you asked for it" sounded like, would he?

He wouldn't dare—but just to be sure, she called in through the window, "Don't you dare open those doors with no clothes on, Devlin Jefferys. If you do, I'll bloody well scream; then you can make your excuses to the servants who come running, *and* my father."

With that warning, she marched to the front of the stable, confident that she had put a stop to what he had intended. And she must have, because he kept her waiting a good five minutes before the doors finally swung open. But he hadn't taken her warning completely to heart. The wait had been to light a lantern, since the inside of the stable was still pitch-dark. For clothes, Devlin had put on only his trousers and boots.

Pink-cheeked that he had obeyed her only in part, Megan swept past him and went straight to Sir Ambrose's stall. It was too much to hope that Devlin would simply go back to bed now and leave her in peace. He didn't.

"Someone ought to teach you a little common decency, courtesy, *and* sense."

Reprimanded by a horse breeder. His gall was utterly astounding.

"What does common sense have to do with it?" she asked without turning to look at him, allowing that she might be a little out of line on the decency and courtesy parts. "I wanted to ride. You had no right to keep me from doing so."

"I still might keep you from doing so," he growled at her back. "You don't wake a man from a sound sleep and berate him for doing his job. Common sense would have told you that you won't get away with it unscathed."

She stilled in the process of reaching for Sir Ambrose's saddle blanket. Her heart, on the other hand, was off to the races.

"You'd better keep your distance from me, Devlin." They both realized, at the same moment, that she'd just used his first name for the first time. "I meant, Mr. Jefferys," she corrected herself quite properly.

"Formality is a bit misplaced by now, don't you think?" he asked, amusement present in his tone again.

Megan continued readying Sir Ambrose for her ride. "No, I don't."

There was a moment of silence before he said, "Even after I've stood naked in your sight?"

She gasped, swinging around to glare at him. "I didn't look!"

"You wanted to."

She didn't answer that, again going back to what she was doing. He chuckled at her silence and the blush that accompanied it.

"I'm sorry I had to disturb you, but you can return to your bed now."

It was the stiffness in her tone which put the disgruntlement back in his. "Which is where you ought to be—in your own bed, that is. You've got no business riding out this early."

"When I ride is none of *your* business, Mr. Jefferys," she pointed out.

"It is when you wake me to do it." And then he sighed. "If you're going to insist on this foolishness, I'll go with you."

That gave her pause and she glanced at him with raised brows. "Whatever for?"

"There's a highwayman working these parts, or has no one told you?"

"I'm not carrying a purse."

He grinned at that bit of lopsided logic. "You don't think he'd find something on you to take? I know I would."

She didn't like the sound of that insinuation. "The hour might be early, but the sun will be up by the time I ride out of here."

"Just barely."

She ignored that. "If I were taking one of my midnight rides, I might worry, but not in—"

"Midnight rides?" he cut in incredulously. "Good God, have you got no sense a'tall, to risk your neck like that, not to mention your bloody virtue?"

Megan was determined not to lose her temper, so she said calmly, "This is a very quiet parish."

"Don't I know it," he replied in disgust.

"It's perfectly safe for me to ride at night when the mood takes me, or it was, before this highwayman chose our area for his robberies. But I haven't ridden at night since he showed up, because, contrary to your belief, I'm not stupid—and why the devil am I explaining myself to you, anyway? You aren't my keeper, Mr. Jefferys."

"Thank God for that."

Her eyes narrowed. Keeping her temper around this man was next to impossible. She didn't know why she'd bothered to try.

"For all I know," she said scathingly, "*you* might be the highwayman. His arrival in this area does coincide with your own, after all."

"I was wondering when you'd get around to making that accusation."

"Well?"

"Well, what?" He suddenly laughed. "Are you expecting me to deny it?"

"If you're innocent, then yes, of course I expect you to deny it."

"And if I were guilty, I'd also deny it, so what's the point of my answering either way? Or were you hoping for a confession?"

His amusement was infuriating her. "I was hoping you'd go away," she bit out caustically. "Since you haven't, I will, *on* my horse, and without you along to further annoy me. *I do not need a keeper!*"

"Is that your final word on it?"

"Absolutely."

"Well, here's mine," he said, and his expression was now implacable. "I've decided not to give you a choice. A spoiled brat like you most definitely does need a keeper. So don't leave this stable until I return with Caesar, Megan. If you do, I'll ride after you, but you won't like what will happen when I catch up, I promise you."

Since he'd glanced down at the area of her derriere as he made that promise, Megan was left with a clear understanding of what it was he was promising to do to her. The last time he'd made that particular threat, he'd managed to intimidate her. Not this time. This time her temper didn't cool, it was brushed to full heat. In fact, she was so furious she was rendered speechless, so he managed to walk away without hearing what she thought of his "promise."

He was bluffing, of course. He was a servant. He might not act like one, but he was, and a servant wouldn't dare lay an abusive hand on his employer's daughter. She could have him arrested, for God's sake, if he so much as tried to spank her. The very idea.

Fortified with her bristling indignation, Megan made quick work of securing Sir Ambrose's saddle and led her horse over to the mounting block. Angrily she mounted and gathered the reins, and angrily she walked Sir Ambrose out of the stable. But, cautiously, she went no farther than to the side of the doors, so she couldn't be seen from inside. And a few minutes later when Devlin, on Caesar's back, came tearing out of the stable to give chase, she let out a trill of laughter that brought him up short and nearly unseated him when Caesar objected to such an abrupt halting.

Seeing that was much better than calling Devlin's bluff. Indeed it was, and Megan rode off grinning, despite the fact that Devlin was swearing a blue streak at her back—or because of it.

Chapter 19

As much as Megan would have loved to let Sir Ambrose gallop across the high meadows, she suspected Devlin would make a race of it, and she didn't care to have her beloved Sir Ambrose shown up by the magnificent Caesar. So, as the sun came up to brighten the dawn sky, she kept to a steady trot. At least, she did until Devlin would ride up beside her. Then she would shoot ahead or fall back, thereby making the point silently that she did *not* care for his company.

Getting rid of him altogether was a hopeless endeavor, so she didn't try. Besides, her mood was much improved after the trick she'd played on him. She still wanted to laugh each time she pictured Caesar rearing up and nearly unseating Devlin. Too bad he hadn't. A humbling experience wouldn't hurt that man one little bit.

As for Devlin's bluff, it could wait to be called the next time he made it—*if* there was a next time. Though there shouldn't be. She was fed up with his attempts to intimidate her, after all, and she'd proved that nicely, if subtly, with the little trick she'd pulled on him. But then she sighed to herself. Who was she kidding? The man was too full of himself to take note of subtle messages.

He's also got something on his mind, Megan, or he wouldn't be sticking to your tail now that the sun has come up.

I've already figured that out for myself, thank you.

But you also know what it is he's going to mention. So get rid of him before he does.

And just how am I to do that?

No answer, but she did finally give it a try, riding through the meadow where Tiffany would meet her, hoping against hope that her friend would be there so she'd have an excuse to send Devlin back to the manor. But she had known Tiffany wouldn't be there this early, probably wasn't even out of bed yet, and she was right.

At that point she headed home herself, and urged Sir Ambrose into a gallop after all. If Timmy had arrived by the time she got to the stable, she would simply turn Sir Ambrose over to him and run back to the manor—and Devlin could sit on his I-told-you-sos and choke some.

He had something to say about the new pace she had set, however. He actually shouted something at her, though she couldn't hear what—probably to stop. She didn't, urging her mare to even greater speed instead. But that only set him after her at a tearing pace. And she had known there would be no contest if it came to racing. He overtook her in a matter of moments, and to her incredible surprise, she found herself being yanked off her horse and onto Devlin's lap.

"Didn't you hear me?" he shouted at her as he brought Caesar under control, then stopped altogether.

Megan didn't answer for a moment. Her landing had been bone-jarring as well as breath-stealing, and she was still amazed that he had resorted to such a dangerous method to get her attention. Good God, he could have dropped her! She told him so.

"You could have dropped me, you dolt!"

"Not on your life, brat!" he replied just as heatedly. "Now answer me!"

She finally glanced at him to see how really angry he was and decided to lie. "No."

"No, you won't answer? Or no—"

"No, I didn't hear you."

"You're lying."

"Prove it," she said unwisely.

"By God!" he exploded. "If you aren't the most obstinate, willful, spoiled-rotten, foolish—"

She cut in resentfully, "As long as we're washing dirty laundry, let's wash some of yours. Arrogant, high-handed, insolent, rude, overbearing, insulting—has the wash water turned black yet?"

It took about five seconds of a totally incredulous look on Devlin's face before he burst out laughing. Megan, needless to say, did not appreciate his reaction.

"That was not meant to amuse you—and put me down," she demanded.

"Too late for that. Your horse has gone on without you—or did you want to walk?"

"Anything would be preferable to this proximity to you."

"Did I forget to mention stubborn?" he said, shaking his head.

"You had it covered with obstinate," she returned waspishly. "But I know I forgot *insufferable*. Now put me down, Jefferys."

"I don't think I will."

"What?!"

"Give over, Megan. It's more than a mile back. Besides, you like riding Caesar."

"Not at the moment I don't. Now, if you don't do as I say this second, I'll—I'll—"

He gave her a moment to finish her threat, but she couldn't come up with anything impressive enough to make him obey her, so he prompted, "You'll what? Scream, maybe?" And then he shook his head in what had to be mock regret. "Afraid it won't avail you much out here. No, that's not quite true. It'd probably annoy the hell out of me, and I would either kiss you to shut you up or . . ."

He didn't finish himself, leaving the rest to her imagination. And there was nothing wrong with Megan's imagination. But it wasn't the word "or" that decided her. *That* she was ready to call him on. It was the "kiss you" part that turned her to face forward.

Coward.

So what?

You liked his kissing.

Not that first kiss I didn't.

It was the second one that counted, or have you forgotten how enjoyable it was?

That's beside the point, and you know it. He's a bloody horse breeder.

A bloody handsome horse breeder who could teach you a thing or two if you'd let him. You ought to take advantage of his experience, at least in the matter of kissing. I can't believe you're passing up this opportunity. All you had to do was scream a little.

Let's not forget that he'd prefer to abuse my backside, so I'd as soon not tempt him either way—and where is Tiffany when I need her? You're no help a'tall.

Megan took her annoyance with herself out on Devlin, snapping, "Well, what are you waiting for, Jefferys? Take me home—or did you plan to stay out here and trade insults all morning?"

Having said it, she was a bit embarrassed at how shrewish she sounded. But more to the point, she should have recalled that Devlin had never let her get away with such behavior without retaliating in kind. He did that now.

"Someone ought to kiss your pants off, brat," he said outrageously as he started Caesar off at a mere walk. "Didn't your duke?"

His sneering tone was infuriating, but the subject made her groan inwardly. And she almost defended St. James, because it had become automatic for her to do so. But she caught herself in time, for she wasn't about to defend that wretched bounder anymore.

She had known this was coming. The only thing that amazed her was that Devlin hadn't mentioned the Duke of Wrothston sooner.

She wondered if she could drop the subject with a simple "No, he didn't." She tried it. She should have known better.

"Could it be you played the haughty little brat with him as you do with me?"

Was that how Devlin really saw her? She *had* been rather curt to Ambrose St. James to begin with. What if he had merely been paying her back for that, as Devlin so frequently did? And what difference did it make? Pay-back or normal behavior on the duke's part, either way she had been gravely insulted, which had ended her aspirations to be a duchess most effectively.

To Devlin, she said, "What happened is none of your business."

"Isn't it? After you shoved your duke down my throat? You didn't even meet him, did you?"

"I met him," she bit out.

"Then he wasn't interested, was he? It's no wonder, with that god-awful hair of yours."

Megan stiffened. "There's nothing wrong with my hair, Devlin Jefferys!"

" 'Course there is. It's red."

"I haven't noticed that preventing *you* from desiring me," she retorted.

"I'm only an ignorant horse breeder, remember, so I don't count. But did you really think a duke, who is constantly in the public eye, would marry a woman with the most unfashionable hair in creation? His friends would never let him live it down, brat."

She said nothing to that. She said nothing more at all. And her stiff back didn't unbend even a little.

After nearly five minutes of silence, Devlin finally asked hesitantly, "Have I hurt your feelings?"

"Would it matter if you did?"

"It might." She merely snorted at that, so he added, "I wouldn't care to make you cry, Megan."

"You could have fooled me."

"Nonsense. You were good and mad. What happened to change that? Good God, you aren't really that sensitive about your bloody hair, are you? Or did your duke remark upon it, too? Is that why you're so touchy on—"

"I'm not touchy, and he didn't remark upon my hair. Only *you* are ill-mannered enough to do that."

"Definitely touchy, and also incorrect. My manners are impeccable."

"Your manners are atrocious."

"I'm keeping my hands off you, aren't I?" he replied in the most reasonable tone.

"Does that imply you wouldn't keep your hands to yourself if you were ill-mannered?"

"Exactly."

"Then let me point out all the times you haven't been so impeccable."

"Don't," he warned her, "or this might be one of those times. Now about your duke—"

"Good God, you're not going to quit until you hear it, are you? All right, Devlin, Ambrose St. James was exactly what you said he was, and I hope I never see him again. Are you happy now?"

"Never see him again?" he almost sputtered in his surprise. "Just because he was a bit of a bounder? What does that matter to you? It was the title you were after, not the man. And let's not forget his stable. You're bloody well in love with his stable."

Megan turned around again to stare at him incredulously. His tone had been chock-full with resentment, too, which made no sense.

"The title would have been nice," she said dispassionately. "But it wasn't as important as you're suggesting, not by any means. I intend to be in love with the man I marry, or at least extremely fond of him, and assured that love will grow from that."

"That isn't the impression you gave," he replied in a tone that was definitely accusatory.

She shrugged unconcernedly. "Whatever impressions I give you, Jefferys, are usually provoked. At any rate, St. James won't do. I've never met anyone as insulting as he was—aside from you."

His disgruntled expression prompted a grin, so Megan quickly turned back around so he wouldn't see it. Damned man should have left well enough alone. She hoped he was choking on his I-told-you-sos.

"So you don't think you could love him?" he had the audacity to ask next.

Why wouldn't he leave the subject go? "Absolutely not," she almost growled.

"Then who have you set your cap for now?"

"No one."

After a few silent moments he declared, "Bloody hell, you're upset about it, aren't you?"

Megan's eyes widened and she swung around again. "What, may I ask, has brought you to that conclusion?"

"You had your hopes set on St. James. You even saw yourself married to him by year's end. You can't be pleased that you're not getting what you wanted."

"Because I'm a spoiled brat?"

"Exactly."

"Why don't you go to hell, Devlin, and stay out of my business on the way?"

"And why don't you admit that you were disappointed?" he shot back.

"So you can gloat over it?"

"I wouldn't do that."

"Like hell you wouldn't. What the devil do you think you've *been* doing? And I wasn't disappointed. I might have been, but I was too furious to notice it."

"I'm glad to hear it."

"Why?" she asked warily.

He shrugged. "Can't abide melancholy females. They're always bursting into tears for no apparent reason. So you didn't enjoy your ball a'tall?"

"On the contrary, I had a wonderful time—aside from my brief encounter with St. James. I even received two new proposals of marriage."

"How many does that make now, or have you lost count?" he said derisively.

"Quite a few, though I would have to think about it to come up with an exact figure, since I *haven't* been counting. But it would seem that some men must find my hair attractive, wouldn't it?"

"It's your little body they find attractive, brat, not your hair."

"Are you going to be crude again?"

"Why not? It goes well with your bragging."

"So I'm a braggart now, too, when all I did was answer your bloody question?"

"Why hasn't your father done something about that foul mouth of yours?"

"Because he's not a hypocrite like you are. And if you say another word to me, I think I *will* scream."

He must have taken her at her word, for he was silent after that, and his increasing Caesar's speed managed to bring them into the stable just a few minutes later. Sir Ambrose had returned on her own, but then Megan hadn't doubted she would. The mare knew every inch of the surrounding neighborhood, but especially the way home.

Megan, not waiting for Devlin to help her dismount, jumped to the ground with only a little difficulty. Timmy had seen to Sir Ambrose's unsaddling, which was fortunate, for all she wanted to do was get to her room to lick her wounds. Trading insults with Devlin was a hopeless endeavor. He went for blood every time, and she didn't have much more to lose.

But she couldn't resist a parting shot. "The next time you think to protect me from thieves, don't. I'd rather meet up with a highwayman than put up with your brand of abuse."

"And here I thought you adored me," Devlin replied sarcastically.

"As much as I adore snakes," she retorted and headed for the door. But her curiosity wouldn't let her leave without knowing what had caused this latest verbal skirmish. She stopped to demand, "What the devil did you drag me off my horse for back there?"

Devlin shrugged before dismounting and sending Caesar toward the back of the stable. "You set off like a house on fire. I thought your animal had been spooked."

"So you were *saving* me?"

"Something like that."

He looked so embarrassed over that admission, she couldn't help laughing. "I'll believe that like I will it's raining outside."

A crack of thunder chose that devil-damned moment to announce a storm coming in from the east. So it was that Megan's laughter was short-lived, while Devlin's followed her out the door.

Chapter 20

Devlin spent the remainder of the day ruining his section of the stable extension, much to his master carpenter's disgust, and Mortimer's undisguised amusement. But he couldn't concentrate on the correspondence that Mr. Pike had sent, and that left him little else to do with his time except interfere in the enlargement he had instigated. But he'd started it to keep himself busy, he reminded himself, so it didn't particularly matter if he was mucking up his own contribution to the project, as long as the project was doing as originally intended, which it was.

At least in part it was. He still couldn't turn off his thoughts. And as he'd found with the hay-pitching fiasco, monotonous activities let his mind drift down its own paths, and nearly all paths today led to Megan.

He was feeling a tad guilty where she was concerned. Well, perhaps a whole lot guilty.

So maybe she wasn't as greedy and heartless as he'd first thought. So maybe he ought to apologize to her for the dirty trick he'd played on her at the Leightons' ball. So maybe he ought to tell her who he really was. And have her hate him even more? There was no reason for her to know. He'd be gone from here soon enough. So would she, for that matter, to her London Season. Bloody hell, what was it about *that* that irritated the hell out of him?

For that matter, what was it about the girl herself that brought out such defenses in him? Was he unwittingly doing what she accused him of, but in the reverse, deliberately causing animosity to keep himself from falling under the spell of her unusual beauty?

How absurd. He was the Duke of Wrothston. He'd like to think he had a little more control over his actions than that. So he desired her. So what? He had only to recall all of her irritating qualities to know that he would not care to spend any more time with her than it would take to make love, for he had no doubt a'tall that once passion was expended, she'd drive him crazy—just as she was doing now.

Still, the attraction was powerful and undeniable, so much so that he hadn't given her a chance to use that devastating smile of hers on him at the Leightons' ball. Good God, but she had been exquisite that night in her green ball gown, with her matching domino adding a touch of mystery. He had been hard pressed to concentrate on what he was there to do, when all he'd wanted to do was take her in his arms and kiss her. Damn Freddy for showing up and preventing him from getting at least one kiss before Megan either exploded in her righteous fury or slapped him.

Just his luck that Freddy *would* have to be her next dance partner that night. Had they danced after he hastily left, or had she been too angry just then to dance with anyone? Freddy, of course, knew how to charm a lady out of a pique. And he had been known to set his scruples aside and seduce an innocent if she was pretty enough. Bloody hypocrite, to get so killing mad just because his lying little sister claimed she was carrying Devlin's child.

He recalled that god-awful day with crystal clarity. He had done no more than he usually did, stopping by Freddy's town house to collect him on the way to their club for dinner. It was typical of Freddy never to be ready on time, so Devlin had drifted into the study to wait. But in had come Sabrina Richardson, all of eighteen now and determined to try out her charms on him, or so he'd thought when she started flirting outrageously.

He had actually been amused. Freddy had been his closest friend for more than ten years, so he'd known Freddy's little sister since she'd been a child in pigtails. She and her many cohorts had been terrible pranksters in those days who had played one-too-many so-called jokes on Devlin for her to have endeared herself to him. Quite the opposite; he could barely tolerate the chit.

But he was a fair man. She was grown now, a young lady, a beautiful young lady at that. He gave her the benefit of the doubt in assuming she had to have outgrown the bad habits of her youth that had made him take pains to avoid her. In fact, he hadn't seen her for the several years that she had attended finishing school.

She was much changed since then, in appearance as well as in manner, demure instead of boisterously loud, flirtatious instead of rudely sticking her tongue out at him every chance she got. Her giggling was still the same, however. There wasn't much hope on improving giggling once a girl started making that irritating sound.

But that day she'd only giggled once, so he hadn't been irritated too much. He'd been more interested in wondering what she was about with her flirting. Actually, when Sabrina was fourteen, she'd told him she was going to marry him. He'd snorted, not taking her declaration at all seriously, and told her he'd already be married by the time she was ready to be. And he should have been, would have been, if he hadn't caught his fiancée making love with her coachman, in her coach no less, but that was another story.

He didn't think Sabrina even remembered that childish declaration. But that day in Freddy's study, she slowly worked her way closer to him until, unexpectedly, she threw her arms around his neck and kissed him. It was a bloody attack, was what it was, but after he thought about it later, he realized that the whole thing must have been planned, that she'd only waited until she heard Freddy approaching down the hall to make her move.

Freddy got an eyeful of the kissing part when he entered the room. Sabrina, to give her her due, appeared embarrassed to be "caught"—for all of five seconds. Then she recalled her scheme and burst into tears.

Freddy, as much a sucker for tears as Devlin was, tried to reassure her that she was making a big to-do over nothing. What was a little kiss? He was only a little shocked, and that because of *whom* she'd been kissing.

At which point she clarified the reason for her tears, wailing, "He won't marry me!"

To give Freddy *his* due, his reaction to that was the same as Devlin's. "Well, why should he?" he asked reasonably, if quite dryly. "Young misses like you are not exactly to his taste."

"That's what you think!" she countered. "I was his type enough for him to get me pregnant, but now I'm not his *type* to marry? Is that what you're telling me?"

"Pregnant?" was about all Freddy could get out at that point.

Devlin, on the other hand, was more vocal. "The devil I did. Is this the level your pranks have risen to, Sabrina? Because this joke is in very bad taste."

She actually looked him right in the eye to reply, "How can you say it's a joke? You know it's not. You seduced me. You let me think you would marry me. And now you won't. Freddy, do something!"

Freddy did. He leapt across the space separating them and plowed his fist into Devlin's jaw. While Devlin was on the floor trying to recover from that, Freddy demanded furiously, "How could you? With my own sister!"

"I've never laid a hand on the girl."

"You were just kissing her!"

"She was doing the kissing, you ass, and obviously for your benefit. I don't even like the girl."

"You liked her well enough to seduce her. Well, now you can bloody well marry her!"

"The devil I will!"

"The devil you won't, or you'll hear from my seconds! I ought to call you out anyway, just on principle, family honor and all that."

"Oh, good God," Devlin said in exasperation. "The girl's lying. If she's pregnant at all, and I doubt even that, it's not mine."

"Is that your final word on it?"

At which point Devlin got angry enough to say, "Yes, by God, it is."

"Then expect my seconds. You leave me no alternative but to kill you."

Devlin would have laughed then, except Freddy was much too angry to appreciate the irony of his statement: they both knew he was a lousy shot, while Devlin was not. Devlin left instead, confident that Freddy would calm down, see the absurdity of Sabrina's accusation, and come around to apologize.

But Freddy didn't cool off, not one little bit. Sabrina had no doubt given him more details to reinforce her tale, and, hot-tempered as he was, he did in fact send his seconds over the very next day. Devlin, not about to agree to meet his best friend on the dueling field, was not "at home" to receive them, and hied himself off to Sherring Cross to give Freddy more time to come to his senses. But the bloody seconds followed him even there, and when he again wouldn't receive them, they managed to get in to see his grandmother instead, forcing Devlin to explain the whole ridiculous affair to her.

The Dowager Duchess of Wrothston didn't find it quite so ridiculous. "Well, you can't shoot the boy," she said in her no-nonsense way. "I'm rather fond of him myself."

"I *know* that, Duchy. But am I supposed to let it make the rounds that I'm a bloody coward who won't meet him? It will, you know, if those damned seconds of his find out that I'm actually here."

"So you won't be here. If you'll recall, I suggested you take some time off after you jilted Marianne, but you insisted you weren't broken up by the incident and saw no need to abandon your work just because she had abandoned faith with you."

"I still maintain—"

"Beside the point, dear boy," she cut in with a dismissive wave of her hand. "I happen to know she's letting it go the rounds that *she's* the injured party."

"I suppose she feels that a little thing like infidelity wasn't grounds to cancel the wedding."

"Don't care what she feels, she hasn't exactly been silent on the subject. And you haven't exactly been correcting the matter with the truth."

"And ruin her good name?"

"She did that herself, which is neither here nor there. The point is, she will probably stop defaming *your* good name if you aren't around to hear about it. And now with our dear Freddy hankering to put holes in your body, you no longer have an excuse to ignore my advice. The House of Lords can get along without you for a while. You, on the other hand, can't get along with your head blown off. So you're going to disappear, my boy. I insist upon it."

"I will *not* leave the country, Duchy, not for any reason. I'm not about to put up with seasickness again that feels like dying, just to avoid dying at Freddy's hand. I'll bloody well shoot him before I—"

"No, you won't, and no one suggested you leave the country. All you need is a place where no one knows you, a change in identity, and an occupation that won't draw notice to you. Give me an hour or so to think about it."

But that evening over dinner, when Duchy had announced the destination she felt would serve perfectly for him, Devlin had laughed his head off. "I thought I was to disappear, not bury myself."

"It won't hurt you to rusticate for a time. Do you good, actually, since you're due for a rest."

"A matter of opinion, that."

"So we're going by mine, not yours," she replied. "And it will only be for a few months. By then Marianne will have—hopefully—got over her grudge against you, and Freddy will have married off his sister—or found out that she was lying, not just about you, but also about carrying a child, which would be my guess."

"But a *stableboy*, Duchy?"

"When's the last time you actually noticed one?" she countered. "They're almost invisible, they're so taken for granted."

Devlin had gone along with everything but the occupation. Mucking out stables was just too much for his dignity to stomach for the sake of friendship. But he did allow that he wouldn't mind working with horses, as long as it was in a position of some authority.

Never could he have imagined, however, that his sojourn in the country would lead to such frustration and aggravation that had nothing to do with his being there. But then he never could have imagined a girl quite like Megan, either.

Chapter 21

Devlin had put Megan in the most horrid mood for the rest of the day. She hadn't enjoyed her morning ride, which she had so been looking forward to. She hadn't given back as good as she got in their verbal battle. She hadn't even been kissed. No doubt about it, that round went to Devlin hands down.

So you did want him to kiss you?

What do you think?

Then why'd you put up such a fuss about it?

If he's going to do it, I don't want to provoke him into doing it.

What do you think the first time was all about?

That was different. I didn't know I was provoking him then. But if I had screamed this morning, after he'd already told me what would happen, that would've been asking for it, wouldn't it? And I certainly don't want him to know I want him to kiss me.

I don't see why not. That would be the quickest way to have it happen.

When the man probably stays up late at night thinking of new ways to insult me? I can just imagine what he'd do with the knowledge that I might want his kisses.

Not "might." You said you did.

Well, I'm starting to rethink the matter.

As usual lately, Megan's discussions with her conscience were more annoying than helpful. Ever since her curiosity had been aroused by Devlin and his sexual innuendos, her common sense started losing the battle. Now, her supposed-to-be cautious inner voice was being anything but cautious, and her curiosity was thrilled that she was going to let it have its way—at least in part.

She did want to experience again the pleasant feeling that had occurred while kissing Devlin, that and a whole lot more. The "more" was wrapped in vagueness, unknown, yet she was nothing if not daring—some of the time. Of course, common sense had not lost the battle completely. She knew where the kind of kissing she was contemplating could lead to. To lovemaking and the ruination of a girl. It was exasperating to know the beginning and the end of a thing, but nothing at all about the middle, and not that much, to tell the truth, about the end either. Still, she would have to place limits on what she was willing to learn from Devlin. Actually, she would have to stop him before she learned *too* much.

I think they have a name for that, and it's not a very nice name.

If they do, I don't know what it is.

You do; you're just ashamed to admit it.

Don't start changing your tune at this late date.

I'm not, but you're not exactly taking Devlin's feelings into account. You ought to be willing to explore every avenue that he has a mind to lead you down. Instead you're already deciding at what point to call a halt to it.

That's because I'm waiting until I'm married to be that *adventurous, and that's final.*

Megan was in that same divided state of mind when she went out to the stable that night. One part of her was still having second thoughts about the wisdom of having Devlin teach her more about kissing—and other things—while the other part was looking forward to it with much too much eagerness. The first part had dragged her feet, waiting until it was late enough that Devlin just might have locked the stable by now and gone to bed, thereby putting an end to her plan—at least for today. The other part was rushing now, hoping she wasn't too late. Neither part expected to see Devlin ride out of the stable on Caesar as soon as she got there.

Well, what the devil, she thought, staring after him because he hadn't stopped, apparently preoccupied enough not to have even noticed her. After the battle she'd had with her conscience just to get her there, it was utterly deflating for Megan to see her quarry disappear into the night. And where could he be going this late, anyway?

A number of answers came immediately to mind. He had an assignation with another woman. Megan had finally annoyed him enough so that he was sneaking off to find employment elsewhere. He was the highwayman on his way to rob more unsuspecting late-night travelers.

Megan pounced on the third answer simply because the first two didn't suit her a'tall. And it made sense. There really hadn't been any robberies until he'd arrived in the area. The hour was ideal right now for such illicit purposes. And for once he wasn't wearing one of those finely made white shirts that he favored and could ill afford—except through illicit means, obviously. And that white shirt could easily be seen at night. His present dark attire could not.

It took her only a few seconds to decide to go after him, a few more to realize that if she was going to catch up with him, she wouldn't have time to saddle Sir Ambrose. The thought of riding bareback was daunting and almost kept her there to confront Devlin when he returned instead. Of course, when he returned, there might not be any evidence of his criminal activities to confront him with, since he could and most likely would hide it elsewhere before returning. And that decided her, since she would very much like to have something like this to hold over that man's head. The thought of it was too tempting by half. She could demand anything of him, put him in his place, make him squirm, make him end his insults.

She ran to get Sir Ambrose without further delay, grabbing only the tack necessary to control the mare, since riding bareback was one thing, but not being able to control a Thoroughbred like Sir Ambrose was another. The slight delay was costly, though. When she reached the road, there was no sign of Devlin anywhere, in any direction.

Megan wasn't about to give up at that point just because there was barely any moonlight and the countryside stretched out dark and ominous around her. She headed in the direction that the robberies had occurred, near the Thackeray estate. In fact, now that she thought of it, the only people who had been robbed were guests of the Thackerays, and each occurrence had been when they were leaving one of Lady Ophelia's parties.

She almost laughed, imagining what vexation the highwayman must be causing old hatchet-face. She did smile. Lady O might even be getting a few no-shows at her parties because of it, at least until the thief was caught. Too bad Megan hadn't thought of it herself.

Her instinct for direction paid off a few minutes later as she caught sight of a movement, just a shadow, disappearing over the next rise in the road. She didn't speed up to catch up with it, however. Knowing the countryside as well as she did, she turned off the road and headed inland, circling around until she finally came upon the small clump of woods that the road passed through just before the Thackeray estate.

A highwayman couldn't ask for a more perfect setting to work in, she supposed. There would be ample concealment for him and his horse, numerous trails in the woods for a getaway that a coach couldn't follow—if the victims even thought to give chase.

Those many trails let Megan come in from the back door, as it were, and stay far enough back from the road so that she couldn't be seen by Devlin or his victims, but she could hear any carriages approaching. Not that she thought she might be lucky enough to have a robbery occur right there in front of her, even though she had chosen to wait in a spot more or less centered in the woods. She still fully expected that she would have to follow the victim for a ways before anything exciting happened, if it happened at all.

This was a weeknight, and Lady O threw her big parties on the weekends, unless she had guests staying over indefinitely. Then every night could be a big "something or other." She was the queen of entertaining, after all. For that matter, she still entertained during the week whether she had houseguests or not, just much smaller gatherings. But a highwayman needed only one or two victims for a profitable night's work.

She settled in to wait, tethering Sir Ambrose and moving a little closer to the road. With the nearly impenetrable darkness of the woods that she had traversed, what she could see of the road seemed much brighter now.

Megan didn't get bored when an hour or so had passed and still no one had come along. She was enjoying herself too much, anticipating catching Devlin and having something to hold over his handsome head.

She finally heard a noise and moved even closer to the road until she could just make out the light flickering from a carriage lantern. The driver of the carriage wasn't very motivated, or perhaps he had imbibed some while his master was being entertained. The vehicle took forever to reach Megan, giving her enough time to decide that she could follow it more easily and more quietly on foot and still keep to the trees.

She did just that, counting her steps so she would know where she had left her horse. But sooner than she expected, the end of the woods was sighted, and for the second time that evening, she was utterly deflated. The carriage would be on the safer open road in seconds. Bloody hell. Either Devlin was letting this one go, or . . .

"Stand and deliver!"

Megan's heart jumped into her throat. He came out of the woods on her side of the road to block the carriage, not ten feet from her. Another few seconds and she might have walked right into him. And if she wasn't mistaken, he was brandishing a pistol to reinforce the order he'd shouted.

The carriage did stand still. The occupants were slower to deliver. Megan was much slower in getting her heart back under control after the fright she'd taken at the sound of that high-pitched voice. High-pitched?

That wretched man, he was disguising his voice. Well, she needed better proof than the sound of his voice, anyway. Actually, she was going to have to confront him the minute he finished. Only how? She wasn't about to unmask him in front of his victims. That wouldn't give her anything to hold over him. It would merely get him arrested, which, actually, was the last thing she wanted to see happen, and that was a surprising thought.

Of course, he still had things to teach her, which he couldn't do if he was carted off to gaol. But was that the only reason she didn't want him arrested? This was no time to probe her motives, however, especially when she hadn't figured out how she was going to stop him from riding off on Caesar as soon as he was through. She'd just have to get closer and be prepared.

Megan did just that, which enabled her to hear more clearly what was going on, too, though that wasn't much. Some low grumbling from the victims, and a nasty chuckle from Devlin, who really seemed to be enjoying the power he was wielding.

But after a few moments more he became impatient. "Toss it down and be quick about it; then you can be on your way. And you'll be quick about that, too, or I might decide I need some practice with this pistol."

"You won't get away with this."

" 'Course I will, you dolt, or were *you* planning to stop me?"

The answer to that was negative. Megan was getting really annoyed with Devlin for his taunting. It was bad enough he was robbing the poor fellow; he didn't have to make sport of him, too.

She was going to tell him that just as soon as they were alone. And since he'd ordered his bounty tossed out on the ground, and would have to dismount to get it, she didn't have to worry about him immediately riding off. She would have ample time to confront him when the carriage left, and it did that now.

They both waited until the carriage was a good distance away to make their moves. But the moment Devlin dismounted, Megan took a step forward—but so did someone else from the other side of the road.

She dropped back, her heart pounding fearfully again. Two of them? Was Devlin involving that nice Mr. Browne in his crimes? But the newcomer was too tall to be Mortimer Browne. And when Devlin noticed him, he was as surprised as Megan.

"Good God, you gave me a fright."

"I'll do more than that, Sanderson, if you don't explain yourself to my satisfaction."

Megan's eyes popped wide open in surprise. *That* had been Devlin's voice, no doubt about it. What the devil? And now she looked more closely at the horse to find that it wasn't Caesar. Did it have to be so dark that she hadn't noticed that little detail sooner? Well, if she had, she wouldn't have stuck around long enough to learn that Devlin *did* know the highwayman, even if he wasn't the culprit himself.

That got proved by Sanderson's reply. "Devlin, is that you? Well, good God, man, what are *you* doing here?"

"I am *not* here," Devlin replied with some very definite annoyance. "I have never been here. You have not seen me here. Is that clear to you?"

"Oh, quite, quite," Sanderson quickly agreed, taking off the kerchief he'd had wrapped over his lower face and stuffing it in a pocket. "Hope you haven't seen me either."

"You, dear boy, aren't that lucky. Now explain yourself, if you can."

The highwayman shrugged, trying to make light of it. "I'm just having a bit of sport, Your—"

"Highway robbery is not sport, you ass. Try again."

"Well, actually, I've had a devilish run of bad luck. Truth is, I needed the blunt."

"It didn't occur to you to ask your father? The earl isn't known to be tight-fisted."

" 'Course it did, but he's a bloody long way from here, and I'm stuck here courting one of the Earl of Wedgwood's daughters. Father sent me here himself. Thinks it's time I settled down. So what was I to do? I sent a letter off to him, but he ain't replied yet. I'm staying with the Thackerays, and my damned hostess thinks she's got to entertain me every bloody day with 'London amusements,' and you know what that means. I lost what little money I came with the first weekend. And I can't bloody well tell Lady Ophelia I'm down and out when I'm here to win one of her daughters."

"You could have suggested other 'amusements' besides gambling, was what you could have done. I would advise you to do that very thing, because your stint as a highwayman comes to an end tonight."

"But I was actually having fun at it."

"You're not thinking of arguing with me, are you, dear boy?"

There was such underlying menace in that question, Megan couldn't blame Sanderson for quickly assuring Devlin, "No, no, I wouldn't think of it."

"You will also return everything you've stolen from these good people."

"But I *can't* do that."

"You can and will."

"But I don't have it all, you see. The trinkets, yes, but there was another game of hazard last night, and, well, my luck hasn't improved yet."

"How much?"

"Eighty pounds."

Devlin made a sound of disgust as he reached into his pocket and came up with a wad of bills that he thrust at Sanderson. The young man took it in good grace, while Megan was flabbergasted that a horse breeder would have that kind of money to just give away.

"You will take that and the rest to the magistrate's tonight. Drop it off with a note saying that you've seen the error of your ways. Do you foresee a problem with that?"

"No, no, tonight it will be."

"Good, because if I don't hear through the gossip mill that everything was returned, and I mean everything, I'll be paying your father a visit. I wouldn't care to do that, he wouldn't care to hear what I have to say, and you wouldn't care for the outcome. I trust we understand each other?"

"Indeed we do. Sorry to put you to the trouble. Won't do it again, I swear . . . I . . ."

His words trailed off because Devlin had slipped back into the woods as quietly as he'd appeared. Megan didn't wait around any longer either, making her way back to where she'd left Sir Ambrose. But she was frowning all the way. Why would an earl's son be so intimidated by a horse breeder?

Chapter 22

The exchange Megan had witnessed between Devlin and the young lord-turned-temporary-highwayman bothered her all the way home. Certainly, she had to allow that there were any number of ways that Lord Sanderson could know Devlin, the most obvious being from the Sherring Cross stables, where Devlin had come from. But just because Devlin had worked for the Duke of Wrothston didn't account for the deference paid him by an earl's son. Sanderson should have put Devlin in his place and done the threatening, not the other way around.

Of course, threatening to go to the boy's father had made an impression, but that hadn't come until later. She supposed, though, that Sanderson might think that Devlin still worked at Sherring Cross and might go to the duke with his tale. He *had* been surprised to see Devlin here in Devonshire, after all. Then, too, she had to allow that Devlin, horse breeder or not, had a presence about him that was definitely formidable and downright intimidating when he chose to portray it. She had been susceptible to it herself.

Regardless, there was still something about that exchange that bothered Megan, and it wasn't until she was nearly home that it came to her. Sanderson's deference had been there from the first, as had been Devlin's command of the situation—as if their circumstances were reversed, with Devlin being the lord and Sanderson the servant. Which made no sense. Working for a duke, no matter for how long, did not give a man prestige above his station, some arrogance maybe, but a servant still ought to know his place, especially next to a peer of the realm.

You're being snobbish again.
But I'm right.

What you are is irritated as hell because he didn't turn out to be the high-wayman.

That was true enough. She really had been looking forward to holding that over him. Now, instead, she was probably in for another lecture about riding out at ungodly hours. Dratted man, why couldn't he act like normal servants and not question his betters?

You're doing it again.

I'm merely getting into the proper frame of mind to face a tyrant.

He's not a tyrant, and hasn't it occurred to you that lectures only come from concerned people, those concerned with your welfare and well-being?

Ha!

In either case, you'd better come up with a good excuse for where you've been, or will the truth do?

You know it won't. But maybe he's not back yet and I can sneak Sir Ambrose into her stall and get out of there before I'm noticed.

I wouldn't count on it.

She didn't, and he was—back, that is—and standing just inside the stable doors with his hands on his hips and one of the most stern expressions she'd ever seen on a man. Megan opted to brazen her way through what was coming.

"So you're back?" she said before he could. "I was going to ask you to accompany me tonight on my errand, but you couldn't be found."

"Accompany you where?"

"One of my father's tenants is doing poorly. I was supposed to visit the family this afternoon to see if they needed anything, only I was otherwise occupied and forgot—but better late than—"

"No sense, no bloody sense a'tall," he said as he hauled her off Sir Ambrose. "And without a saddle!" he added as he noticed the lack thereof. His eyes came back to her. "You actually rode this animal without a saddle?"

Megan groaned inwardly, having completely forgotten about that. But brazenness was working. At least he no longer looked so stern, so she continued in that line.

"You make it sound as if I've never done so before," she retorted. "It's not difficult, I assure you. But I don't know what you're making such a fuss about. The only reason I was going to have you escort me was to avoid this very thing, this bad habit you have of involving yourself in my affairs, but the fact is that I certainly didn't *need* your escort, since I didn't even leave our property. But as long as this seems to be the hour for interrogations, where did *you* go?"

"Out to catch a thief."

She hadn't expected him to admit it. "Did you have any luck?"

"No," he lied.

She knew he lied, but to say so would admit she had followed him. "Too bad. Once he is caught, maybe you'll stop interfering with what I do and when I do it."

"When you do it? I doubt it. Someone has to teach you some sense, and come to think of it, there's no time like the present."

He caught her hand and started dragging her to the mounting block. Megan's mouth dropped open, her eyes widened incredulously, and she was a little bit in shock, knowing exactly what the man intended doing.

"Wait a minute. Devlin, you can't really . . . I'll have you arrested. I'll have you—"

She landed hard across his knees the moment he sat down on the mounting block. She was about to scream her head off when he said, "Making a lot of noise won't stop me, brat. It'll just draw you an audience to watch."

That was perfectly true and out of the question. She clamped her lips shut. She wouldn't make a sound now if it killed her. But, by God, the man was going to regret this. If it was the last thing she did, she'd get even, somehow, and then . . .

The first smack was a revelation. It made a lot of noise when his hand connected with her bottom, though it didn't actually hurt. She'd forgotten that she'd worn one of her thickest riding skirts. Well, the joke was going to be on Devlin, but she'd never tell. Of course, that was only the first whack. By the time he finished, and that was quite a while later, repetition had made silk out of thick wool, and Megan didn't feel like laughing. She was furious that he could get away with doing that to her.

When he set her on her feet, she didn't give it prior thought, she simply swung at him with a closed fist—and missed. If that wasn't enough to make her explode, she noticed his lips curling the slightest bit. Clearly the man found her impotent rage amusing.

"You are the most horrible bastard I've ever met!" she all but screeched.

"And how many have you met?"

His dispassionate reply gave her pause, long enough to inquire with genuine curiosity, "Is there no insult that you won't shrug off?"

"Why should I be insulted?" he asked reasonably. "You're all hot air and brambles, brat—except when you're in my arms. Then you're just hot."

She couldn't believe he'd said that. "You are dismissed! Fired! Exterminated!"

He cocked a brow at the last one. "Is that wishful thinking?"

"You know what I meant."

"Indeed. Shall you be the one to tell your father, or shall I?"

She thought that over for a moment and knew the wretched man had won—

again. She wasn't about to tell her father or anyone else about this humiliating experience.

"Why can't you just get out of my life?" she asked begrudgingly.

"What? Retreat under fire? Desert the war? Wouldn't think of it, dear girl."

That bit of absurdity had her looking around for something to throw at him. But her obvious intention brought him to his feet and his hands to her shoulders.

"I gave you fair warning this morning not to take such stupid risks with yourself," he told her, no longer amused. "That spanking was to reinforce the warning, but perhaps you also need to be shown what happens to reckless females who go traipsing about at indecent hours."

His intent was just as clear and had her drawing back as far as she could, appalled that he could think of kissing *now*. But little good that did her with his hands already gripping her. She was pulled forward, his head bent, and his mouth descended on her uncooperative lips before she could get a word out to stop him.

As soon as she realized that he was playing right into her hands because he thought he was teaching her a lesson but unbeknownst to him it was a lesson she wanted, Megan relaxed her stiffness and immediately experienced a swirl of giddy pleasure. He held her closer and the pleasure increased, as did her pulse, her breathing, and her sense of wonder. So nice, this contact with his body. Who would have thought? But this lesson wasn't over. She decided she'd like it never to end.

She thought he was finished when he stopped the kissing, but it was only to move his lips along her cheek to her ear. And there was another new sensation to savor, and goose bumps spreading down her back.

"Teach me," she said on a gasp as his lips started down her neck.

"What?"

"How to kiss."

Devlin groaned, dropping his head to her shoulder. "I don't think I want you to know how."

Well, that was bloody unfair of him, she thought indignantly. "Why not?"

"I'm having enough trouble as it is, controlling what you make me feel."

"Then let me go."

His head came up, his eyes fixing on hers with an intensity that made her shiver. "Not yet. This was a lesson in what can happen to girls who ride out alone at night, remember? I'm going to finish it if it kills me."

"I got the point."

"Not yet you haven't." And his hand came up to cup her breast.

Megan sucked in her breath, never imagining that such a simple touch could evoke such a wealth of feeling. Of course, she knew he shouldn't touch her there, that this was part of his lesson. But she also guessed that this was some of the "more" that she'd wanted to know about.

He probably thought he was shocking her, or hoped he was, and she wouldn't disabuse him of that notion or he might stop altogether. So she closed her eyes just in case he could see there what she was really feeling. But she wasn't shocked, she was amazed that each movement of his gently kneading palm was sending sensations to other areas besides her breasts, which were already tingling beneath his caress.

She was starting to get urges that she didn't understand. She wanted his mouth back on hers. She wanted to touch him as he was her. She wanted him doing this because he wanted to, not because of a damn lesson he felt she deserved.

And then his mouth was back, but with much more passion than before, and his hands gripped her hips to pull them in to his groin. She whimpered, half in startlement at the heat that shot into her own loins, and half in discomfort from the tight grip he had on her. But the sound took his hands away from her completely, and it took a moment for her to realize that she'd been released, lesson over.

"Megan, I'm going to burn to a cinder in a moment," he rasped out, and the man actually looked like he was in pain. "Get the hell out of here while you still can."

She didn't want to. She wanted his arms back around her, his lips—but prudence and that "while you still can" let her common sense take over for the moment. Only she gave him one last look that was so full of yearning, it made him groan and reach for her again. Megan, startled out of her bemusement, ran like hell.

Chapter 23

❧❧❧

Not until the next day, and only after careful examination, did Megan admit to herself that she might have been a little reckless last night and deserving of a scolding—not a spanking, but a scolding. She had acted impulsively to follow Devlin and to make assumptions about where he was going. The fact was, if Devlin hadn't been after the thief himself, he wouldn't have shown himself right before she was about to, wouldn't even have been there. And she would have confronted a stranger who wouldn't have been the least bit intimidated by her as he was by Devlin. She would also have been quite alone with him, on a dark road, with darker woods on either side of them.

It was entirely possible that exactly what Devlin was predicting could happen *could* have happened. Just because the thief was an earl's son and supposedly a gentleman wouldn't have saved her. A lord acting as a highwayman left his principles at home, didn't he? Confessing who she was probably wouldn't have done any good either. After all, she was out late at night, and without an escort. Why should she be believed?

It was galling to admit that Devlin was right. She had behaved carelessly, recklessly, without a thought to the danger and risk she was taking. Just the idea of a stranger doing to her what Devlin had done made her skin crawl. Aside from that, good God, she could have been seriously hurt.

Maybe you ought to tell him you were wrong and won't do it again.

And feed his colossal arrogance? Besides, Devlin still had no right to abuse my backside. He should have brought my behavior to my father's attention, not seen to it himself. I wouldn't have liked it, but that would have been the proper thing to do.

So tell him that.

I think I will.

Devlin hadn't made an appearance this morning when she'd gone for her ride—at a perfectly decent hour. She'd even lingered over Sir Ambrose's grooming after she returned, but he still hadn't shown himself. Mortimer had, before she'd left the stable, and when asked, he'd informed her that Devlin was sleeping off a "powerful headache." That probably sounded worse than it was, though she'd still spent more time than she ought to today worrying about it.

She could always inquire about his headache if she lost her nerve about upbraiding him for last night. But when she entered the stable for the second time that day, he still wasn't around, but again Mortimer was. The older man was just bringing out one of the new mares for exercising.

Megan stopped to admire the horse, and to ask with what she hoped didn't sound like concern, "Is Mr. Jefferys still sleeping off that headache?"

The little man actually chuckled. "He's starting on another one, is what he's doing now."

Megan frowned. "Another one? How does one 'start' on a headache?"

"By hitting the bottle, miss—two or three bottles, actually."

She wasn't quite sure how to take that startling news. Devlin was getting foxed? And he'd begun the effort last night, obviously, to have had a powerful headache early this morning. And Mortimer's amused look when he'd said it implied it might be because of her. Because of her? That was a thrilling thought, that she could drive the man to drink. Did she really have that much of an effect on him?

Don't be so conceited. His drinking probably doesn't have anything to do with you.

I know, but it was nice to think so for a moment.

At any rate, you don't want to run into that particular man while he's foxed.

Don't I know it. He's nasty enough as it is when he's sober.

That, too, but I was referring to the lack of control intoxicated people have over their emotions. And since his emotions are usually volatile when you're around—

"I get the picture," Megan mumbled irritably beneath her breath.

"What was that, miss?"

"Nothing, Mr. Browne." Megan sighed. "I've just decided to visit my friend Tiffany. I'll take the mare, if it's all right with you."

"Certainly. Saves me putting her through her paces, and she's gentle enough. I'll just change the saddles for you."

Megan nodded, but while she waited, her eyes kept straying to the back of the stable.

Don't even think about it.

Megan flushed guiltily. *Well, aren't you curious about what kind of a drunk he makes?*

Probably an ornery one.

Or a silly one. That I'd love to witness.

You're asking for trouble to find out.

Now you're getting cautious? Must be because I'm going to visit Tiffany. She's always a good influence on you.

And on you. She'll tell you to stay away from inebriated men.

Good God, you don't think I'm going to tell Tiffany about any of this, do you?

You probably will.

Megan had no intention of doing so, not when her own feelings were so confused and, yes, shameful. But she hadn't been with Tiffany for more than ten minutes before this question popped out: "What would you think if I married beneath myself?"

Tiffany responded pragmatically. "How far beneath yourself are we talking about?"

"This is just suppose, now," Megan thought it prudent to point out. "I'm not actually contemplating doing anything so ridiculous—"

"How far?"

"Say he wasn't even a gentleman. Would you be shocked? Would it cause a great scandal, do you think?"

Tiffany stared at her for a long moment before she burst out, "Megan Penworthy, you haven't fallen in love with that horse breeder, have you?"

"Absolutely not," Megan scoffed, though her cheeks were beginning to heat up. "All he and I do is fight. Why, we don't even like each other."

"I'm glad to hear it."

Megan ignored that as she plopped down in a chair in Tiffany's newly redecorated room, then let out a long sigh. "But I have to allow—I find him so exciting, Tiff. When I'm around him I feel so, oh, I don't know, bubbly inside. I'm sure it's just because our fights are so stimulating, and they are, you know. I actually shout at him."

Tiffany was starting to grin. "You don't."

"Yes, I do," Megan assured her. "And he gets just as furious at me."

"With reason?"

"Usually. But I'm beginning to think I might enjoy fighting with him, though it certainly doesn't seem like it at the time."

"You're probably just bored, and he's a handsome man, an incredibly handsome man. Perfectly understandable. But does he have any good qualities?"

"Not a one—well, actually, he does seem to be overly concerned with my welfare. He gets positively livid when I do something he thinks might be a danger to me."

Tiffany's eyes widened. "Megan, what *have* you been doing since we got back?"

Megan shrugged and said offhandedly, "I merely thought Devlin might be our highwayman."

"But haven't you heard? The man's conscience got the better of him. He's returned everything he stole and then some, swearing he'll never succumb to wicked temptations again. It was all in a note he sent the magistrate."

"So he *did* do it."

Tiffany blinked. "What do you mean, he *did* do it? That sounds as if you knew—"

"I did."

"Megan!"

"Well, I can't help it if I happened to be there when he was being ordered to return everything. I *told* you I suspected it was Devlin."

"You mean it was?" Tiffany asked incredulously.

"No, more's the pity," Megan grumbled. "He was out to catch the thief himself and he did just that. I just happened to be following him."

"Hoping to catch him red-handed?"

"Something like that." And Megan briefly explained her late-night adventure, ending with, "He was positively furious when I returned, not that I told him where I'd really been. I can just imagine his reaction if he'd found that out."

"Megan, you have *got* to stop acting so impulsively. Do you have any idea what could have happened?"

She did now, but she couldn't bring herself to confess the rest of what had happened last night, even to her best friend. "I know, and I'm turning over a new leaf. I'll even have one of your footmen escort me home tonight, which will avoid another argument with Devlin, since my going about unescorted is one of the things he objects to."

"You might as well get used to it. In London we don't go *anywhere* without the proper escort. But guess what? Tyler's mother has offered to sponsor us. She's also offered to let us stay with her."

"But that's wonderful!" Megan exclaimed. "I know the major and his wife are dears, and they've known my father forever or they wouldn't have agreed to host us, but to be honest, they don't *know* anyone. But Lady Whately knows everyone, doesn't she?"

"Just about. I'd say we'll have you married before the end of the year after all."

"I hope so, because my curiosity has really been driving me crazy lately about lovemaking. I can't wait to get married and finally find out what's the big to-do about it."

"As long as you *do* plan on waiting for the one before the other."

"Absolutely. I might be thinking about it a lot lately"—an understatement—"but that's all I'm doing."

"Maybe you'd better stay away from your horse breeder altogether," Tiffany suggested cautiously.

Megan laughed. "Now *that's* the kind of advice I'm used to. But you needn't worry in this case. I'm not about to ruin my chances for an excellent match by dallying with a lowborn rogue, no matter how handsome he is."

"And exciting."

"No matter how exciting, either."

"And stimulating."

"You've made your point, Tiffany. I'll never go near him again."

Chapter 24

She'd said it, but Megan knew she'd never stick to it. Staying away from Devlin was an impossibility. Not that she couldn't arrange it. It would be a simple matter to avoid the stable altogether. She need only have her horse brought to her when she wanted to ride, and returned when she was through. Any one of the footmen would be happy to oblige her in that. That she had always done the fetching and grooming herself was actually an abnormal habit, though one she could break if necessary.

The impossibility was that she didn't want to stay away from Devlin.

'Bout time you admitted it.

But tell me why it's so?

Maybe you're falling in love with him after all.

Don't be absurd. There's not a thing about him worth loving.

What about his concern for you?

Not a good enough reason.

His kisses? You can't say you don't adore them.

He can't be the only good kisser around.

What about his unique charm?

What charm? He hasn't any. He's a damned grouch, is what he is.

That's just it. He's not a happy man. He needs a woman to soften him.

I'm not a reformer.

What about what he makes you feel?

I don't know what that is any more than you do. Now forget it. I am not falling in love with that man. Do you think I want to live in a stable the rest of my life?

With someone like him to share it, I doubt you'd mind all that much. What do you love more than horses anyway—besides his kisses?

That doesn't mean I want to live among horses. Good God, do you know what you're suggesting?

Yes.

Megan looked around almost guiltily, but the footman escorting her home wasn't paying the least attention to her, wouldn't know that she was having an argument with herself anyway.

I don't know why I still talk to you. Tiffany puts me in a good mood, and you put me right back into a rotten one. Just because I've agreed to let Devlin teach me how to kiss—

He didn't offer to.

But he will—doesn't mean I would consider marrying the man. I won't consider it. I'm going to marry an earl at the very least.

Stepping down already, are we?

Just being a little more realistic. There aren't that many dukes to choose from, at least not young ones.

Is that grand house to outdo Lady O's still all that important?

Yes.

Stubborn. He hit it on the nose. Too stubborn for your own good.

So now you're agreeing with him, too? I suppose you also think I'm spoiled.

Well, aren't you?

Megan didn't say another word, simmering silently the rest of the way home. When she reached the manor, she thanked her escort and waved him off before dismounting and walking Sir Ambrose back to the stable. Amazingly, considering the conversation she'd just had with herself, she wasn't thinking about Devlin or possibly encountering him.

But he was there, and he wasn't alone.

" . . . but my mum got worried when you didn't come for your dinner," Cora was saying, "so I brung you this basket. Big man like yourself has to eat, don't he?"

"So sweet of you, but food isn't what I need right now." Cora giggled at that, causing Devlin to exclaim, "Good God, when'd you start doing that?"

"What?"

"Never mind. C'mere."

Megan stood rooted to the spot just inside the doors. She couldn't see them, but she knew both voices well enough, and if she thought she'd been angry with herself earlier, that was nothing compared with what she felt right then, imagining Devlin kissing the kitchen maid.

"Cora Lamb," Megan intoned sternly, "just what do you think you're doing?"

There was a muffled shriek, then Cora came stumbling out from behind the hayrick, trying hastily to right her uniform as well as herself.

"Oh, it's you, miss," she said breathlessly. "I swear you sounded like me mum."

"Perhaps your mum ought to be apprised of what you're doing out here."

"No need to do that, Miss Megan. I only brung Mr. Jefferys a bite to eat, is all. And I'll be getting back to the house now."

"You do that, and next time remember that your duties don't extend to the stable. If Mr. Jefferys wants to eat, he can find his way to the kitchen. Don't let me catch you waiting on him again, Cora."

With a bob and a hasty "No, miss, I won't," Cora all but ran out of the stable.

"You shouldn't have done that," Devlin said at Megan's back.

She swung around to glare at him. "Is that so? I'm supposed to turn a blind eye while you seduce the servants? I don't think so."

"If they want to be seduced, it's none of your bloody business, is it?"

She finally noted the slight slur in his words, as well as his appalling condition. Hay clung to his clothes and hair. His white shirt was open to the waist and only half tucked into his trousers. He was minus his boots. And he couldn't seem to stand there without weaving a bit.

"You look disgraceful," she said scathingly.

"I was sleeping when that female started yoo-hooing me. I came out because I thought she was you."

"I don't yoo-hoo, you wretched man."

"You don't giggle either, thank God. All you do is drive a man to drink." He was distracted then by her horse wandering toward the back of the stable. "And what are you doing with that mare?"

Her chin rose defensively. "I was exercising her—with Mr. Browne's permission."

His head swiveled to the open doors to note the darkness outside. Megan could almost read his mind, especially when those blue-green eyes came back to her, narrowed and starting to fill with heat.

She forestalled him coldly. "I spent most of the day at Tiffany's, but I had an escort home, so don't start in on me. *I'm* not the guilty party here who was cavorting in the hay with the wrong woman."

It must have been the contempt in her tone that set him off, because suddenly he was quite furious. "The wrong woman? Let me assure you that I have reached such a state of need, thanks to you, that *any* woman will do!"

"You're blaming *me* for your licentious behavior?" she asked incredulously.

"You're damned right I am!"

Having said it, or more to the point, snarled it, he surprised Megan by turning away. But he must have moved too quickly because he swayed again, and it was no straight line that he walked to the stable entrance.

He's still foxed, Megan thought smugly. She almost smiled, wondering if she ought to tell him he was going in the wrong direction. But he stopped on his own, and her eyes widened as she watched him close the stable doors and drop the bolt into place.

Amusement fled, replaced by wariness as she remembered what had happened to her the last time he'd been this angry, just last night. There might not have been any lingering evidence this morning that she'd suffered his wrath, but she'd gone to bed with her bottom still smarting. And the man wasn't himself right now. He'd been drinking a good part of the day, if Mortimer could be believed. He couldn't be thinking clearly if he'd thought *she* was Cora. By God, if he spanked her for interrupting his lovemaking, she'd— she'd shoot him.

"What are you doing?" she demanded, backing up as he started in her direction again.

"You should have turned about and gone back to the house without interfering. Should have stayed away from me today altogether. But I suppose I should thank you, since I didn't really want her, and now that you've sent her off, you can bloody well take her place."

Megan backed into the hayrick, losing her balance against it. She was only lying back on it at a slightly slanted angle, but that allowed Devlin to lean over her, one hand placed on either side of her shoulders. She shook her head wordlessly. He smiled down at her.

"What, you no longer want a lesson in kissing?" he asked lazily. "Or did I dream that, your asking me to teach you how to do it?"

Was that all he was talking about? Suddenly there were new possibilities to this situation, and the mere thought of these sent a warm thrill straight to Megan's belly.

"You're willing to teach me now?"

"If you tell me why you want to learn."

"I don't want my future husband to be disappointed in me," she said truthfully.

She thought for a moment he was going to laugh. Instead he leaned closer until his lips were just a hairsbreadth away from hers. She could smell brandy, but mixed with the scent of hay and musk, it wasn't unpleasant.

"Open your mouth, brat."

For once she didn't mind the name he persisted in calling her, because he said it tenderly this time, giving it almost the sound of an endearment. And she really couldn't think about that now, when his lips were so close to touching hers.

"Do you want to start slow, or do you want to find out what a real kiss is like?"

He had to be teasing her. What had he been doing those other times if not really kissing her?

"I want to know all there is to know about it," she assured him.

"Remember you said that if this shocks you," he warned just before his tongue invaded her mouth.

Megan would have gasped if her breath weren't locked in her throat, not from shock, but from a deluge of unanticipated sensations converging on her all at once. It felt like her blood was soaring, her legs were melting, her insides were coming apart. This was that pleasant feeling she'd felt before, only now it was magnified a hundred times, and she didn't know if she could withstand so much feeling all at once. Then there was more.

His body pressed slowly into hers and liquid heat spread into her loins. He groaned deep in his throat and her breasts responded by tightening. His hand came to assuage the feeling there and her heart slammed against her chest.

"Don't hide your tongue from me," he said against her lips. "Give it to me, Megan. Taste me."

It seemed like she no longer had a will of her own, she obeyed him with such eagerness. But then she wanted to taste him. She simply hadn't known that she could until he ordered it. But if she could copy him in the kissing, could she also copy him in the touching? Because that was another overwhelming urge she had, and this time she didn't wait to be directed.

When her hand slipped between them as his had done, he moved slightly to the side to give her access, which gave him more access as well, which he took swift advantage of. Suddenly there was no cloth between his hand and her breasts. He'd somehow worked her blouse open and got beneath her camisole, and she discovered fire. Good God, his hand couldn't be that warm, but it was. His chest under her own palm couldn't be that hot either, but it was. He'd talked of burning to a cinder last night. Was it possible?

Megan didn't care at the moment, not one little bit. She felt as if she were falling, falling . . . Good God, they *were* falling!

Devlin tore his mouth away from hers to say, "Bloody hell, we're—" He landed with a grunt, mostly because Megan landed on top of him. "—Falling," he finished after the fact.

At which point he started to laugh, deep laughter of the like she'd never heard from him. It was infectious, especially in light of what had happened. This was not precisely the best time to slip off a hayrick. Fortunately, they'd fallen onto a bed of hay, the remainder of what had been pitched earlier in the day. Still, it wasn't how she would have imagined a lesson in kissing to end.

She was laughing as hard as he was, then harder when the shaking of his chest caused her to slip off him as well. She rolled onto her back, holding her belly until her humor finally wound down. But her eyes had watered, and she tried to find the pocket of her jacket to get a kerchief when she noticed one dangling in front of her.

She made quick use of it, then lowered it to see that Devlin had rolled onto his side and was leaning on one elbow, grinning at her.

"That fall was not part of the lesson."

She grinned back at him. "Thank you for telling me. I wasn't quite sure."

He chuckled, but then his eyes lit on her open blouse and they seemed to kindle with heat again instantly. "Actually," he said in the most sensuous tone, "we're in a much better position now for kissing. Do you want to learn more?"

"There's more?" she replied in wonder.

"Most definitely."

"Show me."

He bent toward her, but then he stopped and shook his head as if to clear it, and suddenly he was frowning. "No, I—good God, I must be mad. Go home, Megan, and do it now. This lesson is over."

Her disappointment was almost too keen to bear. "Why?" she whispered.

"Because I lost myself in that last kiss. I forgot for a moment that you're an innocent miss with too much curiosity for her own good."

"Are you saying you would have made love to me?" she ventured.

"Yes, damn it."

She hoped that was all that was bothering him. "But I wouldn't have let you. I would have stopped you. You *would* stop if I told you to, wouldn't you?"

"Certainly," he said indignantly.

"Then I don't see a problem."

"Don't you? I'm not exactly sober, you know," he said, as if she hadn't noticed.

"I don't mind." She leaned toward him then and implored softly, "Show me."

He groaned and gathered her close. "Give me your tongue again." She did, but this time he didn't let her explore with it, but gently sucked on it instead for a while, then said, "There are other places to do that."

"Where?"

He moved to draw her earlobe between his lips for the same tantalizing treatment. She shivered deliciously, gasping. "Where else?"

She tried to concentrate on the path his mouth was taking so she could anticipate his destination, but she was enjoying the sensations that he was evoking on the way too much. And then she sucked in her breath as one nipple was drawn deeply into the heat of his mouth. She was incredulous and a little shocked that this could be part of kissing, but she didn't stop him. God, no, she wasn't about to stop him—not yet.

When she later felt a coolness on her legs, it didn't register that her skirt was being raised. When she felt a tugging on her drawers, that didn't make much sense either, but she finally asked, "What are you doing now?"

His mouth came back to hers for a deeply stirring kiss before he said, "Showing you everything. Isn't that what you wanted? Or are you afraid now?"

"A little."

"You should be."

It was the wrong thing to say, or the right thing, challenging her stubbornness and curiosity at once. "Don't stop, Devlin, not yet."

He kissed her again, so that she barely noticed her drawers coming off completely. But she couldn't miss warm fingers slipping between her legs. She shrieked in surprise, but the sound was muffled by his mouth. Then she was moaning, and gripping him to her, and reveling in the most startling sensations yet. Her legs parted of their own accord, her body and its responses were taking over, and she didn't care.

"Is—is this part of kissing?" she gasped out when his mouth returned to her neck, then her breasts.

"Yes," he lied without the least qualm.

"Then I have to do that to you?"

"No," he croaked, knowing he'd never survive it.

"But I want to."

"I'm going to die."

She thought she was, too, especially when he moved on top of her, placing his hips between hers, and that hard part of his body was pressing into the place he'd heated with his fingers, giving her the same pleasure as before.

But then a sharp pain swiftly pierced her and there was nothing pleasurable in that. Her eyes flew open in shock. How? No, maybe not. Maybe that pain and fullness inside her now wasn't him, but still his fingers. Yet she could feel his hands, both hands, beneath her back, holding her tightly to him. She felt shock again. This wasn't supposed to happen.

"Tell me you aren't making love to me," she demanded in rising panic.

He became very still, suffering some shock of his own. "I'm afraid it's too late to tell you that."

"But you can't be!"

"I'm sorry, Megan, truly, but the damage is done."

Her shock turned rapidly to resentment as all the repercussions bombarded her. "I won't marry you."

That wasn't the wisest thing to say to a man who'd just broken every scruple he possessed. "I bloody well wasn't going to ask you to—"

"Good!"

"—but now I have to."

"Well, aren't you fortunate that you already have my answer," she retorted acidly. "Now get off me!"

His face dropped into the curve of her neck with a groan. "I can't, Megan."

She wasn't interested in his problem. "Of course you can. You said you would."

"That was when I could. Now—oh, God." He thrust once, twice, then was still again.

That hadn't hurt, but she was too furious to notice. "I'm getting hysterical, Devlin. If you don't want a crying, screaming woman on your hands, then—"

"In all fairness, I owe you a climax. You've come this far, you might as well—"

"I didn't mean to come this far and you know it!" she hissed.

He rose until he was leaning over her and she was able to see at last his own upset. Guilt was tearing into him much more sharply than her verbal abuse, and in his present inebriated state, he couldn't handle either too well.

"Then you should have left when I warned you to!"

"That's right," she bit out. "Absolve yourself of guilt, why don't you?"

"If I was doing that, I wouldn't have offered to marry you."

"You know very well I can't marry a horse breeder! My father would never allow it, either."

"On the contrary," he said with a full measure of his arrogance. "Once the circumstances are explained, your father will give his wholehearted approval, I do assure you, so don't use that as an excuse for refusing me."

"Don't you dare tell him what you did to me! Don't you dare tell anyone. This did not happen."

"Megan, you can't pretend—"

"I can do anything I please, and if I please to go on with my life as if this didn't happen, I damn well will."

"Fine! You do that!"

He rolled over and got to his feet without swaying. Megan scrambled to her feet just as quickly, then spent a few moments gasping over each proof of his crime that she could see—and feel. She had been made love to and she was still fully clothed—well, almost. She swiped up her drawers and marched to the doors, throwing back the bolt. Devlin she didn't spare a glance for, but he was watching her with brooding eyes.

"When you come to your senses, brat," he said to her back, "you know where I'll be."

"You'll be in hell before I come to you again for anything," was her final retort before she stomped out, still without looking back.

Devlin turned and, with a growl, smashed his fist through the nearest wall, then went back to his room and smashed his remaining stock of brandy.

Chapter 25

Megan stayed in her room for three days brooding, though the word went out in the household that she was merely under the weather. But there was only so much brooding someone of her exuberant nature could tolerate. So she'd made a mistake. It wasn't the end of the world, at least not yet. And the fates couldn't be so cruel as to visit upon her clear evidence of her one and only fall from grace. She believed that wholeheartedly—but she'd wait until she had actual proof of that before celebrating.

In the meantime, she got back to her daily routine, with one major exception. She gave up riding for a while, or anything else that would cause her to send to the stable for anything. That, of course, kept her housebound, and there was only so much of that that she could stomach, too.

Finally, she packed a trunk and went for an extended stay with Tiffany, giving her father the excuse that they had innumerable plans to make for the upcoming trip to London, and that could be done more easily if they were together—which was nothing out of the ordinary. They had frequently, through the years, spent weeks at a time at each other's houses. It was nothing to cause comment about, nor did it imply she was running away from something. Only an arrogant horse breeder might get the latter impression, and she wasn't the least bit concerned about what he thought.

At least she wasn't until he showed up at Tiffany's house her second day there, requesting to speak with her. Apparently her absence from the stable hadn't bothered him as long as she had been at home and accessible, but now that she'd left home, he had something to say about it.

Of course, she refused to see him. And he went away—what else could he do?—without leaving a message, which told her it couldn't have been anything serious that he wanted. But he came back the next day, and the next, and that told her something else. The man wasn't going to give up until he'd said his piece. But Megan was nothing if not stubborn. She wasn't going to hear it.

The trouble with that was that this new, uncommunicative war they were having couldn't be fought privately. Tiffany's servants were beginning to talk, Tiffany was dying of curiosity herself, and Tiffany's butler, male that he was, was taking sides and starting to give Megan reproving looks.

But she could withstand all that easily enough. Obstinacy had its uses, and she had plenty to spare. It was her own urges that she was having trouble dealing with, for ironically, despite what had happened, she was beginning to miss Devlin. She missed their fights. She missed the sight of him, which was always, no matter how angry she might be with him, a pleasure to her senses.

But she still wouldn't receive him at Tiffany's. And she wasn't going to go home, where he had access to her house and could search her out, until she could tell him, truthfully, that he had nothing to worry about, that there would be no unwelcome results from their indiscretion.

She didn't even blame him anymore for what had happened. She blamed her curiosity. She blamed her body for liking too much what he'd been doing to it. And she blamed that part of her that had talked her into letting him teach her about kissing, when her common sense had been against the idea from the start.

"Are you ever going to say why you're so mad at him?" Tiffany asked one day over lunch, after Megan had given the order, for the ninth time, to tell Devlin she wasn't available.

"Do I look mad?"

"Well, no—but you must be. Why else don't you want to talk to him?"

Megan tried to shrug the matter off. "You advised me to stay away from him, remember?"

"And how often do you follow my advice?" Tiffany countered. "Now come on, why are you hiding here?"

"I'm not hiding."

"This is your best friend you're talking to."

Megan sighed. She was amazed that Tiffany had held her tongue this long. But at least she had two shameful experiences to choose from for this confession, and the first was no longer as shocking as the second one.

"The man thinks he's my father."

"Oh, come now," Tiffany scoffed. "His interest in you *can't* be paternal."

"In this one instance it most definitely is," Megan insisted. "He claims

I need a keeper, and he's backed up that contention by assuming the role, complete with disciplinary measures. He—he—"

"He what?" Tiffany prompted impatiently.

Megan looked down at her plate, her cheeks starting to scald. "He spanked me."

"He did *what*?!"

"He put me over his knees and—"

"I know how it's done! But he's a—he's only a—how could he dare?"

"Easily. Devlin doesn't behave like he ought to, nor has he ever done so. The fact is, there's not a subservient or deferential bone in his body. I suppose that's one reason he's so fascinating. He just doesn't fit into the standard order of things. He's a servant, but a servant who won't take orders, who can't be dismissed, who's got more arrogance than ten pompous lords."

"You're making excuses for him?"

Megan glanced up to see that Tiffany's shock was mounting. "Absolutely not," she assured her friend, then shrugged. "But you asked how he could dare. That's how."

"Then he must have been surprised when he got dismissed despite that ridiculous stipulation in the stallion's sales contract," Tiffany said, drawing the wrong conclusion. "Is that why he's trying to see you? To beg your forgiveness so he can get his job back?"

The thought of it was so preposterous, Megan couldn't help laughing. "Devlin beg? He wouldn't know how."

"He doesn't think he can force you to reinstate him, does he?"

Megan squirmed now, seeing no way to avoid admitting, "He wasn't—"

She was saved for the moment when the Robertses' butler knocked and opened the double doors to announce in an aggrieved tone, "He's back, Miss Megan. He says he won't leave this time until you see him."

Tiffany shot immediately to her feet. "Of all the—*I'll* see to this."

Megan rose, too. "Tiff, no—"

But Tiffany was already out the door, and Megan could hear her accosting Devlin in the hall. "Your gall is astounding, Mr. Jefferys. How you can dare come here after what you did is beyond comprehension. And even if Megan would agree to see you, I wouldn't permit it, so leave this house and don't come—now just a—you can't—"

Megan braced herself, expecting to see Devlin marching into the dining room, and he did, not stopping until he towered over her. Even though this was a situation she had tried to avoid, her senses still ate up the sight of him.

"You *told* her?"

She knew what he thought. "Not about *that*," she replied in a furious whisper. "About the other."

"What other?"

"That you abused my—my posterior."

"Oh," he said, the heat going out of his expression, to be replaced, incredibly, with genuine concern. "Are you all right, Megan?"

"Certainly," she said uncomfortably.

"We have to talk."

"No."

"You can't avoid me forever."

He said that with such confidence that Megan's stubbornness reared its ornery head. "Actually, I can—at least until I'm safely married—to someone else."

That answer wasn't to his liking; it made him so furious, in fact, that Megan cringed to see his reaction. But he made no reply to her. He stalked out instead, though not before he growled at Tiffany's stiff figure in the doorway, "She deserved it."

"Well, I never!" Tiffany said huffily and slammed the door shut behind him. "Is that the kind of behavior you had to put up with?"

"Constantly."

"He should have been dismissed sooner, regardless of any stipulations."

Megan sat down, a strange kind of dejection coming over her that made her feel like bursting into tears. Dispassionately, she said, "He wasn't dismissed."

"You can't be serious! What *is* your father thinking of?"

"My father doesn't know anything about it. I never told him."

"Megan! What can *you* be thinking of? If that wasn't grounds for dismissal and worse—"

"Even if I did deserve it?"

"Yes, even so. It wasn't *his* place to correct you—Did you?"

"Sort of—yes. But I told you that he gets overly concerned about me, and he was furious that I'd put myself in danger that night."

"That night? This wasn't the night you followed him, was it?"

"The same."

"And you kept that to yourself when you told me about it?" Tiffany said reproachfully.

Megan was feeling worse and worse and finally gave in to the urge to cry. "I didn't want to mention it now, either," she said miserably. "I'm not exactly proud of the fact that I was treated like a child."

"Oh, Meg, don't," Tiffany said contritely. "I shouldn't have pried."

"Don't be ridiculous," Megan retorted. "What are friends for if not to pry?"

It took a few seconds before they were both grinning at that bit of nonsense. Megan wiped at her tears before adding, "Devlin was just trying to open my eyes to the fact that the most horrible things can happen when you recklessly ignore good common sense."

So why didn't I pay closer attention? she asked herself bitterly. But her inner voice was conspicuously silent on that one, and a week later Megan couldn't ignore the truth any longer. The fates had been cruel after all.

Chapter 26

Devlin dove under the water, swimming the length of the pond twice before he surfaced for air. He had taken to coming here each morning for a swim because he couldn't stomach the stable at this time of day, since Megan had stopped showing up for her morning rides. He didn't like it that he'd driven her away from not only the stable but also her home. He didn't like the guilt she was making him feel, when he didn't have all that much to feel guilty about. And he certainly didn't like it that he could barely remember what had caused it all. If she hadn't clarified the matter that one time he was able to see her at her friend's house, he still might be convinced that he'd dreamed the whole thing.

But he hadn't dreamed it. He'd made love to Megan Penworthy. And it had been unbelievably nice—up to the time of penetration when he'd realized what he was doing, and so had she. The shock of it had ruined it for them both. Even his climax, uncontrolled and unwanted at that point, had been the worst he'd ever experienced. Yet he knew instinctively that it could have been the best.

But it shouldn't have happened at all. He'd been fighting his emotions since he met her, and succeeding admirably, or so he thought. And if he hadn't put so much brandy into his system that day, he would bloody well have insisted she leave the stable, rather than just suggesting it. Of course, he wouldn't have tried to drown himself in drink if she hadn't driven him crazy with lust the night before.

And now she wouldn't even let him do the honorable thing. Not that he wanted to marry a temperamental, spoiled redhead. He certainly didn't. So why did it infuriate him that she'd refused him? Simple wounded pride that she'd prefer anyone but him? Probably.

He dove under again, pressing it for three lengths this time, but didn't quite make it, surfacing with burning lungs in the center of the pond. A toss of his head got the hair and most of the water out of his eyes, but the sight that greeted him left him doubting his vision. Megan, dismounting from Sir Ambrose and walking up to the edge of the pond—and right into it, clothes and all. Nor did she stop until she reached him, and the second she reached him, she cracked her palm against his cheek, then slammed both fists against his bare chest.

Devlin let her beat at him for a moment before he asked, quite reasonably under the circumstances, "What the devil do you think you're doing?"

She shouted her answer. "You bloody rotten bastard, if you weren't so tall, I'd drown you!"

"Why?"

"Because I want to murder you!" She hit him once more to stress her point, then said, "Why couldn't you just kiss me like I asked you to?"

"When?"

"You know when! Why did you have to ruin it by making love to me?"

He almost laughed at the absurdity of that question. Any other woman he had been kissing like he had been kissing Megan would have been furious if he *hadn't* finished by making love to her. Of course, none of those other women would have been virgins.

"The kind of kissing we were doing that night generally does lead to lovemaking, brat," he explained. "And why the sudden fireworks over it? You weren't this mad when it happened."

"I was, too," she insisted. "But I was still in shock then."

His brow rose at that sulky reply. "It's taken you three weeks to come out of shock?"

She hit him again. "It's taken this long to find out that you've ruined me! I'm going to be disgraced!" she wailed. "I'm going to be a scandal!"

The dramatics suddenly made sense to him. He'd been expecting it; she obviously hadn't. "Is this your pleasant way of informing me that you're enceinte?"

"Yes, you stupid—"

"How do I know you're telling the truth?" he asked reasonably.

She stared at him incredulously for a moment before she turned and walked away in disgust. But she couldn't do so very quickly in the water, and he had only to reach out an arm to grab her back, which he did.

"I'm sorry, Megan, but there have been other females who've made the claim that I'd fathered their babes, and I bloody well hadn't."

Her eyes narrowed. "Are you trying to say it's not possible that I could be carrying your child?"

"Not at all. If you are carrying a child, it most certainly is mine, and I'll take full responsibility for it. Only, are you sure?"

"No, I'm not sure!" she shouted up at him. "How can I be sure this soon? But I'm a week late for my—I'm late, and I'm never late!"

"There's no need to get hysterical. I offered to marry you whether there was a babe or not, if you'll recall." Then he frowned. "Didn't I?"

Megan started at the question, her eyes rounding. "Don't you remember?"

"Until I saw you at the Robertses' house, I wasn't sure if I hadn't dreamed the whole thing. Apparently not, but I'm still not crystal clear on everything that happened."

"Well, don't expect me to remind you. I'm trying to forget it myself."

His other hand joined the one holding her to give her a little shake. "One thing I am certain of is that you refused to leave when I advised you to, because you were enjoying yourself too bloody much. The only thing you'd like to forget is the end, and frankly, so would I. But as that's not possible any longer, there's no point in bemoaning it further."

"I'll bemoan it if I—"

He shook her again. "Megan, don't provoke me. D'you think I want to marry a spoiled brat who doesn't care a damn about me? But I've got no choice and neither do you."

"But it's not fair!" she cried. "You can't give me the big house I wanted so I could impress Lady O. All you can offer me is my own stable. And you don't love me either. You probably just want to marry me because you think it will bring you a step up in the world. But it won't, you know. It's not going to make you a gentleman. That takes—"

"That's quite enough, brat," he interrupted coldly. "All that self-pity is turning my stomach. Did it occur to you even once that I might have had other plans for my life that didn't include you? Do you ever think of anyone but yourself and what *you* want?"

That was unfair and he knew it. What Tyler had told him about her proved she did occasionally consider other people's feelings. But her near hysteria over the possibility of marrying him was shredding his pride to bits. Of course, from her point of view, he had no prospects, was below even untitled gentry, and was therefore utterly unsuitable as husband material. And if he was who she thought he was, that would be perfectly true.

He knew he ought to tell her the truth, which would turn her distress into a cause for rejoicing—at least for her. Damned if he would. It was the horse breeder she'd come to to satisfy her sexual curiosity. It was the horse breeder she could bloody well marry.

She'd been glaring at him after his question and turning quite red in the face because he'd dared to criticize her. "Who says I'm going to marry you, anyway?" she demanded now. "Do you know how many gentlemen of this parish have asked me to marry them?"

"And you burned your bridges, turning down every one of them."

"Which doesn't mean I can't change my mind, does it? So you can get on with the great plans you have for your life. I have no intention of complicating them."

She looked like she just might mean it, which made Devlin angry enough to shake her again. "Self-sacrifice doesn't suit you one little bit, brat. And you aren't marrying anyone else while you're carrying *my* child. We're going to elope to Gretna Green."

"What?!"

"Your father will give his approval after I speak with him."

"No, he won't. You're mad!"

"It will give the marriage a romantic aspect. Otherwise the gossips will tear you apart, counting the days until you give birth."

"They're going to tear me apart, anyway, for marrying a horse breeder."

"Then you agree?"

"I didn't say that," she grumbled. "I won't live in a stable."

"You'll live where I live."

"I suppose we could share my room."

"I'm not moving into your father's house!" he said with clear finality.

She went on as if she hadn't heard a single word. "And it will be costly, but we can improve your wardrobe. And—oh, what's the point? No one is ever going to mistake you for a gentleman. For one thing, you're a damned bully. Have you been listening to yourself?"

"I was beginning to think I was the only one who was," he replied dryly.

"I'm trying to find a compromise here, but you're not letting me."

"No, what you're doing is what you have a bad habit of doing, thinking you can have everything your own way. I hate to be the one to break this to you, Megan." He didn't sound the least bit distressed. "But the wife does what the husband tells her, not the other way around."

"Which is a good reason why I can't marry you. If you loved me, you'd try to please me, but you don't love me, so you're going to make me miserable."

"I'm not going to make you miserable," he gritted out between clenched teeth. "I'm going to make you my wife. The two are *not* synonymous!"

"In your case they will be," she maintained with infuriating stubbornness.

Devlin took his hands off her before he *really* shook her. "Go home, Megan. Pack a bag. We will leave directly after I speak to your father."

"You're serious, aren't you?" she said with some surprise. "You really think you can get my father's permission to marry me? You're dreaming, Devlin. The only way he'd agree is if I tell him it's what I want. And the baby won't make a difference, if that's what you're thinking. He'll find me another husband."

"Then shall we leave the decision to him? If he agrees, you'll go along with it?"

Her eyes narrowed suspiciously. "You aren't planning to bully him like you do me, are you?"

"I don't bully you, damn it!" She snorted, as if his response merely proved her point, so he continued with a little less volume. "I have no intention of bullying your father. Do we have a deal?"

"Yes," she snapped with ill grace, only to add loftily, "But there's no point in my packing. You won't get his permission without my help, and I still don't think I want to marry you."

"But you will if he says so?" he demanded, wanting it clarified.

"I've already answered that."

"Good. Then consider yourself engaged." He picked her up and gave her a short, hard kiss before setting her back in the water, turning her, and giving her a little push toward the bank.

She went, but she was only halfway out of the water when she turned back to say something else, only to finally notice his condition. "Good God, Devlin, you're naked!"

Her surprised expression was priceless. To have been so angry with him that she hadn't noticed a body she'd previously been fascinated with—he started laughing and couldn't stop, not even to tell her, "And you're wading in a pond with your clothes on."

Just as well. She wouldn't have appreciated having that pointed out any more than she did his humor.

Chapter 27

It wasn't possible that she was on her way to Scotland to be married. Only how many times did Megan have to repeat that to herself before it became true? The countryside they passed through continued to change. The miles continued to fall behind them. They were traveling steadily north—to Scotland—to be married.

They'd brought a footman along to take the carriage back, because Devlin planned to rent a coach as soon as a decent one could be found. In Somerset he'd found better than decent; he'd left her at an inn and come back with the Earl of Sedgemeer's sumptuous private coach, complete with a coat of arms emblazoned on the doors, and the earl's own driver.

Megan had looked the vehicle over dubiously, prompting Devlin to explain, "I told the earl we'd been set upon by robbers, had all our money and clothes stolen, as well as our carriage."

"And out of the goodness of his heart, he hands over his own coach to you?" she scoffed.

"I also told him I was the Duke of Wrothston. The man couldn't do enough for me after that. Even threw in the driver. I do look like St. James, you know."

"I've met him, remember? And you don't look anything like him." Which should have told Devlin that if he said the sky was blue, Megan would insist it was green.

But the luxurious coach at least made the trip tolerable, if her traveling companion didn't. Having Caesar along also helped: it got Devlin out of the coach for long stretches at a time.

Megan had wanted to bring Sir Ambrose along, too, but Devlin had flatly denied her request. Bossing her around already, and not even married yet. The man was going to be impossible to live with. Traveling with him was just as bad. And it was a long trip, with more than three hundred miles to reach Scotland and the renowned Gretna Green, where eager-to-be-marrieds had been going for decades; couples too impatient to wait the three weeks for the posting of banns, or couples who didn't have parental blessing—which Megan did.

That parental blessing still confounded her. No, what confounded her was that her father had seemed so genuinely *happy* when he'd come out of his study with Devlin to congratulate her and say how delighted he was that she'd chosen such a "fine man" to be her husband. He'd gone on to say other things appropriate to the moment, but Megan got stuck on that "fine man" and looked at Devlin as if he were suddenly a devil capable of casting spells of enchantment. Too bad he hadn't cast one on her.

She was too upset to accept this monumental change in her life happily. She might have been contemplating that same change, but having it forced on her *and* Devlin wasn't the same. She intended to keep silent about it, however, because she knew her upset would come out negatively and that certainly wouldn't help.

The trouble with that decision was she couldn't stand the silence beyond the second day and waited only until Devlin was about to doze off in the afternoon to say, "I don't understand it. What could you possibly have said to my father to make him so happy about a union between us?"

He didn't bother to open his eyes to reply. "I told him I loved you, of course, and that my only wish is to make you deliriously happy."

The words caused a pang in her heart, because she knew they weren't true. "I see nothing funny in this situation."

"That's one of your problems, brat. You've got a rotten sense of humor."

"Well, you've had your little joke—tasteless, by the way. Now answer my question."

"I told him the truth, Megan."

"That you seduced me?"

"I believe it was the other way around."

"It was not," she retorted indignantly.

He opened one eye to say, "I asked you for kissing lessons, did I?"

"My point exactly," she pounced. "Kissing lessons I asked for, not lessons in that other thing you did."

He sighed. "I've accepted responsibility for my part. Obviously you're not going to do the same."

"Why should I when the fault is entirely yours?"

"Have it your way," he replied tiredly and closed both eyes again.

Megan brooded silently for several minutes before she said, "You still haven't answered my question."

"Perhaps because talking to you is too infuriating to continue for any length of time." When she didn't respond, he looked over to see her staring forlornly out the window. "Bloody hell," he swore. "What the devil do you think I told him? I confessed that I'd got you with child. He happens to be of the firm belief that a child belongs with both parents—both *real* parents—so my offer of marriage was readily accepted. He would have preferred the marriage to come first, naturally, but he understands how these things can happen."

"Did you have to tell him about the baby?"

"You're the one who said it wouldn't make any difference, that he'd merely find you another husband. Well, you were wrong, Megan. He'd prefer you have the father of your child. And yes, I had to tell him about the baby, to explain the reason for a hasty elopement."

"That doesn't really say why he was so *happy* about it," she grumbled.

Devlin shrugged. "Unlike some people whom I shall refrain from naming, the squire happens to like me. He's not displeased with your choice."

"*I* didn't choose you."

"I believe he sees it differently—considering your condition."

Megan made no response to that, but settled for simply glowering at him, which he chose to ignore by once again closing his eyes. It didn't take long for her to slump back into dejection again.

This was *not* how she had imagined her wedding all the times she had fantasized about it. Granted, the man of her dreams was sitting across from her, the most handsome man she'd ever encountered. That part was fine, better than even she could have imagined, actually. And he was determined to marry her. That part was all right, too. So why was she miserable instead of ecstatic?

Because he doesn't love me.

What's there to love about you lately?

Are you taking his side again?

Are you saying you haven't been the veriest bitch since he first showed up?

Possibly, but with a great deal of provocation, or are you forgetting all the times I've been insulted, offended, or otherwise goaded into losing my temper? Besides that's not the only reason. Am I supposed to be delighted that he's being forced to marry me?

I didn't hear him complaining about it until you started blaming him for everything. And I thought you weren't going to do that.

I wasn't when it was only my life that was going to be ruined. But I'm not about to take full responsibility for ruining his life, too.

Shouldn't he be a bit angrier than he's been if he really felt his life was being ruined by you?

You'd think so, wouldn't you? But when does he ever do anything that you might expect?

You haven't been doing much of the expected, either, lately. You won't even admit you're getting what you want—him.

Megan snorted without realizing it, then wondered why Devlin was suddenly looking at her with raised brows. "What?" she said disagreeably. "Haven't you anything better to do than stare at me?"

The unprovoked attack amused him for some reason. "I was trying to sleep, but you seem determined to see that I don't. Bored, Megan?"

"Certainly not. I've been having a perfectly stimulating conversation with myself."

"There's no need to be sarcastic."

"I wasn't. In fact, you may as well know that you're going to marry someone who frequently talks to herself. It's not too late to change your mind and take me home, you know."

"And miss my only chance to step up in the world?"

Megan frowned, sensing his sudden rage as if it touched her physically, yet his expression hadn't changed. And then his eyes closed once more, and she wasn't about to protest, a bit unnerved by his anger this time.

But she complained to herself, *Can't he ever do what's expected? I give him the perfect out, that I just might be crazy, and he gets angry.*

Don't look to me for answers this time. I'm as baffled as you are.

Chapter 28

❧❧❧❧❧   ❧❧❧❧❧

They spent their last night of unmarried bliss in the town of Carlisle on the English side of the border. The next morning, Devlin, in one of the rare times he'd spoken to Megan voluntarily on this trip, said they'd be married before noon that very day, since Gretna Green was supposedly just over the border. Megan thought to wonder aloud if their Somerset driver could find the place—he'd already got them lost twice—but decided to keep her mouth shut this once.

With the intimidating moment so near to hand, she was feeling a bit subdued, at least in no mood to start an argument. She was afraid the mood wouldn't pass, either, but grow worse. It wasn't just prenuptial nerves, though she definitely had those, too. But she'd been thinking too much the past few days about the unbelievable amount of control Devlin was going to have over her life after today. With any other man, that wouldn't be a worry, but Devlin . . . he didn't even like her. He didn't want to marry her. And he was going to make her life a living hell.

"You aren't going to cry, are you?"

She glanced over to find those turquoise eyes intently studying her, and wondered how long he'd been doing so. "Certainly not."

"It looked like you were about to."

"I'm not, I tell you," she insisted, but her lower lip was trembling.

"Is the thought of marriage to me that horrible, Megan?" he asked gently.

"Yes!" she said, and burst into tears, hiding her face in her hands.

So she didn't see his pained expression, or the firm resolve that took its place. And it wasn't until she quieted down to sniffles that she heard, "I don't know what you're blubbering about. I can assure you ours will be a marriage in name only."

She glanced up in surprise to demand, "What does that mean?"

"It means that I found making love to you as unsatisfactory as you did, so we won't be repeating that mistake."

Megan stiffened, her cheeks suffusing with color. So she could now add no-longer-desired to her list of complaints against him?

"That suits me just fine."

"I thought it might."

Before either of them could add to that, the coach rolled over something that sent them nearly bouncing out of their seats, there was a yell of alarm from the driver, and then, incredibly, the coach seemed to be sliding sideways.

"What the—?" Devlin began, only to end in a shout to Megan. "Get down!"

"Get down where?"

"The floor!"

"Don't be—"

He didn't give her a chance to finish her protest, reaching over to yank her to the floor, where he joined her, on top of her actually, and that so surprised her, she had nothing more to say for the moment. But Devlin didn't stay there. The crazy sliding picked up speed; then suddenly the coach was tilting at an odd angle, and Devlin was thrown to the side, hard against the wood casing of the seat. Megan followed him, rolled over him and up onto the seat, an easier, cushioned landing, until she crumbled headfirst into the side panel as the coach settled and was finally still.

"Are you all right, Megan?"

She wasn't quite sure. It took her a moment to get her skirt out of the way so she could right herself, then another moment to ascertain that she'd merely lost her bonnet.

"I think so, yes," she replied. "And you? Was that your head I heard crack?"

"Very funny," Devlin snorted as he sat up himself. "I believe it was one of the wheels you heard. Stay put while I investigate."

The coach wasn't lying completely on its side, but almost. When Devlin opened the lower door, it hit the ground beneath it, leaving only about a foot to squeeze through, not enough room for a man of his size. The other door had to be thrown back and crawled out of, but he managed that easily enough. Megan had a less easy time of it just trying to stick her head out of the upper door to see what was going on. She wasn't tall enough to stand there and look out, but had to pull herself up to the opening.

The coach was sitting in a deep ditch off the side of the road, which ran down a small hill. Coming down the hill could have accounted for the sliding they'd experienced, only it wasn't that steep a hill. And looking toward the top of it now, Megan could see that something wet covered the surface. It was that wetness that Devlin and the driver were both presently investigating.

Megan looked further around. At least the horses were all right. Even Caesar was still standing up on the road, but only because his lead rope had been long enough not to drag him into the ditch with the coach. And apparently they'd have help in a moment, for she could see three men riding up the hill toward them.

Her arms gave out then and she slipped down to sit wedged in the lower corner again. She could hear their help arriving, and a pretty thick brogue. Scotsmen, then. She hadn't realized they'd crossed the border.

After a few moments more, she grew impatient waiting for Devlin to return and get her out of there. The lower-door opening had been too narrow for him, but it wasn't for her. She squeezed right out to the ground, coming out on the down side of the coach. Crawling out of the ditch was another matter, with skirts to hamper her.

"Pig's fat?" she heard with a laugh. "Can ye imagine that, Gilleonan?"

"Some farmer got careless taking his fat tae market, I dinna doubt. What d'ye think, Lachlan?"

"Oh, aye, there's that, tae be sure. There's also reavers bold enough tae set traps for the unwary in broad daylight these days."

"Reavers?" That from the coachman.

There was amusement in the voice that explained. "Robbers, mon. Where're you from that you havena heard of Scottish reavers? 'Tis a pleasant enough activity for laird and crofter alike, though usually enjoyed late of a night."

There was a bit more laughter that Megan frowned over. Scots humor was definitely beyond her, but then she wouldn't be in this country long enough to need to understand the oddities of its people.

"D'ye smell a trap, then, Lachlan?"

"Blast you, Ranald, dinna be in such a hurry. When I smell a trap, I'll be letting you know. Give these gentlemen a hand now."

"That won't be necessary."

Megan was dusting off her hands, having finally achieved the road, when she heard Devlin say that. She stood behind everyone, unnoticed. The Scotsmen had yet to dismount. All she could see of them was some very broad backs. Devlin, on the other hand, or at least his face, which was all she could see of him beyond the horses, was looking too serious by half—which didn't explain to her satisfaction why he was refusing the Scotsmen's help.

"And why not?" she asked, drawing his eyes to her, and turning three horses about.

"Bloody hell, can't you ever do what you're told, Megan?" Devlin demanded as he pushed his way through the horses to confront her.

She blinked at the amount of anger she detected in his tone. "Apparently not," she replied stiffly.

"Then try it now and get back in the coach," he hissed so only she might hear.

"After I just fought my way out of it, no thanks to you?"

"Megan—"

"No," she cut in. "You're being unreasonable as usual. The coach has to be righted, doesn't it? Do you expect me to be bounced around in it while it is?"

"I expect you to do as you're told."

"Well, we aren't married yet, Devlin Jefferys, so you can save your ordering—"

"Och, but those are pretty words. So you're no' a wife yet, darlin'?"

The question came as a horse unexpectedly nosed its way between Devlin and Megan, so smoothly done that Devlin was nudged out of the way, the animal completely separating them now. Megan looked up as a giant of a man slipped from the horse to land next to her, immediately reached for her hand, and bent over it, just brushing the back of her knuckles with his lips. Her instinct was to snatch her hand back and upbraid the fellow, but when he straightened, his sheer size gave her pause, as well as his startling good looks.

He had light green eyes and the darkest auburn hair that had mere hints of red glimmering in the sunlight. His well-tailored navy-blue jacket fit snugly over shoulders likely twice the width of her own, and a barrellike chest, yet it seemed to be, amazingly, all lean muscle. Legs like tree trunks were covered in buff trousers and knee-high riding boots. An old-fashioned frilly cravat lent an abundance of lace to his throat. He was quite the second most handsome man she had ever encountered, and he was staring back at her as if transfixed by what he saw.

"Faith and be—such flaming glory, and the face of an angel tae be going with it," he said, his eyes touching on her hair, then on every inch of her face.

Megan automatically brought a hand up to straighten a bonnet that wasn't there, was still in the coach. She was flustered, but in a pleasant way, not accustomed to such boldness in a man who obviously found her attractive— *including her red hair.* The urge was strong to glance at Devlin and say, "Did you hear that? Flaming glory—ha!" but she managed to restrain herself.

"Lachlan MacDuell, at your service," the Scotsman was saying. "Can I be offering you a ride tae—Gretna Green, would it be?"

"Why, yes—I mean, that is our destination."

He grinned widely, quite an engaging grin. "They say a great many eloping couples dinna make it tae Gretna Green because they'd ne'er spent so much time together as they do getting here, and by the time they're getting here, they despise each other. Dare I hope that is your case, darlin'?"

He was too perceptive by half, but Megan wasn't about to air her grievances to a stranger. "You may not. And I'll thank you—"

"Are ye smelling that trap yet, Lachlan?" one of his companions called out.

"Not *yet*, Gilleonan," Lachlan replied with clear impatience. "Canna you see I'm courting here?"

Megan blinked. Gilleonan shot back, "Nay, it doesna look that way tae me."

At which point Lachlan dropped down to one knee. "*Now* does it?"

"Oh, aye, now it does indeed. Will ye be long at it, then?"

"As long as—"

"Not long a'tall," Devlin interjected as he came around the Scotsman's horse.

Lachlan sighed, but other than that, he completely ignored Devlin's presence and continued to stare at Megan. She in turn was embarrassed, yet undeniably flattered.

"Do get up, Mr. MacDuell," she urged.

"I canna, no' until you ken you've stolen my heart, darlin'."

"I certainly didn't mean to."

He grinned at her. "Aye, I know you canna help it, but there it is, in your hands. So I'll be plighting my troth in the proper manner, and you'll be so impressed you'll be giving me the answer I'm hoping tae hear."

She couldn't help grinning back at the outrageous fellow. "I will?"

"Aye, that you will. But then look at your choices, darlin', a stuffy Englishmon or a bonny Scot who'll give you laughter, joy, and ne'er a dull moment."

Megan laughed. "You can't seriously be proposing marriage."

"I am," Lachlan assured her. "Is that no' what you're here for?"

"Well, yes, but—"

"Marry me. I swear you'll no' regret it."

Megan was loath to disappoint the charming fellow, but disappoint him she must. "I—"

"This absurdity has gone on long enough," Devlin cut in tersely. "The lady is marrying me, Mr. MacDuell, with her father's blessing."

Lachlan came slowly to his feet. Devlin was tall, but the Scot had a good four inches on him and a lot more brawn. And he likely thought his sheer size ought to make Devlin back off. It should have, but it didn't.

"That's Laird MacDuell tae you, English. And what does the lass have tae say about it?"

Megan jumped in before Devlin answered that for her, too. "He's right, Lord MacDuell. I struck a deal of sorts with him that is binding."

"But do you love him?"

"That, sir, is none of your business," Megan retorted indignantly.

Lachlan laughed heartily. "But I'm making it my business, darlin', and I'll interpret your answer as I see fit. You're needing more time tae rethink the matter, and that I can give you."

Megan frowned. "I beg your pardon?"

"Nay, I'll be begging yours, I dinna doubt, for stealing you away. *Now*, Gilleonan."

Chapter 29

Megan was so angry she could spit. They were thieves, highwaymen—Scottish reavers, as they termed themselves. What transpired after Lachlan MacDuell's startling statement proved it beyond a doubt. Pistols had been immediately drawn, and Devlin's purse had been demanded.

But Lachlan had surprised his companions in crime in the last instance. "Leave the rest," he'd ordered as he tossed a struggling Megan onto his mount. "I've found all the treasure I'm needing today."

"But what about the horse?" the one called Gilleonan had protested. "There's a fortune tae be made in selling an animal like this."

Lachlan had stared at Caesar for a long moment before he chuckled. "Leave him. I'm feeling generous today. But spread the sand, Ranald. I dinna want tae be disabling vehicles I'm no' here tae plunder."

Devlin had known what was going to happen, had tried to get Megan out of notice and harm's way before the reavers owned up to what they had come for. But she'd stood there and argued with him until it was too late, until she'd drawn the leader's amorous attention. Laird MacDuell indeed. A pretension, no doubt, and irrelevant under the circumstances. She'd been abducted. Devlin and the coachman had been bound hand and foot and rolled down the ditch.

Devlin's one bit of resistance, slamming a fist into young Gilleonan's face, hadn't got him shot, thank God, but it did get him a good-sized headache from Ranald's pistol butt cracking against the back of his head. A hard head, since the blow had merely dazed him, rather than rendering him senseless, and his shouted curses and promises of retribution could be heard as they rode away, again irrelevant, since he couldn't give chase any more than Megan could get loose of the thick arms locked about her waist.

She was indeed furious, abduction a new experience she could have done without. There was nothing romantic or exciting about it. The wild ride over rough terrain that did not include roads quickly became quite torturous, especially since Megan absolutely refused to relax against her abductor, and was also sitting at a twisted angle in front of him. When he'd make a sharp turn, the breath would be squeezed out of her—damned Scot didn't know his own strength—but she said nothing, saving up her complaints to let him have them with both barrels once they alighted—if they ever alighted.

She became quite cold after the sun set. The horses were merely plodding along now considering the speed they'd given throughout the afternoon. She was beginning to wonder if the Scots meant to run their animals to death when they finally stopped and dismounted by a small stream. In quick order a fire was started, some food was dug out of saddlebags, and blankets were tossed on the ground. Camp. They actually meant to sleep—outdoors.

Megan groaned as she was lifted off MacDuell's horse, the stiffness in her joints screaming to attention. But even though she could barely stand on her own, she immediately slapped away the hands that had helped her down. Lachlan was amused by that and even chuckled. Megan stepped back so she could better scowl at him.

"You won't get away with this," she said.

"I already have," he replied cheerfully.

"Just where do you think you're taking me?"

"Home."

A lot that brief statement told her, so she tried a different tack, warning him, "I won't stay there, wherever it is."

"You're no' getting into the spirit of the thing," he complained. "I'm doing you a favor, giving you this opportunity tae devote a wee bit more thought tae your choice of husband."

"What you're doing is showing me that I prefer an uncouth Englishman, who isn't the least bit stuffy, by the way, to an uncouth Scotsman."

He clucked his tongue at her. "You're angry wi' me, I take it?"

"Absolutely."

"But you shouldna be, darlin'. How else can you make the right choice unless you get tae know me better?" She just stared at him, prompting him to add, "Dinna fash yourself, lass. You'll no' be hurt, I swear it."

"I already hurt all over. Do you Scots *always* run your horses to ground?"

He grinned at the direction in which her complaints had turned. "They're sturdy mounts, bred for endurance, no' like your fat English horses. It's sorry I am that you're a wee bit sore, but the speed was necessary."

"You don't really think you're going to be followed, do you?" she scoffed.

"For you, darlin', oh, aye, he'll come—at least he'll try tae find you. No mon in his right mind would give you up wi'out a fight. But I promise you he'll no' be having any luck. There isna a Scotsmon who can find me when I dinna want tae be found, much less an Englishmon."

Which made Megan want to sit down on the ground and cry. She was supposed to have been married by now. Granted, nothing would have changed with Devlin insisting they'd be married in name only, but still, she couldn't *not* marry with a baby on the way.

Lachlan was spreading a blanket on the ground for her. His two companions, neither as big as he was nor as finely turned out, were bemoaning the loss of Caesar loudly enough for Lachlan to hear—and disregard. He bowed, offering his hand to Megan to help her to sit. She pointedly ignored his hand and dropped stiffly to the blanket on her own.

"You're no more than a common thief, aren't you?" she asked boldly when he started to sit next to her.

He paused, but it was only a moment before he started laughing so hard he fell to his knees in front of her. "Common? Never, darlin'. There've been reavers in my family for generations gone by. So who am I tae deny such an honorable undertaking?"

There were hoots and snorts from his friends over that answer, which got them a scowl that lasted no longer than it took Lachlan to gaze at Megan again with another of his engaging grins.

"You actually see nothing wrong with stealing?" Megan ventured curiously.

"Och, now, I didnae say that. But you must know it's been many centuries that the Scots and the English have had the pleasure of raiding each other. I've merely started up the practice again."

"You're saying you only steal from the English?" she demanded, indignant on behalf of her countrymen.

He shrugged indifferently, pointing out, "We willna be reaching my home until tomorrow afternoon, so as you can see, I go out of my way tae make sure it's only English pockets I'm emptying."

"How patriotic of you," she sneered. "There are no English near where you're from?"

"A few. But can you no' see my dilemma in that? I'd have tae stop every carriage tae demand, 'Are you English, mon, or Scottish?' But Scotsmen dinna like tae be detained for silly reasons like that, you ken. So 'tis much easier tae go where I'm guaranteed a great many English will be roaming, and that's near the border."

"To my own misfortune."

"Nay, dinna say so, darlin'. You're upset, naturally. I'm confused and amazed myself at the feelings you provoke in me as well. But dinna think I make a habit of absconding with bonny lassies. You're the first."

"Lucky me."

He laughed at her continued sarcasm. "Nay, I'm the lucky one. You canna imagine how long I've been searching for a woman like you."

Since he didn't appear to be that old, no more than in his mid-twenties or thereabouts, it couldn't have been all that long, but Megan merely said, "You still haven't gotten lucky, MacDuell, since I'm already spoken for."

Which didn't daunt him in the least. "You canna really want that sour-faced Sassenach," he admonished with firm conviction.

"I most certainly can."

"But you dinna love him," he replied confidently. "That was as plain as—"

"Of course I love him. I love him so much I'm going to have his baby."

He smiled, humoring her. "A fine goal that, tae have a mon's bairn."

"You mistake me," she told him. "It's not something intended for the future—well, it is, but it's also an accomplished fact."

She said that without the embarrassment she'd expected to feel. And his expression of surprise was worth all the discomfort she'd experienced in that race across the wilds of Scotland. Only it didn't last long, and suddenly he was laughing uproariously. It took her a moment to realize the man didn't believe her.

Now what?

The devil if I know. I thought you were convincing, by the way.

Then why didn't he believe me?

Maybe because he doesn't want to.

Well, that's just dandy, isn't it? He didn't believe my lies either.

What lies?

Notice I'm not laughing.

But Megan was frowning at herself. Lachlan noticed and thought her displeasure was directed at him—which it would have been if she hadn't gotten distracted by her deluded inner voice.

"I'm sorry, darlin', but you must see how unlikely it is for a fine young lady like yourself tae be having a bairn afore you're wed, especially the bairn of a mon you dinna even like." Then suddenly he wasn't amused anymore, his expression turning dark with suspicion. "Unless he—"

Megan caught the drift his thoughts had taken and cut them off before they were completed. "He didn't, and I resent your even thinking it!"

"Och, now, there's nae need tae be losing your temper," he said with a degree of embarrassment.

"Losing it? I lost it this morning, you dense man. You had no right to steal me away from my fiancé. I was to be married today!"

Lachlan actually squirmed a bit, thinking she was getting near to tears, which he couldn't abide. "You still can be. I'm sure we can find a kirk around here somewhere."

"I won't marry you! In fact, I demand that you take me back right now!"

"Courtin's no' going tae well, Lachlan?" Gilleonan asked straight-faced, though it was obvious the man was fighting not to laugh.

"I could've told ye kidnapped brides are a passel o' trouble," Ranald added.

Megan joined her scowl to Lachlan's until both his friends turned back to face the fire. He then tried to smile at her, but she wasn't having any more of that.

"Charm has its place, but this isn't the place," she said shortly. "Now, I'm sure you're a nice man for a reaver. You might even make some girl a fine husband if you ever give up thieving. But it won't be me."

"Why dinna we sleep on it?" he said, as if her little speech wasn't to be taken seriously.

"Why don't you take me back instead?"

"Have a heart, lass. The horses couldna manage it even if I was of a mind tae let you go so soon."

"So soon? Just how long will it take you to understand I mean what I say?"

He did grin this time. "After you admit I'd make a fine husband, reaver or no'."

"Incorrigible," she said in exasperation. "Absolutely beyond redemption, too. And I thought Devlin was pigheaded," she added in a mumble for herself.

"What was that?"

"I'm not speaking to you anymore, so don't say another word to me."

"Then let me feed you and—"

"I won't eat your food either."

"Och, now, I willna let you starve, darlin'," he said quite firmly.

Megan's eyes narrowed, warning him clearly to forget whatever good intentions he had about forcing her to eat. "Just try and stop me."

"Faith, but you're a stubborn lass," he said with some exasperation of his own, but then he sighed. "Verra well, but when you get hungry, just tell me."

She snorted and turned her back on him to lie down, hitting the blanket as if it were a soft mattress, regretting that bit of temper instantly as her hand throbbed. Damn, damn, damn. This had to be Devlin's fault. If she gave it enough thought, she was sure she could find some way to blame him for her sorry plight, or at the very least, for not rescuing her. Never mind that he had been tied hand and foot. He should have been resourceful enough to get out of that and come after her.

Why don't you consider getting out of this one on your own?

How?

You aren't bound hand and foot. Once they're asleep, you can just walk away.

Are you under the mistaken impression that I know where the devil I am? I don't, you know. I could wander about lost indefinitely and really *starve.*

Or you could find help just around the corner.

What corner? I'm out in the middle of nowhere, if you haven't noticed.

You won't even consider it?

Certainly I will. I'll be stuck in Scotland forever if I wait for Devlin to rescue me. But if I get lost and starve, it'll be your fault.

I didn't just refuse food when my tummy was already growling.

That was a matter of principle.

What has principle got to do with escaping?

"MacDuell, I'm hungry."

Chapter 30

"Are you sleeping, lass?"

"Would it matter?" Megan grumbled, keeping her back to Lachlan, whose voice was coming unnervingly from directly behind her.

He ought to be sleeping. She'd been waiting patiently for what seemed like hours to hear some sign that he was. His two companions were snoring away. But Lachlan had been suspiciously quiet, and Megan wasn't taking anything for granted in her bid for freedom. She'd been determined to wait until she was positive he was asleep, so it was beyond aggravating to find him most definitely still awake.

"I've been thinking—"

"That's a bad habit you have, MacDuell," she cut in dryly. "You ought to give it up."

"And that's a bad habit *you* have, trying tae provoke a mon's temper."

"Is it working?"

He didn't answer for a moment, tempting Megan to turn over and look at him. She resisted. And then she heard his soft chuckle. Was there nothing the man *wouldn't* find amusing? He was as bad as Devlin, not taking insults to heart, but worse, always being in such infuriating good cheer. It was almost impossible to stay mad at a man who was constantly grinning or laughing— almost.

"It's come tae me, lass, that you might be thinking I'm no' sincere in my desire tae wed you."

"Not at all. Being tossed up onto a horse is quite clarifying."

"I didnae toss you," he protested.

"My bottom disagrees."

There was a long pause, then: "I'd be happy tae massage the—"

"Don't . . . even . . . think . . . it!"

Another chuckle had Megan gritting her teeth. "Verra well, but you should know I wouldna make that offer tae just any lass."

"Is that supposed to tell me I'm special to you?" she scoffed. "After all of a few hours' acquaintance, you find me special?"

"After all of a few seconds. I warned you that you'd stolen my heart."

You'd better redirect his thoughts real quick. Hearing things like that is liable to turn your head.

My head isn't turnable, and stay out of this.

"I don't happen to believe in love at first sight, MacDuell." Which was a lie, since Tiffany was proof that it was definitely possible. "Lust, now—"

"You're wounding me, darlin'."

"About time."

He burst into laughter. "I wish you could see as clearly as I do how well we'll deal together just as soon as your temper calms down."

"What makes you think my temper's up? It's not, you know. This is how I always am, perpetually disagreeable. It comes from being spoiled rotten, which I also am. Just ask Devlin—well, it's too late to ask him, but he would have told you it's true. He even calls me brat."

"Och, it's nae wonder you dinna like the mon," Lachlan replied in an I-just-figured-it-out tone.

"I *told* you," Megan bit out, rolling over in her frustration to castigate him royally, "I love—"

His mouth swooped down the moment she was on her back. She'd forgotten how close his voice had sounded, but he'd merely been biding his time, waiting to provoke her into facing him, in the perfect position to kiss her once she did.

Megan was shocked, not that he was kissing her—she wouldn't put anything past a damned thief—but that it was so nice, almost as nice as—no, not quite that nice. She didn't feel the surge of exciting sensations that she did when Devlin kissed her. Which wasn't to say she felt nothing, it just wasn't overwhelming.

"That'll be enough of that, MacDuell," she said as she pushed the Scotsman back.

He was grinning down at her unrepentantly. Now why didn't that surprise her?

"You canna say you didnae like it."

"I can—but I won't," she allowed. "However, that's quite irrelevant. Or have you forgotten that I'm carrying another man's child?"

"I havena forgotten that you said so, but perhaps you're forgetting that I dinna believe it. Admit it, darlin', you're as innocent as they come."

"Naive, yes, but no longer innocent," she maintained staunchly. "Now, I know there are men who would overlook that to marry me anyway, despite the baby, but somehow I doubt you'd fall into that category. So give it up, MacDuell. My condition isn't going to go away, it's just going to get disgustingly—noticeable."

"Noticeable, but not disgusting, brat."

Megan gasped at the sound of that familiar voice. Lachlan's response was to swear quite ungentlemanly. And for a really large man, he moved incredibly fast in getting to his feet. But he had no more luck than Megan did, as she stood up more slowly, in trying to locate where Devlin was. It was just too dark beyond the immediate area of the fire to see anything but dense shadows.

"If you're waiting for an invitation tae join us, mon, it willna be forthcoming," Lachlan said. "I canna say I'm pleased at your arrival."

"What a shame," Devlin replied. "And here I was sure you were expecting me."

They swung around to find him coming slowly out of the shadows from the north, rather than from the south. Megan ate up the sight of him, overjoyed that he'd actually come for her. She wanted to run to him, throw her arms around him, shower him with kisses, but the cursory glance he gave her kept her where she was.

Lachlan was more interested in the pistol Devlin had pointed at him. "I dinna suppose you'd be considering this an unfortunate mistake?"

"Would you?"

Lachlan had the audacity to grin. "Nay, I'd no' be that stupid."

"Neither am I," Devlin said as he paused by Ranald to toss aside the gun the Scot had laid near to hand, then did the same with Gilleonan's weapon.

"Are you sure, mon?" Lachlan dared to taunt. "You seem tae have come alone."

Devlin shrugged. "A necessity, since no one else could keep up with Caesar."

"Ah, the stallion. So I made a mistake, after all, in leaving him behind."

"Generosity coming back to haunt you?"

"That it is."

Megan had heard quite enough. "Do you two think you might get beyond this idle chitchat? I'm cold, hungry, and I'd like a decent bed before I attempt sleep again."

"And here I thought I was keeping the wind off your back, darlin'."

"Is *that* what you were doing?" she asked, her tone thick with sarcasm. "I'd never have guessed."

The man *still* wasn't abashed. "She says you call her a brat," he said to Devlin. "I'm beginning tae see why. 'Course, it doesna matter a'tall when a mon looks at her," Lachlan ended with a dramatic sigh.

Megan snorted her lack of appreciation for his wit. Devlin gave her a warning look. She noticed then that Gilleonan and Ranald had been awakened by the sound of their voices, and both were eyeing Devlin with not a smidgen of the nonchalance Lachlan was displaying. Foolish of her to have forgotten that this was still a situation on the dangerous side, and she and Devlin had yet to make their escape from it.

"I won't kill a man for making a fool of himself over a pretty face," Devlin said now.

" 'Tis glad I am tae hear it."

"But daring to take what's mine deserves a black eye or two."

Megan hadn't heard that correctly. She couldn't have. Lachlan didn't doubt what he'd heard, though, and threw back his head with great guffaws. Gilleonan and Ranald were now smiling. Was she the only sane one there?

"Devlin, you don't want to do that," she pointed out in what she hoped was a perfectly calm tone.

"On the contrary, my dear," he said with an underlying determination that made her groan inwardly. "I can't think of anything I'd like to do more at the moment."

"But—"

"Do you know how to shoot a pistol?"

She blinked at the change of subject and started to retort, "Certainly," but that would have been prideful boasting, and this was no time for that. "No."

"Good," he surprised her by saying and handed his weapon over to her, but not before he had placed her finger on the trigger and aimed the gun in the direction of Lachlan's two cohorts. "You'll be more likely to shoot them if they even blink, won't you? And watch *them*, Megan, not the fight. Can you do that?"

She was too upset at that point to do more than nod. She'd never held a gun before, never shot a man before, never had a fiancé about to get pounded into the ground by a veritable giant. Watch the audience instead of the fight? She'd probably faint if she had to watch Devlin getting hurt. How was *this* going to get them out of there?

The first blow was heard, making Megan cringe. Despite Devlin's admonishment not to, and her own determination not to, she glanced swiftly toward the two combatants, then right back to the two she was supposed to keep from interfering. They didn't look the least bit inclined to interfere, hadn't even done more than sit up. And in that brief glance toward the fight, Megan hadn't been able to determine who'd been hit, though she assumed it was Devlin.

Another solid blow, another cringe, and another swift glance. But again she couldn't tell who was taking the punches, who was receiving them. All she saw was the two men circling each other, searching for openings. Not surprising was that Lachlan was grinning. Devlin wasn't. But Devlin's form, fists raised, one arm slightly extended, straight-as-a-board stance, *was* surprising.

Megan had witnessed two other out-to-really-hurt-you fights in her life, one at a fair between a local blacksmith and a traveling fighter who was there to take on all comers for the entertainment of the crowds, and another between two of her suitors who were minor lords with some small knowledge of the gentleman's art of college boxing. Devlin wasn't fighting like the blacksmith, as she would have expected. Lachlan was, but Devlin was fighting like a gentleman. Now where the devil had he learned how to do that?

She had to be mistaken. Her glances had been too brief for her to be certain. Three more fists-to-skin-and-bone sounds were heard. She resisted looking. But the two men she was watching were telling. Gilleonan winced at one point. Ranald just looked amazed.

Megan couldn't stand it anymore. She turned to watch the fight in earnest, and she hadn't been mistaken. Devlin was indeed fighting like a gentleman, with straightforward punches, lightning jabs, and not a single wild swing or wasted movement. He was also, incredibly, the one landing all the punches. His ducks and retreats were simply too fast for Lachlan. Of course, one punch from Lachlan would probably bring Devlin to his knees. The Scotsman just wasn't getting a chance to demonstrate that fact.

On the other hand, Devlin's unusual advantage didn't seem to be doing him much good. Lachlan was still grinning, for God's sake, and didn't seem to be feeling any of the damage Devlin was inflicting. And there was some visible damage now. One of Lachlan's eyes was most definitely going to turn black by tomorrow, was already red and starting to swell. His lower lip was a bit puffy. And was the left side of his jaw starting to swell, too?

Megan made her swift glances toward Gilleonan and Ranald now, continuing to watch the fight with distressed fascination. She ought to put a stop to it. Devlin had gotten what he had claimed to want, so why were they still going at it? And then it happened, what she'd feared would happen. Lachlan faked a left swing and connected with a right, squarely on Devlin's jaw. Amazingly, Devlin staggered back only two steps before he caught his balance. His form remained the same, both fists raised, which clearly said he was prepared to take more damage. Megan wasn't prepared to watch him do so.

"Enough!"

Lachlan glanced at her with an aggrieved look. "Have a heart, darlin'. I've only hit him once."

Megan stared at the Scot incredulously. By the look of him, you'd think she'd snatched a favored toy away from a little boy. Devlin didn't look too pleased either. Well, that was just too bad for both of them.

"You two might be having a great deal of fun, but I'm not having any. I'm about to have hysterics, actually, and I'll probably shoot someone by accident while I'm at it, but what do I care?"

Devlin's response to that was, "Can't you *ever* do as you're told?"

Since this was the second time in one day that she hadn't done as she'd been told by him, and the first time had put her in this predicament, she naturally turned defensive. "When you're my husband, Devlin Jefferys, you can give me orders to your heart's content, but until you make that a fact instead of an intention, don't expect me to obey you without a damn good reason."

"I *had* a good reason, brat, which you are amply demonstrating. But did you just promise to obey my every command once we're married?"

Megan opened her mouth for a quick denial, but snapped it shut, appalled that she might have done just that. "You can't hold someone accountable for what they say during hysterics," she pointed out reasonably.

Devlin snorted. "I didn't think so."

Lachlan was laughing by then. "I dinna think I'll be envying you after all, Jefferys. I could manage a week or two of her blathering, but no' much more'n that. Would you be swapping the horse for her?"

"How quickly your *sincerity* changes colors, MacDuell," Megan sneered. "And he doesn't own Caesar, he only borrowed him from my father."

"I dinna care who owns him, dar—"

"Call me darling once more and I'll shoot you!"

Since she'd turned the pistol toward him as she yelled her threat, Lachlan made no reply, and for once he wasn't grinning. But Devlin walked slowly toward her and took the weapon out of her hand.

Quietly, dryly, he said, "If you're going to shoot him, my dear, you'll have to take the safety off." This he did, then handed the pistol back to her with a smile. "Now you can shoot him."

She stared at the man she was supposed to marry and thought about shooting him instead. She didn't. She gave him a hurt look and dropped the gun at his feet, then turned and walked away from him.

"Bloody hell," he said behind her. "You didn't *want* to shoot anyone, Megan."

"That's not the point," she tossed back. "And see if I'll ever protect you again."

The Scotsmen were laughing again, all three of them this time. Megan didn't care. She'd entered the shadows beyond the camp to look for Caesar, and if she found him, she had every intention of leaving by herself.

Chapter 31

Megan's stiffness had lasted all of two minutes after Devlin had placed her on Caesar and mounted behind her. Then she'd relaxed against him and a few minutes later fallen fast asleep. She hadn't spoken to him, however. Her annoyance with him had been as plain as her red hair, but nothing new for him to worry over.

He supposed his rescue of her was not the romantic affair she might have been hoping for. She ought to be grateful he'd found her at all, for he'd had a devil of a time following their trail after the sun went down. Stumbling upon them had been pure luck, aside from the fact that the landscape provided very little in the way of obstruction to block his view of their campfire, which he'd seen from miles away.

Devlin flexed his jaw and winced. He supposed *he* ought to be grateful Megan had stopped that fight, which had been nothing but sheer folly on his part. He should have gotten her straight out of there instead of seeking revenge because his damned pride was a bit lacerated over losing her in the first place. But no, he'd thought he could take the man, despite his size. MacDuell had disabused him of that notion quickly enough. Damned Scot had a cast-iron jaw.

And the audacity of the fellow, to stand there grinning when he had had a gun pointed at him. If Devlin weren't still smarting over the whole affair, he would probably admire the chap.

MacDuell had even had the gall to ask Devlin before he left, "Do you and the lass ever get along, mon, or are you after arguing with her all the time?"

Devlin had shrugged. "I'm coming to the conclusion that she enjoys arguing. You didn't notice?"

"That I did, but do you enjoy it?"

"Not particularly."

"Then why do you want tae marry her?" Lachlan had asked baldly.

An excellent question. Devlin had merely smiled, answer enough for the Scotsman, as far as he was concerned. But the question had stayed with him as he'd gathered their horses to take with him—he was determined *not* to meet up with MacDuell again if he could help it—and gone to collect Megan. It had stayed with him after he'd found her and been given a dose of her silence, so complete that she hadn't even asked why she had to ride Caesar when he had the other horses. And she was asleep when he let the other mounts go several miles away, which would have answered the question she had stubbornly refused to ask.

But the Scot's question wouldn't go away. Why did he want to marry her, aside from it being the honorable thing to do? And he did want to. There was no denying that, after the fear and rage he'd felt when she was taken from him. He wanted her to be his wife. He wanted to have the authority over her that marriage would grant him. He wanted her in his house. He wanted her near at hand. He wanted to know where she was every minute of the day. He wanted her in his bed, though that was one thing he wouldn't insist on until she wanted it, too.

He wanted her to love him.

Good God, he'd fallen in love with Megan Penworthy!

How the devil had that happened? And no wonder his mood was so bloody rotten. Loving a girl like Megan was asking for nothing but heartache and an end to his sanity. She was beautiful, certainly. He'd give her that. But the only good thing he could say about her quirky temperament was that she didn't hold a grudge. The girl might explode frequently in anger, but her tantrums didn't last long. Although why should they, when she always had something new to get mad at the next time around.

He must be mad. On second thought, he must be trying to put a nice face on his lust. That was all. He still lusted after the girl. One visit to his mistress ought to take care of that; then he could start dealing with Megan a little more impartially. At the very least, he'd stop losing his temper, stop letting her emotions wring his guts, stop thinking about her constantly—stop wanting her so much.

'Course, he'd have to go to London to visit his mistress, but why not? He'd rusticated for nearly two months. Freddy's sister had to have married by now, or been found out for the little liar she was. And what would that matter anymore when he'd be coming back with a wife himself? Except Freddy

166 *Johanna Lindsey*

still might want to blow his head off, but that could be dealt with when the time came.

It was nearing dawn when Devlin found the town he'd noticed on his race north. It wasn't Gretna Green, but it had a Scottish kirk, so it would serve.

The proper thing to do would be to register at the inn and get some much-needed sleep, then get married at a decent hour. But Devlin wasn't thinking of proper just then; he was thinking more in line with getting the thing done before anything else happened to prevent it.

The Scots clergyman didn't appreciate that. Neither did Megan. But a hefty donation to one, and a little bullying and prodding to the other, and Ambrose Devlin St. James, fourth Duke of Wrothston, had himself a new wife and duchess.

Megan woke to the sound of children shrieking in play and someone whistling a cheery tune. It took some time for her to realize the racket was coming from below an open window in the room where she'd finally gotten some undisturbed sleep—undisturbed until now.

She still didn't feel like getting up. She even thought about marching to the window and shouting down for some quiet. Some people had no consideration a'tall. But then she noticed the brightness in the room and decided it might be too late in the day for that kind of consideration.

How long had she slept? She had no idea, but she didn't exactly feel rested. There'd been too many interruptions—every time Caesar would slow to a trot, then when Devlin had dragged her into that church . . .

Good God, she was married! And her husband hadn't spent the night with her.

Megan looked over at the space beside her in the bed to make sure, but it was most definitely empty, the sheets still smooth. And then the memories started returning with a vengeance: the fight, the dirty trick Devlin had played on her with the gun, the dirtier trick he'd played in marrying her while she was half asleep.

He'd asked for two rooms at this inn this morning, and had escorted her to hers, leaving her with a curt good-night and an admonishment to lock the door. She'd still been too exhausted to think anything was strange in that. Strange? No, he'd simply meant it, a marriage in name only.

Did you think he was joking?
Yes.
Well, I for one don't blame him. You never give the man any peace.
The man doesn't deserve any peace.
Then why are you crushed by his rejection?
I'm not.

You are.
Bitch.
Are you cursing yourself?
Megan turned over and hit her pillow.

Chapter 32

Megan had slept in half of her clothes. But after all the riding done yesterday, the rest were in as deplorable a condition as what she'd slept in. When she would be able to change she couldn't guess. She didn't even know if her trunk was still in that ditch with the coach, or if the coachman had managed to get the vehicle back on the road. Hopefully they would meet up with him today.

It was a splendid room that she'd been given, now that she was awake enough to notice. Scotland certainly outclassed England in the way of inns, and she'd stayed in enough this last week to know. She wondered if Devlin was throwing away good money again on account of it having been their wedding night, even though they hadn't shared it, or because this was the only hostelry available in this town. Probably the latter. But not for the first time, she wondered how he came by so much money to waste.

There was a vanity replete with perfumes, cosmetics, and everything necessary to repair her hair, but Megan was starting the day in a peevish mood because of her embarrassment over the rumpled state of her attire, especially since the expensive furnishings in her room declared the inn to be an elegant establishment that only the rich could afford.

It didn't help her mood any to realize, when she left her room, that she had no idea which closed door along the corridor would lead her to Devlin. And she couldn't just go knocking on each one until she happened to find him. The other guests certainly wouldn't appreciate that.

She was forced to go in search of someone who could direct her, but she slowed her steps halfway down what was a grand staircase, amazed at the opulence below. So much for thinking this was merely an inn. It had to be a hotel, though she certainly hadn't noticed the size of it last night. Of course, the lower lobby had been dark when they'd arrived at dawn, with only one light burning.

The more Megan looked around, the more her reasoning faltered. It didn't really look like a hotel; it looked like the foyer of someone's home. In fact, the innkeeper who had admitted them could have been a butler. Admitted? Devlin *had* knocked to gain entrance, now that she thought about it.

"Good afternoon, Your Grace. May I direct you to the dining room?"

It was the man who had let them in this morning, more fully dressed now, and definitely behaving like a butler. Your Grace? Megan groaned inwardly. Surely Devlin hadn't lied again about who he was.

"You may direct me to my husband, if you would," she replied.

"If you will follow me?"

She expected to be taken back upstairs, but instead he headed for a double set of doors at the end of the foyer. It turned out to be the dining room after all, a very large dining room, and Devlin was there, sitting at the head of a long table, being served lunch by not one but three uniformed maids who couldn't take their eyes off him, and were almost fighting for the honor of bringing him what he wanted.

Megan was struck by that same emotion she'd experienced when she found Devlin frolicking in the hay with Cora, and she didn't like it one bit. She waited for him to notice her. When he didn't, her temper snapped.

"Out! All of you," she said, looking straight at the maids. "There's more food before him than he can possibly eat, and the man knows how to serve himself."

The three servants weren't very quick to obey a stranger, especially one so rumpled-looking, but one look at the butler and they were gone. "What would you like, Your Grace?" he asked Megan.

That damn title again made her wince. "Just some privacy, thank you." When he nodded but just stood there, she added, "And I'll seat myself."

The poor man seemed so appalled by that notion that Devlin stood up. "I'll seat her, Mr. Mears. But you can bring her an extra cup."

"Very good, Your Grace."

Megan waited until the butler was gone to say, "I'll seat myself," and marched down to the end of the table to do just that.

Devlin resumed his own seat. "Got up on the wrong side of the bed, did you?"

She gave him a disgruntled little smile. "You mean that splendidly comfortable bed that belongs in a bloody palace? That bed?"

Devlin sighed. "Very well, brat, get it off your chest. What are you in a snit about this time?"

Megan chose merely the most recent transgression. "You're telling that lie again, aren't you?"

He opened his mouth, closed it, then shrugged. "It seemed convenient at the time."

She frowned as she drew a basket of hot buttered muffins toward her. She could swear that wasn't what he'd been about to say.

Nonchalantly, though with some definite malice, she asked, "Can't you get arrested for impersonating a duke?"

"I should hope so."

Her frown increased. The dratted man wasn't making the least bit of sense this morning.

"Then why do you keep taking that risk?"

One of his brows rose slightly. "Are you thinking of turning me in, Your Grace?"

"Don't call me that, and yes, I ought to, and I *will* give it some thought."

He pushed a plate of ham and boiled sausages toward her. "When you do," he said as he went back to eating, "you might want to consider that you'd be turning yourself in, too, since you happen to be my wife now, and these people think you are my duchess."

Megan stared at him openmouthed for a moment before snapping, "You might have thought of that before involving me in your crime."

"Yes, I might have, but I was too bloody tired to think beyond finding us a place to sleep. The only lodgings this town boasted burned down last week."

"Oh," she said, fixing her eyes on the crumbs she was scattering from her muffin. "In that case, thank you for the comfortable bed."

Devlin put down his fork and did some staring of his own. Megan conceding a point? And actually *thanking* him for something?

"Did you get enough sleep?" he asked.

"Yes."

"Are you running a fever, then?"

She looked up, blushing slightly. "That isn't funny. You're making me out to be a monster."

"No, just a nag and a termagant, and, don't let us forget—a brat."

She gave him a furious glare. "You're not exactly per—" She had to stop as the butler returned with a cup for her. Her fingers drummed loudly on the table while the man made a production of pouring coffee and offering cream and sugar. But the second the door closed again, she said, "I'm beginning to think you're a worse bounder than that bounder you're impersonating, Devlin Jefferys."

"Good God, then there's no hope for me a'tall," he exclaimed.

He was actually smiling at her. Megan was getting angrier by the minute.

"Can you be serious for two seconds?" she demanded.

"I will if you will."

The man was impossible this morning. Megan almost got up and walked out, but her curiosity wouldn't let her. "Whose house is this, anyway?"

"It belongs to a Margaret MacGregor. She's an Englishwoman and a countess in her own right."

"Living in Scotland?"

"She married a Scot in her younger years. When he died, she elected to stay on."

Midnight-blue eyes narrowed in disapproval. "You've been gossiping with the servants, haven't you?"

"Servants don't gossip with dukes," he replied in a perfect imitation of a pompous nobleman, then spoiled it by grinning. "On the other hand, clergymen will gossip with anyone who will listen, and the one who married us happened to mention Lady MacGregor, and that she was putting up travelers until the inn is rebuilt."

But not in her best rooms, Megan didn't doubt, and with a passel of servants to wait on them. Unless, of course, they claimed to be the Duke and Duchess of Wrothston.

"You don't remember?" Devlin added.

That was another sore subject better left alone, but Megan wasn't inclined to. "No, I don't remember," she grumbled. "The one and only time I'm ever getting married, and all I have is vague memories of a ceremony in a dark church. When I'm finished being mad about it, I'll probably cry."

"The one and only time, Megan?"

She was too agitated to notice the softness of his tone. "The gentry don't divorce, Devlin Jefferys," she informed him haughtily. "If that was what you were hoping to do at a later date, you can just forget it. You're stuck with me until death do us part, and I don't intend to die so you can go about your merry way."

He laughed at that point. "Good God, the notions you get astound me sometimes. For your information, divorce isn't permissible in my family either, though why a woman who just got married should even think about—"

"I don't feel married," she interrupted him in a small, bitter voice.

Devlin became very still, not daring to even look at her. Keeping his glance on his plate, he asked carefully, "Do you want to feel married?"

Her head snapped up, but all she saw was his nonchalance. What else did she expect? He'd said that he hadn't enjoyed making love to her any more than she'd enjoyed it. Not exactly the words of a man eager to come to her bed, now that he could. But if he thought she'd ask him to after that crushing rejection—well, he could rot before she would.

"No," she said. "Whatever gave you that idea?"

His fork clattered loudly on his plate as he stood up abruptly. "A stupid question, wasn't it?" he said and headed for the doors.

"Wait a minute! Are we leaving?"

"We might as well," he replied curtly without looking back at her.

Chapter 33

Megan quickly swiped up a napkin to fill with the food she hadn't gotten a chance to eat. Wretched man. What had set him off all of a sudden? Could he possibly have wanted her to say yes? After he had rejected her? Not likely. And she wasn't about to leave herself open to another rejection. If he wanted her, he was going to have to say so.

Megan blushed furiously when the butler came in with a picnic basket full of food for them to take along, but like any good servant, he deigned not to notice. "Have a pleasant journey, Your Grace."

Her blush increased. She was really starting to hate that title that she'd once coveted.

She stuck her pilfered food into the basket as if she did such things every day and marched out into the foyer, where Devlin was waiting. As usual, he was a convenient target for her annoyance, this time over her embarrassment.

"You're going to drag me off before I even get a chance to thank our hostess?" she asked.

"Lady Margaret is visiting friends in Edinburgh and isn't expected back until tomorrow," he informed her rather stiffly. "Did you want to wait?"

"And risk the chance of her knowing the real duke?" she hissed in a whisper, since the butler was still there, though he had moved over to the front doors. "Certainly not. You can send for Caesar."

"I already have, as well as a carriage for your convenience."

"You found a carriage for rent?"

"I'm borrowing one of Lady Margaret's."

Megan groaned. "Not again." Then she added sternly, "I'm really going to have to insist that you not take advantage of this lady."

Devlin glanced down at her with a supercilious expression that would have done a duke proud. "How, pray tell, am I taking advantage?"

Megan leaned closer to whisper, "You know very well she'll think you-know-who has borrowed her carriage and not mind in the least, even be thrilled to oblige such an exalted personage when that isn't the case a'tall."

"Why deny her that gratification, then, since she's not here to miss the carriage anyway?"

That was a very good point, though entirely self-serving. "It still isn't right," she insisted.

"Then let it rest on my conscience, my dear, and be grateful you won't have to carry that cumbersome basket on your lap atop Caesar."

Another excellent point which she hadn't considered, so she said no more, though she made sure her expression told him she still wasn't happy about it.

After another moment when their transportation still hadn't shown up, she set the basket down and remarked, "That's the first time you've ever mentioned a family."

He gave her a wary glance, but she was staring across the way at the butler and didn't notice. "When did I mention family?"

"In the dining room, in reference to divorce. You can't have forgotten that quickly."

Devlin relaxed. "So?"

"So do you have family, brothers and sisters, that sort of thing?"

She appeared only mildly interested, but he knew her better than that by now. Her curiosity was more powerful than most people's. It had even led them indirectly to this state of marriage. And Devlin was sure that now that it was aroused, she'd find a hundred other ways to get that question answered if he tried to avoid it.

He should have come to that realization sooner, for there were several ways that he could use her curiosity to his own advantage. He'd have to give that more thought, but right now he said, "A grandmother, a great-aunt, and numerous distant cousins."

"No one closer than that?"

"Not for some time."

"Where is your family from?" she asked next.

"Kent."

"Near Sherring Cross?"

"Very near," he said dryly.

"I suppose that's how you ended up working in the duke's stable?"

"You could say that. Now, why are you suddenly so interested in my past?"

"It's something I ought to know about, don't you think, now that we're married?"

"I don't think. A wife doesn't need to know, nor should she know, everything about her husband."

Megan's mouth fell open. "Who says so?" she practically sputtered. "Men?"

He shrugged. "I suppose."

"And you agree with that nonsense?"

It was hard to keep from grinning, she was so incredulous.

"I believe I was a man last time I looked."

Her eyes narrowed suspiciously. "Are you teasing me, Devlin?"

"You finally noticed?"

It was his turn to be incredulous when she gave him a full smile, the one that brought out both dimples and made him want to grab her and kiss her. "That's all right, then," she told him. "I don't mind being teased." Since he was too speechless to reply, she added, "Now where were we? Oh, yes, your previously undiscussed past."

"No," he disagreed after a moment, "we were going to get to yours, or did you think this exchange of information would be one-sided?"

"But my life hasn't been all that interesting," she protested, then sighed. "Oh, very well, what would you like to know about?"

"Nothing for the moment."

Her eyes went back to narrowed. "I believe I'm going to develop a new habit—screaming. Consider yourself warned, you odious man."

Devlin burst into laughter. Megan opened her mouth to begin her new habit. But Mr. Mears opened the front doors first. The carriage had arrived. Only it wasn't their carriage, they found as they went outside. An elderly lady was being helped from it by two attendants who were quickly shooed away the moment she was firmly on the ground. And then she noticed Devlin, and a pair of faded turquoise eyes widened.

"I don't believe it," the woman said to herself. "After all these years—what the devil are you doing here, Devlin? I just had a letter from your grandmother last week, and she didn't mention you were coming."

"Because she didn't know. I didn't come for a visit, but to get married, which I've just done, and you have only to look at my bride to see why I was in such an all-fired hurry. She was planning a Season. I wasn't about to let the rest of the ton get a look at her before she was safely mine."

"How divinely romantic, Dev," Margaret exclaimed, "and so unlike you."

Megan was already blushing over his nonsense, meant to put everyone off from wondering about the real reason for such a hasty marriage. That this sweet-looking lady believed it was obvious by her answer, and Megan blushed the more. But worse and worse, the lady's eyesight must be nearly gone, for she actually thought Devlin was someone she knew. An odd coincidence, however, that both men were named Devlin. Or was it? Could the lady possibly know him somehow?

Megan was introduced. The old lady welcomed her into the "family" with a great deal of warmth and sincerity, which was making Megan feel simply horrible about the ruse Devlin was playing. But was it a ruse? Half the things Margaret MacGregor was saying didn't make a bit of sense. Then she was speaking to Devlin about people they supposedly both knew, and he was coming up with a satisfying answer for every question she asked.

Now that was just too damn coincidental as far as Megan was concerned. Something definitely wasn't right here. And Devlin kept giving Megan the most probing looks, which only increased her suspicions. But Margaret MacGregor was so genuinely pleased to see him, Megan didn't have the heart to ruin their "reunion" if she could help it. But she would have some answers the very second they were alone.

"What's this?" Margaret said now as the borrowed carriage and Caesar were finally brought up. "Don't tell me you're leaving?"

"I am."

"No, you're not."

"Yes, I am."

"You're not," Margaret insisted stubbornly. "After all these years of promising you'll visit—you're here, you'll visit a while."

"I'm not alone, Margaret," he reminded her pointedly. "And I have obligations. Duchy doesn't even know yet that I've married."

"Oh." She thought about that for a moment, then laughed. "You mean for once I actually know something about you before my sister does? She'll be furious with me for that." She laughed again, enjoying the prospect, then ended with a sigh. "Very well, it looks like I'll have to do the visiting as usual, but then I've got nothing better to do, whereas you never have enough time for anything. Don't know how you found the time to meet your bride, much less elope with her, but mind you, I expect to hear all about it when I come to Sherring Cross."

"Sherring Cross?" Megan said in a small voice that wasn't heard, since Margaret hadn't quite finished with her admonishments.

"Now that you have a wife," the old lady continued, "you can't spend *all* your time in the House of Lords, dear boy. I'll expect lots of great-great nephews and nieces to carry on in the St. James tradition—"

Margaret paused now because Devlin was suddenly groaning for no good reason. But before she could ask what was wrong, his beautiful young wife was calling him a nasty name and kicking him in the shin, quite viciously, Margaret noted with a sympathetic wince.

He yelped, and lifted his leg to squeeze the injured area. Hopping around on one foot for a moment, he didn't notice that his wife wasn't staying around to be reprimanded.

"I say, Devlin, should she be riding that animal?" Margaret asked.

"What animal?" He swung around only to see Megan setting Caesar into an immediate gallop. "Bloody hell. Megan, come back here!"

He didn't exactly expect her to obey him. She didn't.

Chapter 34

Since she wasn't paying any attention to where she was going, Megan came upon another town quite by accident. It was more a village, no bigger than Teadale, but the sight of its one eating establishment reminded her that she didn't have her purse or anything else that would buy her a meal. Like her bonnet, what little money she had brought with her had been left behind in the coach yesterday.

No money for food or lodgings. How was she supposed to get home? But the thought of returning to her husband was out of the question. She'd rather go hungry. And she had Caesar. With him she could reach home in half the time, only three days likely. She wouldn't starve in just three days, would she?

But what was the point? He'd only show up a few days later, so she'd have gone hungry for no good purpose. Then she'd simply leave again, and be better prepared the next time.

The trouble with that plan was that he had the right to drag her back if he wanted to, as many times as he wished. He could even lock her up if he got tired of chasing her around the country. She'd given him that right by marrying him.

But she hadn't married *him*, she'd married Devlin the horse breeder . . . Maybe he hadn't put the right name on the marriage paper, so she might not be married to him after all. That was wishful thinking that she couldn't count on. He'd done the noble and responsible thing in his mind, after all, so he'd have made sure he'd done it right.

Only she didn't want to be married to him now. She hated him and meant it this time. He'd lied to her, deceived her, misrepresented himself, and who knew what else.

Shouldn't you be telling him all this?

Yes, by God!

Megan turned around and headed north again. And again she was too deep in angry thoughts to pay attention to where she was going. But Caesar stuck to what road there was, and it wasn't all that long before the carriage was there and was almost upon her before she even noticed it.

Megan stopped. Devlin did the same. She didn't dismount. He leaped out of the carriage and yanked her off Caesar, not giving her an opportunity to leave again on the one animal he'd have no chance of catching up with. Megan, too intent on her fury, didn't even notice his precaution.

"I have a number of things to say to you, *Your Grace*," she began while in his arms—he was carrying her from the horse to the carriage—putting all the contempt she could muster into his title.

"You can say them in the carriage," he began calmly enough, then abruptly released some of his own anger, growling, "Don't you *ever* take off on my horse again, Megan, when I'm not on him with you!"

"*Your* horse? He happens to be—"

"*My* horse."

"I see," she replied stiffly. "Another lie, and one you even involved my father in."

"Actually, your father confessed he'd have difficulty with subterfuge, so for the duration of my stay, he did in fact own Caesar in what you might call a short-term, cashless sale, to terminate with my leaving—which I've done."

"I don't care how nicely you twisted it around for my father's honest scruples. It was still another lie, *Ambrose St. James!*"

"Ambrose *Devlin* St. James," he corrected her, dumping her into the carriage none too gently. "No one calls me Ambrose, brat, so don't you start."

She had to yell after him, because he'd turned to tie Caesar's reins to the back of the carriage. "I don't care what everyone else calls you! I have a few choice names that are more appropriate. Care to hear them?"

"No!"

That deflated her for a moment, long enough to notice that he was limping as he came back to get in the carriage. She looked pointedly at his leg and said, "If that's to make me regret kicking you, it's not working. I'm thinking of doing it again—in the same spot—only harder."

"Appreciate the warning, so I'll return the favor. Kick me again with those pointed little shoes of yours, and you will travel across England barefoot."

"You wouldn't dare!"

He cocked a brow at her. "I thought we had established the extent of my daring."

"You are exactly what you claimed you were—probably the only true words you ever said—a bounder, a cad, and I am not going to speak to you for the rest of my life!"

"Do you promise?"

Obviously not, for she wasn't done railing at him. "You are the most wretched man who ever breathed breath. The most despicable man in all of England—no, make that the world. And you're probably a terrible duke, too."

"You might want to reserve judgment on that, since you haven't actually met him yet."

"Met who?"

"His Grace, the Duke of Wrothston."

Her eyes flared. "Are you telling me I was mistaken in what I heard, that Margaret MacGregor isn't your great-aunt, and she didn't say she was expecting some St. James nephews and nieces from—"

"Yes, yes, you heard exactly right," he cut in impatiently. "I *am* the fourth Duke of Wrothston. But kindly recall that I've been playing a role since we've met, which is what you're in such a snit about. Naturally, my behavior had to conform to that role, and that behavior was my interpretation—what I'm trying to say, Megan, is the way I've acted with you is completely different from how I normally am. I am usually quite circumspect, utterly proper, and I've even been called stuffy, though I can't imagine why."

But that wasn't the man she had fallen in—*I wasn't going to say that.*

Yes, you were.

Stay out of this.

"Are you claiming you're not the least bit arrogant or bossy?" she asked.

He flushed slightly. "It's called leadership, not being bossy, and so a few of my own traits got mixed up in the role. I didn't say I'd got the horse breeder down perfect."

"Oh, I agree absolutely. If you had, you might not have been so provoking."

"Actually, I enjoyed our verbal skirmishes—some of the time, since I so rarely get to let go like that. Are you saying you didn't?"

She would be lying if she said no. "That's entirely beside the point," she answered primly. "The fact remains that you misrepresented yourself from day one. I did *not* marry a duke."

"But you wanted to," he reminded her with a good deal of smugness.

Megan's face went up in flames of mortification as she recalled the day she'd told him, *him*, that she was going to marry the Duke of Wrothston. How he must have laughed over her vain presumption and . . .

"My God," she said, appalled as the rest came back to her. "You rode all the way to Hampshire just to humiliate me with an improper proposition so I would no longer want to marry you. I didn't realize you despised me that much."

She was no longer angry, she was deeply hurt, and Devlin was horrified that he'd caused it. "Dammit, that is *not* why I went to Hampshire. I was merely annoyed because you were so bloody determined. I thought you were a scheming opportunist out to marry a title no matter how despicable the man holding that title might be. What I did was in the way of a lesson. I certainly didn't think it would work to put you off the idea altogether."

"How delighted you must have been to find out otherwise," Megan replied bitterly. "And appalled to end up caught anyway. I suppose you now think I got myself in my present condition on purpose."

"Don't be ridiculous," he snapped. "It takes two to get you in that condition."

"But you were foxed at the time, and I, of course, am a scheming opportunist who would have taken quick advantage of that."

"Bloody hell, weren't you listening to me? I said I thought that previously. I don't think it now."

"And you're a very good liar, Your Grace, proven once again."

"You don't believe me?" he asked incredulously.

"Of course I don't believe you. Or are you going to tell me you would have asked me to marry you if a baby weren't involved?"

She was infuriating him as usual. "How the bloody hell should I know what I would have done down the road, which is entirely irrelevant now. You *are* expecting. We *are* married. And you're being unreasonable."

"I'm not surprised *you'd* think so. Any time *I'm* right, I'm unreasonable."

"You're wrong, dammit!"

Her chin went up in the air as she looked away from him. "I don't care to discuss it anymore."

"Then I'll bloody well count my blessings."

Chapter 35

Megan didn't know the English countryside well enough to realize that the coach that had been retrieved in Scotland had changed directions midway through the return trip. She had assumed she was being taken home to Sutton Manor. By the time she noticed a few landmarks that seemed vaguely familiar, it didn't occur to her that she might have seen them years ago, rather than last week. But not long after that, she had no trouble in identifying the magnificence of Sherring Cross, which suddenly loomed on the horizon.

She was as spellbound as the first time she'd seen this ducal estate spread out across the land, but not for the same reason. It really was a grand edifice worthy of royalty. The trouble was that *her* husband owned it and she shouldn't be his wife.

Devlin was napping across from her—or pretending to. He'd been doing a lot of that lately, to avoid her sulky looks, she supposed. He'd given her his explanation of why he'd assumed the guise of a horse breeder. "Freddy" and "Sabrina" meant nothing to her, and so she hadn't been all that impressed that there had been a dire reason for his subterfuge.

But she had made a guess and said, "You told my father you were a duke, didn't you? That's why he was so pleased to have me marry you, isn't it?"

"I told him merely to expedite the matter."

"But you couldn't tell me?"

"When you were so enjoying your resentment over having to marry a horse breeder? Why spoil it for you?"

Answers like that had kept their conversation to a minimum, but Megan wasn't used to keeping her unhappiness bottled up, and she'd done so long enough. She leaned forward to wake Devlin, only to hesitate.

Not in your present mood, or are you going to start a fight with him only minutes away from being descended upon by his servants?

I don't suppose that would make a good impression, would it?

Definitely not. It's bad enough that you pity him for marrying you; at least let his servants be happy for him—until they get to know you.

Well, aren't you the bitch today. And he deserves to be pitied. I've ruined his life, remember?

What about your life? It's just as ruined.

But it was my fault—

Aha! 'Bout time you remembered that.

I hadn't forgotten. But before, I'd only ruined Devlin's life, which didn't have all that far to go to be ruined. And there was every chance that marriage to me would have improved his lot, despite his contrary opinion. But now I've ruined a duke's life, which is a whole different matter. It's no wonder he hates me.

You know, you ought to be finding some good in this mess, instead of nursing all the dreary aspects.

There isn't any good to find.

What about your getting just what you originally wanted—a duke?

The original plan included him loving me.

All right, scratch that. What about the fact that you're going to get to live at Sherring Cross?

I don't care anymore.

Liar, you fell in love with this house.

It's a bloody mausoleum like Tiffany said.

It's better than a stable.

That's true.

"You're awfully quiet." Devlin's voice came to her softly. "Nervous?"

She gave him only a brief glance before looking back out the window. "That's convenient timing you have, waking just as we arrive."

"What can I say? I have an excellent inner clock."

Megan snorted. "And no, I'm not nervous. Nor was I quiet. You forget, I talk to myself."

"You're right, I did forget. And anyone who talks to herself never lacks for company, does she? You'll have to let me listen in on one of those conversations sometime. They must be fascinating."

She recognized humoring when she heard it, but decided that was better than the anger he'd displayed at the last mention of this subject. "I suppose you would find them fascinating, since they're usually about you. But I'm afraid I'll have to refuse your eavesdropping. My conversations are private—and quite silent."

"You mean you don't talk aloud to yourself?"

"Of course not."

He frowned sternly. "That's not the impression you gave me, Megan."

She shrugged, remembering that she'd encouraged him to think she might be a little crazy in order to give him an excuse to call off the wedding—and he'd been furious about it then. "It's not my fault if you misinterpret what I say."

"Isn't it?"

The coach stopped, saving Megan from answering that incriminating question. Devlin usually opened the door, but he wasn't quick enough for the bevy of footmen who appeared instantly. More started pouring out of the house as soon as it was realized that this wasn't a guest arriving, but the duke. And between the coach and the house, Megan heard more "Your Graces" than she ever hoped to hear again, and that was nothing compared with the commotion once they reached the mammoth entry hall, where it seemed every servant in the house wanted to welcome home the master. At some point Devlin got around to introducing his wife, and then the "Your Graces" started all over again.

Megan didn't know how she managed to get through it—it seemed the butler, John, and Mrs. Britten, the housekeeper, were determined to give her the name and duty of everyone present—but that they were all so genuinely welcoming quickly alleviated the nervousness she'd denied having.

Devlin had a moment to stand back and watch her interact with his people, and he was frankly dumbfounded to witness a Megan he'd never seen before. He'd done the unthinkable and brought a bride home without giving the household any warning to prepare for her, yet she was putting the frantic ones at ease by swearing she'd like to view the grounds first, then some of the house—which was undoubtedly true, since the *stables* were on the grounds—before she was shown to her rooms, giving them the time they needed to prepare those rooms.

He'd been too nervous when she'd met Margaret to notice her behavior or even what she'd said to his aunt. But this time he listened to her every word and watched her conduct herself graciously, like the perfect lady, and finally his amazement got the better of him and the words just tumbled out. "Good God, where did my brat go?"

He knew it was a mistake instantly. He saw Megan's back stiffen, watched her swing around to face him, felt the pain explode in his shin, then watched her eyes widen at the realization of what he'd provoked her into doing before his entire household. He wasn't surprised that she then burst into tears and ran out of the hall. He felt like doing the same.

He knew as well as anyone that first impressions were lasting impressions, and he'd thoughtlessly ruined Megan's introduction to his household, possibly undermining her authority. He had no excuse except that he'd been under the same strain as she this past week—and he hadn't been behaving normally since he met her.

Short of replacing the entire staff, which was displaying various degrees of shock and embarrassment, he offered an explanation. "We've been traveling continuously for two weeks. My wife, naturally is exhausted because of it, and so not quite herself."

"You surely must be exhausted as well," John said beside him, and it was thirty-some years in the household that made him bold enough to add, "Because I don't believe I've ever seen you do anything so stupid—Your Grace."

Devlin heard several murmurs of agreement, enough to realize that the blame was going where it belonged. He almost laughed in relief, but managed a serious "Quite right, John. Truth is, I haven't been at all myself since I met the young lady."

"That's love, sir, if you don't mind my saying so," Mrs. Britten volunteered.

"Is it? Then I'd better get used to it, hadn't I?"

The staff was back to smiling at that point, which was an excellent time for Devlin to take his leave to search for his furious wife. He owed her a thoroughly contrite apology this time, though he'd be lucky to get it out before she kicked him again. No doubt about it, he was definitely going to have to buy that girl some softer shoes.

Chapter 36

Megan was nowhere to be found in the stables. Devlin had hoped otherwise. He knew she adored horses. He had counted on the sight of so many Sherring Cross Thoroughbreds to charm her out of her current mad, or at least lessen it somewhat, so she'd listen to what he had to say.

One of the gardeners finally mentioned he'd seen her heading for the lake. Devlin had a moment of panic, considering the state of upset she'd been in, and treated the man to the unprecedented sight of the Duke of Wrothston racing hell-bent down a tree-lined path.

He saw her from a distance, sitting on the bank away from the boating dock. She looked like a veritable hoyden with her bonnet removed and her hair released from its constraints to form a bright red cloak down the dull gray of her traveling jacket. She had her skirt raised to her knees, and one foot dangled in the icy water.

Devlin could perhaps thank the icy water for dissuading her from jumping in, if she'd been of that mind, but now that he saw her, he knew how ridiculous that notion of his had been. Megan wasn't the type to hurt herself when she was upset. She was spoiled enough to prefer making her antagonists suffer right along with her. No, maybe not spoiled in that. It was human nature to retaliate. He'd caught himself doing it lately. She just did it with such a flair.

He approached her cautiously. She heard him and stiffened, but didn't turn around to see who was disturbing her peace. Was she still crying? God, he hoped not. He'd prefer her volatile temper anytime to her tears, for, like most men, he became a blithering idiot when faced with them.

With that in mind, he said the one thing guaranteed to provoke her. "Stubbed your foot, did you?"

Devlin groaned inwardly when all she said was a quiet "Yes."

He dropped down to his knees behind her in the soft mulch of the bank. His hands rose to draw her back against him, but he stopped himself, afraid she might tumble into the water in an effort to get away from him.

"I'm sorry, Megan."

"For what?"

"For putting my leg in the way of your foot."

She made him wait for a reply while she put her stocking and shoe back on, but finally she encouraged him with a surly tone. "You won't be forgiven for that."

"For my thoughtless words?"

"Nor for that."

"For being so surprised at your impeccable behavior?" he tried.

"Possibly for that."

Even though she couldn't see it, he kept his relieved grin to himself. "You were doing splendidly, by the by, and no one faults you for—for stubbing your foot. All censure has been directed where it belongs. In fact, my butler has assured me that I've never behaved so stupidly."

"I disagree. I can recall any number of—"

"One apology at a time, brat."

At that she stood up abruptly, so abruptly her derriere bumped into his chin. She swung around with a startled "Oh," but then remarked with what he could swear was a touch of humor, "Daring, weren't you, getting so close to me?"

"Not at all. Cold water isn't just good for cooling off lust. It also cools off tempers."

She amazed him by actually laughing. "You wouldn't throw me in."

"Possibly not. With that cumbersome train on your skirt, I'd probably have to jump in to save you, and I'd rather not, since I can assure you that my lake is much colder than your pond."

"I don't recall your even having a lake."

"Undoubtedly you couldn't tear yourself away from my stable to explore further."

She detected the ill humor in that statement, but chose to ignore it. "Actually, I saw a great deal of your house. One of your maids was having a fine time impressing Tiffany and me. Even showed us your private suite—well, only a peek."

"Were you impressed?"

"Oh, absolutely. Why do you think I wanted to marry the Duke of Wrothston?"

The taunt cut him to the quick. He should have realized she wouldn't let the matter of his embarrassing her go so easily, that she'd be getting even in some other way. And she'd chosen a truly sore spot to strike at.

"I recall your saying it was because of my stables," he replied with deceptive mildness.

"That, too," she said with a smile, then sauntered away, unaware of the black mood she was leaving him with.

He didn't attempt to follow her, too angry to trust what he might say. For a good hour he sat there brooding over his misfortune. And not once in that time did it occur to him that Megan might have been teasing him. The subject was too touchy for him, too painful, so he naturally assumed she must know that.

"I hear you made an ass of yourself upon your arrival," the Dowager Duchess of Wrothston said without preamble as she entered Devlin's office—also without knocking. "Sorry I missed it, but—good God, Devlin, what have you done to yourself? You look positively disgraceful—and have your valet cut that hair immediately."

Devlin leaned back in the chair behind his desk and twisted an overgrown lock around his finger. "You don't like it? This is what happens when one rusticates. Would you like to hear a few other things that can happen?"

"Am I getting the impression that you're annoyed with me, dear boy?"

"Quite possibly."

"Very well, we'll do this your way." And she sat down across from him to visibly brace herself. "Tell me what other things can happen."

"One could go insane."

"That hadn't occurred to me, but I suppose it's possible. What else?"

"One could get married."

"So John *wasn't* ribbing me? You actually came home with a bride?"

"There are a number of things I'd call her, but bride isn't necessarily one of them."

Lucinda St. James cocked a silver-white brow at him. "Trouble already?"

Devlin snorted. "Already? Never anything but."

"I believe I'll form my own opinion, since you're in such a tetchy mood. Where is the gel?"

Devlin shrugged. "The stable would be as good a guess as any."

Duchy's brow shot a little higher, since it was after ten o'clock at night. "This late?"

"The time of day or night is never an issue when *she* wants in a stable."

She started to say something, then changed her mind. "I'm not going to touch that one."

"Don't blame you a'tall," Devlin retorted dryly.

"Very well, you've kept me dangling long enough. Who is she?"

"Squire Penworthy's daughter."

"Well, I'll be damned," Duchy said with a grin that told Devlin what he'd suspected.

"You ought to be. What maggoty reasoning gave you the notion that I would take to that redhead?"

"Now how could I possibly know that?" she asked with perfect innocence.

"But you hoped."

"I suppose I did."

"Care to tell me why?"

"I met her a number of years ago."

"So I've learned to my regret."

She gave him an annoyed look for that cryptic interruption. "Then you know her father brought her here to purchase one of our Thoroughbreds."

"And guess what she named that mare?"

"Something silly, no doubt. She was only a child, after all."

"I've always thought the name was ridiculously silly myself, which is why I never use it."

Both of Duchy's brows shot up. "You don't mean—not Ambrose?"

"*Sir* Ambrose, actually," he replied, at which point his grandmother burst into laughter. "I fail to see the humor in that."

"You wouldn't, dear boy, but then you're as stuffy as your grandfather was at seventy. Comes from too much work and little time for anything else, which I have been *trying* to break you of. You were under his wing too long, that's your problem. But I'm here to tell you he *wasn't* like that when I married him, and you're too damn young to be taking after him."

"I do *not* consider myself stuffy—nor does Megan, for that matter."

"Delighted to hear it, but then that's one of the reasons I'd 'hoped.' The gel makes a lasting impression—at least she did on me. I've found myself thinking about her quite often over the years."

"What'd the minx do, set fire to the furniture with her temper?"

Duchy chuckled. "Didn't notice any temper. But I did notice a great deal of enthusiasm and precocious charm. She was a delightful little chit, with an outspokenness that was quite amusing. It was also vividly apparent that she was going to be a great beauty. Is she?"

"Without equal," Devlin allowed grudgingly.

"Then where's the harm done? I certainly saw none in putting you where you could meet her and might be influenced by her vivaciousness."

"Playing Cupid doesn't become you, Duchy," he said disagreeably. "You'd met Megan Penworthy only once, six years ago when she was no more than a child, and on that one meeting you throw your only grandson to the wolves. I'm disappointed in you."

"So I gather. Wolves, Devlin?"

"Vixens, then."

"I take it you're trying in your ambiguous way to tell me she's not the girl I thought she was."

"Not at all. I'm sure that girl is still there and a great many people get to meet her quite frequently. I'm just not one of them."

Duchy sighed in exasperation. "Kindly remember that I didn't create the necessity for you to disappear for a while. I merely took advantage of it. The fact remains that you've gone through most of your adult life expecting to marry Marianne, so, quite correctly, you weren't looking around for anyone else. But that marriage did not take place as planned, and when it didn't, you should have immediately started a search for another bride. Did you? No, you did not. You were too set in your ways already, and too immersed in your work, even though you know full well that you have a responsibility to marry and produce a son for Wrothston."

"Why does this sound all too familiar to me?" he asked dryly.

"Because I have a duty to harp on it, and at least I know *my* duty."

"Haven't I seen to mine?"

Duchy lost patience with him. "You're pulling teeth, is what you're doing. If you don't like the gel, what'd you marry her for?"

"Who says I don't like her? No, actually, just now I *don't* like her, but what the hell's that got to do with it? It certainly doesn't stop me from lusting after her every time she comes near me, even when she's not near—bloody hell, any damn time of the day, for that matter!"

"I'm going to pretend you didn't say that."

"Beg pardon."

"As well you ought to," she retorted indignantly. "Now, before I expire of exasperation, what, exactly, is the problem, Devlin?"

"She doesn't love me."

Chapter 37

"He doesn't love me."

Lucinda St. James sat back, amazed to hear those familiar words in answer to her question. She had been expecting something else entirely, the hot temper Devlin had spoken of, possibly some haughty indifference. After all, the chit had far surpassed Lucinda's predictions in the way of beauty. She certainly hadn't expected to find the same dejection that her grandson had displayed—to the same question.

She had called on the new Duchess of Wrothston early this morning, and was received in the formal sitting room, a grand chamber where Devlin usually conducted his less official business. It divided his suite of rooms from his wife's, a division that apparently was much wider than the thirty-foot length of the room.

Megan had been reserved at first, understandably, but after they'd reminisced about their first meeting, she'd relaxed enough to show Lucinda glimpses of the vivacious child the elderly woman remembered from six years ago. But she could also see the unhappiness Megan was trying to hide, which was what had prompted her to ask the same question she had put to Devlin last night. Getting the exact same answer was a revelation.

Carefully, because the situation called for delicacy—matters of the heart were so damned touchy—Lucinda asked, "What makes you think so?"

"If a man loves you, he'd tell you so, wouldn't he?" Megan replied.

"He ought to do that, yes."

"Well, Devlin's told me that I've ruined his life. He didn't want to marry me, you see. He went to a great deal of trouble to put me off the idea."

"The idea?" Lucinda said. "Then you'd already decided to marry him?"

"The duke, not him."

"But, my dear, he *is* a duke."

"I know that now, but I didn't know it before I married him."

"Then who did you think you were marrying?"

"A horse breeder. Didn't you know he'd been masquerading as one?"

"He was supposed to be a stableboy, but that's neither here nor there. So weren't you the least bit pleased to end up with a duke instead of a horse breeder?"

"Pleased?" Megan exclaimed. "He deceived me. I was bloody well furious—oh! I beg your pardon, Your Grace."

"My dear, we're family now. I'll expect you to call me Duchy, and to feel free to speak your mind to me, good or bad." And then she leaned forward to confide in a whisper, "I've been known to swear a little myself on occasion. Not in public, mind you, nor where that stick-in-the-mud grandson of mine might hear me. He thinks I can do no wrong, which is as it should be. Can't very well chastise him for his swearing if he knows I do, now can I?"

Megan shook her head in agreement, grinning, and in that moment they became fast friends. "Wish I'd thought of that. But then Devlin takes such delight in complaining about my bad habits, it'd be selfish of me to mend my ways."

Lucinda burst out laughing. "You're just what that boy needs," she stated positively. "Someone to shake him out of his stuffed shirt."

"He doesn't think so," Megan replied with a return of her dejection.

"Are you still angry that he's a duke instead of a horse breeder?"

"Yes—no—I don't know," Megan ended with a sigh.

"He happens to think you're delighted with the title—and his stables."

Megan made a face. "Shows what a dense man he is. I'd told him I was going to marry Ambrose St. James merely to impress him into ending his antagonism and insults, which is all I'd been getting from him since he showed up. 'Course, he couldn't leave it at that and be impressed. He had to know why I'd decided on Wrothston. But I wasn't about to tell *him* the real reason. It was none of his business. So I mentioned that I liked the duke's stable, just to put him off the subject." Megan's eyes widened with the realization. "I can see now how that might have annoyed him, him being the duke in question."

"That wouldn't be the half of it, my dear," Lucinda said with a chuckle. "The boy's had women making fools of themselves over him for as long as I can remember. Same thing went on with his father, and my husband, for that matter. Damned St. James looks *are* extraordinary. It must have been a shock to the dear boy to find a woman who wasn't instantly enamored of him, and who might even prefer his stable to him. Good God, I wish I could have seen his expression when he heard that. 'Course, you weren't even aware that you were bending his nose out of joint."

"A shame, since that is one of my little pleasures," Megan said, straight-faced.

"Thought it might be." Lucinda grinned. "But what was the real reason you were after a duke, if you don't mind my asking?"

Megan shrugged. "It was a good reason, an excellent reason, though it would probably seem quite silly to you. I was snubbed, you see, cut to the quick, actually, by our reigning hostess, Lady Ophelia Thackeray. For two years I'd been waiting and hoping for one of her coveted invitations, but she finally made it quite clear that I'd never get one. Tiffany is sure that it was because of this damn face of mine—you remember Tiffany, don't you? My dearest friend, who was with me the day we bought Sir Ambrose?"

"Yes, but—"

"Now there's another thing Devlin got all huffy about, what I named my horse. I'd been paying the duke a compliment, because I thought there was no horse finer than mine, but Devlin didn't see it that way."

"He wouldn't," Lucinda said dryly.

"But anyway, Tiffany is sure that Lady O wouldn't have me at one of her parties because she's got three daughters she's trying to marry off. That's well and fine, but to never get one of her invitations, when the whole parish has got one at least once, implies there's something wrong with me. That's when I decided to marry a title more lofty than hers—she's Countess of Wedg-wood—and bend *her* nose out of joint with it. That might sound petty and vengeful to you—it really does, doesn't it?—but I was angry and hurt at the time."

"But why Devlin?"

"He was the grandest lord I could think of, and I *do* happen to like his stable. But he was only a goal to work toward. I'd have to meet him first, and fall in love with him—that was a priority that Tiffany and my conscience weren't going to let me overlook, because I wasn't planning on ruining my life just to set Lady O on her ear. I wouldn't marry a man I didn't love, or wasn't sure that I could love, no matter how lofty his title. 'Course, I saw no reason to tell Devlin that. And he was determined to put me off the idea of *him* as my choice."

"How exactly did he do that without revealing to you who he was?"

"He told me the duke was a bounder, a cad, a seducer of innocents."

"He most certainly is not," Lucinda said with a good deal of huffiness.

"That's what I said. 'Course, I hadn't met the duke yet, so I was defend-ing a man I didn't know. Well, Devlin then arranged to prove it to me. He showed up at a masked ball I attended as himself, the duke, and promptly propositioned me to be his mistress."

"He didn't!"

"He did."

"But that's so unlike him."

"I'm afraid I have to disagree. That was just one of many insults I've had from that man. At any rate, he then had the gall to be surprised when I returned and told him—the horse breeder—that I hoped I'd never see the duke again."

Lucinda sat back, nearly speechless. "How, might I ask, did you two ever manage to get through all that muck to an altar?"

"I'm entirely to blame for that, though I'm not about to admit it to him. But the truth is, I unknowingly *and* unintentionally instigated my own seduction. Damned curiosity of mine did it. And it was so nice, the kissing part, but I didn't care for what came after. He didn't either. He said so. In fact, he so disliked it, he said we'd have a marriage in name only."

Lucinda got over her embarrassment with this subject quickly enough upon hearing that last. "The devil he did," she said angrily. "He can't do that. He's got a responsibility to produce the next duke. He can't very well do that if he doesn't—well, if he doesn't."

"Actually, he can, if the child I'm carrying turns out to be male. Didn't he tell you I'm going to have a baby, and that's why we were forced to marry?"

"No, the damned boy must have forgotten to mention that little tidbit."

Chapter 38

It was two days before Megan visited the stables to discover that Devlin had arranged to have Sir Ambrose delivered to Sherring Cross for her. She was pleased to see her mare again, but she was actually even more pleased to have a reason to seek Devlin out, to thank him for his thoughtfulness. She shouldn't need a reason to speak with her husband, but she felt she did.

She had barely seen him since their arrival, much less talked to him. She had been led to the formal dining room to dine alone with him last night— Duchy was conspicuously absent—but eating at different ends of a twenty-foot-long table was not conducive to conversation.

She'd noted the change in him without comment, the elegant attire, the very correct posture and movements. He was every inch the duke now—well, not quite every inch. He hadn't cut his hair yet. Duchy had complained over breakfast this morning that he was leaving it long just to annoy her. Megan decided it was for her own benefit so she wouldn't forget that he was the man she'd married—as if she could.

She'd only had one remark for him last night before they parted to go to their separate bedchambers, and that only because two hours of formal silence at that long table had gotten on her nerves, and she wasn't up to attacking his *new* self yet.

"It's patently clear now why you made such a lousy horse breeder. The next time you think to impersonate a member of the working class, leave your fine shirts at home, as well as your arrogance."

She'd gone to sleep regretting those sulky words, which hadn't even gotten a reply other than a condescending lifting of his brows, meant to exasperate her, no doubt. Then again, his grandmother possibly had the right of it. Megan had confided to her that the Devlin she knew was argumentative, disagreeable, and disrespectful, only to be told that simply wasn't Devlin St. James, that such behavior had to have been part of the role he'd been playing.

Megan sincerely hoped not, for the very proper, unflappable Devlin she'd dined with last night was a bore. Still, she was simply going to have to make an effort to get along with him, and to stop trying to provoke him into the same state of unhappy feelings she was in. Which was why she was glad of an excuse to speak with him now. She would be pleasant. She would offer an olive branch. He was her husband, for better or for worse. She was tired of the worse.

Megan entered the house by a side entrance, where the corridors were almost mazelike, though they eventually led to the main block where Devlin's office was located. She was nearly there when she heard a voice that was vaguely familiar raised in anger.

" . . . won't do you a bit of good to tell me he's not here when I bloody well know he is. I've had spies watching the house day and night to inform me exactly when he returned, so get out of my way, John!"

Megan came around a corner in time to see Devlin open the door to his office and ask mildly, "Were you looking for me, Freddy?"

"Come out of hiding at last, have you?" Frederick Richardson shot back in hot temper. "And where the devil did you go, Dev, that a hundred bloody runners couldn't find you? Clear to America?"

"You ought to know me better than that. I wouldn't put up with seasickness again for any reason—even to preserve your rotten hide."

"Preserve?" the Marquis of Hampden exclaimed with a good deal of indignation. "Let's not forget who intends to shoot whom."

"Have you brought your pistol with you, then?" Devlin was still showing a marked lack of interest, which was causing a marked excess of alarm for Megan.

"Yes, by God—I've got it here somewhere."

While Freddy was searching through several of his pockets, Devlin stepped forward and socked him one, catching him so off guard that the marquis was knocked off his feet. "I believe I owed you that," Devlin said, finally showing a bit of emotion, in this case satisfaction.

"The devil you did!"

"The devil I didn't, and I'm not referring to that blind punch you gave me. You cannot begin to know what your sister's false accusation and your pigheadedness have cost me. I never would have gone to the wilds of Devonshire if it weren't for your damned temper that needed time to cool off. It's *your* fault I'm so bloody miserable now, thank you very much!" And having displayed ample emotion at last, Devlin went back into his office, slamming the door shut behind him.

"Well, what the devil did he mean by that?" Freddy asked as he picked himself up off the floor.

"I couldn't say, my lord," John replied quite correctly, only to spoil it with an opinion. "Possibly he refers to the difficulty he is having adjusting to married life."

"Married life?" Freddy replied in shock. "Married! He didn't!"

"I assure you—"

Freddy didn't wait for the butler to finish, but barged uninvited into Devlin's office. Megan turned around to retreat unnoticed, heartsick to know that she didn't just have the ruination of Devlin's life on her conscience now. She was also making him miserable.

"How dare you marry someone else when my sister—?"

"Lied, Freddy," Devlin cut in curtly without pausing in the act of pouring himself a large snifter of brandy. "When are you going to get that through your thick head? Good God, it's been two months!" On second thought, he left the glass and brought the bottle back with him to his desk. "Didn't Sabrina own up to it yet?"

"Own up to it?" Freddy blustered. "She still maintains you seduced her."

"Why that little—Duchy tells me she's not married yet. If you tell me you were waiting for me to show up and do the honorable thing, I think I'll hit you again."

Freddy rubbed his jaw with a wince and dropped into one of the chairs across from Devlin's desk. "Rather you didn't, and no, I wasn't. Found her a groom, though. Carlton is knee-deep in debt and so is quite agreeable. They were to marry on the quiet next week."

"Were?"

"She lost the baby last week, so she's canceled the wedding."

"Lost it?" Devlin frowned. "Then she really was?—wait a minute," he said suspiciously. "Did you see her lose it, or did she just tell you about it after the fact?"

"Well, actually, she did tell me, but she was quite broken up about it."

"They're all experts at crying at the drop of a hat. Haven't you figured that out yet?"

"Well, that's damn cynical of you," Freddy protested. "I had no reason to doubt her, Dev."

"Except that I'm your best friend, and I *told* you I never touched her."

"She's my sister, dammit. What would you have done in my place?"

"I wouldn't have been so quick to believe a habitual practical joker, which you bloody well know Sabrina is. And I would have had a little more faith in my best friend, who doesn't go around seducing innocents—at least he didn't used to," Devlin ended in a mumble.

Freddy pounced. "I heard that. Who else have you been seducing?"

"I certainly wasn't talking about your damn sister, who, by the by, is going to get her neck wrung if I ever see her again. And you—I'm seriously thinking about sending *my* seconds round to pay *you* a visit."

"That's twice now you seem to be blaming me for I don't know what."

"Then let me enlighten you," Devlin offered. "Because of you, I was forced to bury myself in the country, where I met the most beautiful girl I've ever set eyes on, and my life has been hell ever since."

"I beg to differ," Freddy replied smugly. "*I've* recently met the most beautiful girl you're ever likely to set eyes on. Haven't been able to get her out of my mind. I don't mind telling you, I'm seriously contemplating returning to Hampshire to court her."

"Hampshire? She wouldn't happen to have red hair and blue-as-midnight eyes, would she?"

"How the devil did you know?"

"You can forget about courting her," Devlin said in a near growl. "And you will bloody well get her *out* of your mind. I've already married her."

"That isn't funny, Dev."

"Am I laughing?"

"Not Miss Penworthy?"

"The same."

"Well, I like that!" Freddy said huffily. "And you're *complaining*? You ought to be thanking me."

"When she despises everything about me, except my title—and my horses?"

"Well, at least she's got good taste. I like your horses myself." When Devlin just stared, he added, "Sorry, but it can't be all that bad."

"Can't it?" And Devlin proceeded to tell him just how bad it was.

Chapter 39

The situation was intolerable. Devlin was obviously avoiding her. That much Megan had figured out before she had been at Sherring Cross a full week. If she saw him at all, it was only in passing.

He never even made another appearance for dinner after that first night. And when Megan did see him, he was so disgustingly polite she wanted to hit him to find out if the old Devlin was still there, or if he really had been no more than a creation for a role he was playing. She didn't. The new Devlin was just too intimidating, and so bloody imperious that she couldn't even think of starting an argument with him without feeling utterly childish.

The situation was definitely intolerable. Megan was crying herself to sleep at night. And for no good purpose, since Devlin didn't even know about it. But he was just as miserable as she was. She'd heard him say so. He was just making the same effort she was to conceal it.

The situation was *absolutely* intolerable, but Megan had finally figured out what she could do about it. Overhearing Devlin tell Duchy that Freddy's sister, Sabrina, was claiming to have lost her baby gave her the idea. She was going to tell Devlin the same thing, that she'd lost their baby. It wouldn't be an easy lie to tell, for the mere thought of something like that actually happening brought tears to her eyes. But it would solve both their problems by allowing him to get a quick annulment.

Even her conscience couldn't change her mind. And with the decision firmly made, there was no time to waste, what with Duchy planning a formal ball to officially announce the marriage. And Devlin's grandmother was determined to do that, since she'd complained of being denied the opportunity to arrange his wedding. So Megan had to act before those plans progressed to the invitation stage. The fewer people who knew about her, the quicker Devlin could get on with his life—and she could forget that she'd been foolish enough to fall in love with a man who wasn't real.

Megan waited nervously in the formal sitting room that night until she heard Devlin enter his chambers directly from the hallway. She paced, waiting for the sound of the door to close again, signaling the departure of his valet. Then she started crying—loudly. Within seconds the door connecting the two rooms slammed open and Devlin was rushing toward her.

"Why are you crying?"

"I—I'm not," Megan said, her mind going blank with him standing so close. "I—oh, never mind. Go away."

"Megan!"

"I don't know how to tell you," she cried into her hands. "I've been trying not to think about it, because every time I do, this happens. But I suppose you have to know."

"What?!"

"I lost the baby."

Utter silence greeted that statement, so Megan wailed louder. But she couldn't look at him. If he said one kind word to her, she'd be crying for real.

"I require proof," was what he finally said, quite *un*kindly. "Are you still bleeding?"

Megan blanched, never having imagined that he might actually doubt her. Fortunately, he couldn't see that, because her face was still buried in her hands.

But she quickly recovered, improvising. "It didn't just happen. It was on the return trip from Scotland. And I haven't told you sooner because—because I've been in shock. Are you so insensitive that you haven't even noticed?"

"You have been unusually . . . quiet."

A nice word to describe her present lack of temper, but uttered so dryly, she knew something wasn't going right. He either didn't believe her or— could he possibly think she had lied to begin with, that there had never been a baby, and so no reason to get married?

"Why are you badgering me?" she demanded. "Can't you see that I'm upset?"

"I would have thought you'd be relieved."

She gasped at what he was implying, her head coming up so she could glare at him. "I wanted that baby!"

"No, you didn't."

"Don't you tell me I didn't when I did!"

He sighed over her increasing dramatics. "Megan, there obviously wasn't a baby. It was a mistake."

"That's beside the point."

"We'll have others."

"No, we won't!" At which point she finally had something to really cry about, and her tears began in earnest.

His expression changed instantly from put upon to genuinely concerned. "Megan—"

"Don't touch me," she said as he reached for her and drew her unresisting against his chest.

"Megan, don't—please."

"I hate you," she cried into his neck, gripping fistfuls of his robe. "You don't know anything about what I want. I may not have wanted this baby before, but I do now." She didn't even realize she'd stopped using the past tense.

"Then I'm sorry. Tell me what I can do."

"Nothing. There's nothing you can—hold me, Devlin." Megan's eyes widened at the strength of his comforting, which went from awkward patting to a near death's grip. And she took advantage of it shamelessly, aware that he would probably never hold her again, for any reason, and desperately wanting those arms around her one last time.

When the soft nonsense he was murmuring in an effort to quiet her turned to kisses along her temples, her forehead, her wet cheeks, she knew she was really taking advantage now, but she didn't care. Just a little while more. She'd never ask for another thing.

But suddenly she was tasting her tears on his lips as his mouth brushed over hers by accident, only to come back once, twice, and when she didn't protest, to settle there for a gradually deepening kiss. She gripped his robe even harder, in case he thought to come to his senses and let go of her. He didn't. His tongue delved into her mouth with a deep groan, his, which drowned out her own.

The maelstrom of sensations that he so easily evoked with such kisses was there again, more overwhelming than ever after such a long absence. Megan forgot about her plan, forgot that she was supposed to be grievously upset. Concerns became nonexistent, thinking impossible, with such pleasure clamoring for notice.

Which was about all she noticed. Softness was suddenly beneath her. She had been fully clothed; now she was not. But she didn't become aware of these things until the heat of his skin covered her. And then it was only a vaguely curious awareness, because all the while, Devlin kept up those magical, drugging kisses that wouldn't let her think.

What had been previously offered as comfort became hot brands, his hands no longer soothing, but stirring new fires wherever they roamed. And they roamed all over, teasing, thrilling, causing shivers of delight on her neck, across her breasts, down her belly to what had become the center of her universe, that place aching for his touch.

She was not to be disappointed. Deeply his fingers caressed, bringing whimper, moan, gasp, whimper again, and need, burning, consuming need that was answered with remarkable astuteness. At the precise moment she was sure she could bear no more, she was filled with the thickness of his manhood thrusting to her depths, and the resulting explosion of relief nearly did her in, it was so electrifying. Nor did it end, delicious spasms of pleasure continuing with each additional thrust, until he reached his own shattering climax. Even then the aftermath kept her spellbound and so sensually languorous, there was no thought but to savor every last incredible sensation. If only the first time had been . . . The first time?

Megan's eyes flew open with the realization. "Dammit, Devlin, why did you make love to me?"

The question was so absurd, he could be forgiven the dryness of his tone as he leaned up to say, "I was comforting you in a very old, very reliable way."

"But you've ruined everything. You were supposed to get an annulment. Now you can't!"

He lifted himself off her with stiff, jerky movements that were indicative of anger. It wasn't until he'd yanked on his robe and turned to face her that she saw her guess was correct. He was definitely angry.

Megan reached for something to cover herself with, as if that could shield her from the fury in his eyes, but there was nothing. He'd made love to her on the sofa in the sitting room. Her own clothes were in a pile on the floor a goodly distance away.

"Is that what you were hankering for?" he demanded. "An annulment?"

"Certainly," she replied uneasily. "It's what *you* want, isn't it?"

"At this precise moment, it would be my fondest wish. But as you pointed out, it's too late now."

"Not—not if you forget this happened."

"Oh, no, my dear, I'm not *about* to forget this," he replied coldly. "Besides, you could well be with child again."

"That's not likely to happen twice in a row," she retorted, but she was groaning with another realization, that she was going to have to tell him she *was* still with child. Not tonight she wouldn't.

"Then let me put it this way, and this ought to sound familiar, brat. You're stuck with me until death do us part, and I'm not about to die to convenience you."

"Well, that's a fine attitude!" she shouted after him as he stalked from the room.

But he turned in the doorway for one last rejoinder. "You couldn't have taken the title of duchess with you if you'd got your bloody annulment."

"I know that, you stupid man," she replied, but he'd already slammed the door shut.

Chapter 40

Devlin left for London the next morning. Megan found out about it after he'd gone, when Duchy joined her for breakfast in her small sitting room, which was much more cozy than the formal one. The lavender shades in the wall coverings and furniture would have to go, however. She ought to consider changing it now that she was staying, but she wasn't in the mood to spend Devlin's money.

"You shan't be parted long, however," Duchy informed her, "since we're going to London, too."

"We are?"

"Yes. Told Devlin I was taking you shopping. He should have waited to escort us, but he got testy when I mentioned it. No matter. We'll join him at the town house."

I run him off, but the poor man just can't get away from me.

You're assuming. He's been away from his work a long time. You know how men love their work.

And how that man despises me.

He didn't despise you last night.

So he liked me long enough to make love to me. It wasn't intentional. It just happened.

Then why don't you work on getting it to "just happen" again?

Because that won't solve anything.

It can't hurt either.

" . . . at least thirty dresses to start," Duchy was saying, "And, of course, the new ball gown."

Megan hoped she hadn't missed more than that, because that was too much. "I don't need a new wardrobe, Duchy. I've already sent home for the rest of my things, and my complete wardrobe is extensive."

Duchy waved a dismissive hand. "No wardrobe is *ever* large enough. And besides, after the official announcement at the ball, you'll be deluged with callers, and the Duchess of Wrothston has an image to uphold. Haven't you seen the size of your closet?"

Megan had wondered why that room was so large. "If you say so," she conceded grudgingly.

"I do." Then the dowager duchess frowned. "I'll be dropping you off for your selections and fittings. I find it too boring by half these days. I trust you know what colors suit you? I mean, you don't favor pink, do you?"

Duchy looked so worried, Megan assured her, "Pink gives me freckles."

The old lady's eyes widened. "Didn't know that was possible."

"It isn't."

"You minx." Duchy chuckled.

But now Megan was worried. "It's going to be a problem, isn't it—my hair? Devlin calls it god-awful red. He said once that the duke—he was talking about himself, though I didn't know it at the time—wouldn't be seen in public with a redhead. I believe his exact words were 'a woman with the most unfashionable hair in creation.' "

Duchy sighed. Love had turned her grandson into an utter ass, it seemed. "There is nothing wrong with your hair, child. I find it incredibly lovely, and I don't doubt for a second that Devlin does, too. If he said otherwise, he probably had some contrary reason for it. In fact, I'll wager that if I tell him you plan to dye it, he'll forbid you."

"That's not such a bad idea."

"Then I'll tell him."

"No, that I dye it."

"Don't you dare," Duchy scolded. "You'd be doing it for the wrong reason, and you know it."

Megan didn't try to deny it. "But *he'd* be happy, wouldn't he?"

"The only way that boy is going to be happy is if you tell him you love him."

"Do *what*?"

Duchy had promised herself she wouldn't interfere, so she shrugged. "It was just a thought."

But Megan's conscience had had the same thought. *So why* don't *you tell him?*

You know very well why. He'd laugh, and I'd never forgive him.

You know the old Devlin might laugh, but the new Devlin would . . .

Yes? He would what?

I don't know.

Neither do I, and I'm not going to embarrass myself to find out.

Well, something has to be done. You could offer a truce in the bedroom for a start, and see where that leads.

I'll think about it.

Why don't you not think about it for a change, and just do it?

That's easy for you to say. You're not the one facing possible rejection.

I'm not the coward either, but one of us sure as hell is. Or do you like the way things are?

Megan sighed. She really did hate it when her conscience was right.

Two days after arriving at the St. Jameses London mansion, Devlin barged into Megan's dressing room, where she was preparing for dinner. Her maid was so startled, the girl rushed out before she was dismissed.

Megan was just as startled, the more so when her husband said without preamble, in a don't-argue-with-me tone, "You may *not* dye your hair."

She had forgotten that Duchy had planned to tell him that. And it was apparently a good thing she hadn't accepted that wager. But this was the first time she'd seen Devlin since she'd come to London—he kept appalling hours when he was attending to ducal business—and her conscience wasn't going to let her back out of her newest decision, to bury her temper and charm the man into liking her.

So she gave him a smile, merely reminding him, "But you don't like my hair."

The smile threw him off, unexpected, and so suspect. "It's grown on me," he said grudgingly.

"But it's not fashionable."

That annoyed him, hearing his own words thrown back at him. "The Duchess of Wrothston makes her own fashion. She doesn't have to emulate it."

"But I wouldn't want to embarrass you in public. And besides, it clashes with the pink ball gown I've ordered."

"Oh, God."

She pretended not to hear that. "Black, I think. Yes, black. Blond is so common, after all, with everyone favoring it."

"If you dye one lock on that beautiful head of yours, I'll put you over my knee again, and you know bloody well that's not an idle threat!"

"If you say so, Devlin."

"I mean it, Megan," he warned, suspicious of her compliance.

"I know you do."

She confounded him with another smile. He had come anticipating a fight.

After their last parting, he needed one. But she wasn't obliging him, and she wasn't behaving the least bit like the Megan he knew.

She must want something. Had she figured out another way to get out of their marriage?

Bloody hell, it infuriated him every time he thought of that damn annulment idea of hers. After making love to her, finally, as he'd dreamed of doing, and knowing that she had found it as incredibly satisfying as he had, Devlin realized that for her to tell him she wanted an annulment proved without a doubt how much she loathed him, so much so that she was even willing to give up the title she'd hankered after.

Then why hadn't she stopped him from ruining her goal? Her curiosity? He had wondered how he might use it against her. Had he done so without even knowing it? Or had she simply been so caught up in her own passion that her goal had temporarily been forgotten?

He ought to tell her that he wouldn't have given her an annulment even if they hadn't made love again. Maybe that would get him the fight he wanted.

He opened his mouth to do just that, but she turned her back toward him, revealing an only half-closed gown, and asking over her shoulder, "Since you're here and my maid isn't, would you fasten my gown for me?"

Devlin was appalled to hear himself say, "I'd rather unfasten it."

She swung back around in surprise. "Now?"

"Anytime."

"All right."

He couldn't have heard that correctly. "Liked it that much, did you, that even I will do?"

"*Only* you will do," she replied softly, her cheeks rosy with a blush.

Of course she had to say that. He was her husband. But he wasn't going to spite himself just because he couldn't comprehend what she was up to.

He made love to his wife right there in her dressing room, swiftly at first, because he was afraid she might change her mind, then with exquisitely slow thoroughness when he was sure she wouldn't.

But they were really going to have to try this in a bed sometime.

Chapter 41

It made a difference, their new relationship. By mutual agreement, silent though understood, a sort of truce was declared for lovemaking. It was an unusual concept, but it worked very well.

Devlin would come to her room at night, and without a word, Megan would move into his arms. She came to understand that despite what he might think of her as an individual, he absolutely adored her body. That she was still fascinated by his wasn't in doubt either. And although silence wasn't demanded or even encouraged, anything of a serious nature was expressly forbidden, for absolutely nothing was to disturb what was becoming a necessity for them both.

Outside the bedroom, it was like they were meeting for the first time. He no longer deliberately avoided her. She no longer searched for ways to tweak his nose when something annoyed her. They spoke to each other with growing ease. They asked questions about their pasts and answered them without the least hesitancy.

His superior-than-thou attitude was also less noticeable, though not completely diminished. He was still the duke, after all, not her horse breeder. Accordingly, he never raised his voice to her anymore. And she continued to dazzle him with her smiles.

They were getting along.

It wasn't quite enough.

Megan still had to tell him that she'd lied about losing the baby, and hope she could make him understand that she'd done it for him. She still had to get up the nerve to tell him she loved him. And she knew she wouldn't be able to continue being pleasant indefinitely, at least not *all* the time, or keep watching her every word to avoid arguments. It simply wasn't her nature to be so guarded with her emotions.

And she still wanted her horse breeder back.

"I can't believe it worked out exactly as you planned it," Tiffany said on a happy sigh as she and Megan strolled through Hyde Park. She had arrived in London yesterday, for her own wedding was less than a week away. "You got your duke. You love him. And he adores you."

"Two out of three isn't bad, Tiff."

"What's that supposed to mean?"

"It means, what makes you think Devlin loves me back?"

"Of course he does," Tiffany insisted. "He must. He married you, didn't he?"

"Yes, but not because of any great affection, or any affection at all, for that matter." Megan looked off toward the lake before reluctantly adding, "There was a little something I didn't mention when I wrote to you, Tiff. I'm going to have a baby."

"But that's wonderful news!"

"I agree, now, but I didn't think so when I first found out—since I wasn't married at the time."

Tiffany stopped walking to exclaim, "But—good God, d'you mean to say you *had* to get married?"

Megan turned back to face her friend, but she still couldn't meet her eyes. "Yes."

"No wonder you doubt his affections. But certainly he's told you he loves you since then?"

"Not once."

"Then what does he say when you tell him that you do?"

"I don't."

"What do you mean, you don't? You just got through telling me that you do."

"No, I mean that I don't tell him."

"Megan! Whyever not?"

"As long as my letter was, I still didn't tell you the half of it, Tiff." She did now, with little embellishment. It was still quite a while before she concluded, "So you can see why I've been reluctant to put him on the spot with a declaration, especially since—since I've so been enjoying our unusual truce, and don't want to do anything to ruin it."

Tiffany's cheeks were about as red as Megan's locks. "Is it really that nice?"

"Better than nice," Megan said as they continued strolling, nodding every once in a while when a gentleman would pass and tip his hat, ignoring those who simply stopped and stared. "Just don't expect to enjoy the first time, at least not all of it. Men do, which is bloody unfair, if you ask me. But it's our lot to not only face it in fear and ignorance, but to also have to deal with the pain of it."

"My maid says the pain is excruciating," Tiffany confided, her face a bit pale now.

Megan snorted. "The girl doesn't know what she's talking about. It was more annoying than terrible, and over before you know it. In my case, it merely brought me to my senses, which effectively ruined it for me. Actually, unlike me, you could go on to enjoy the rest."

"I can't tell you how relieved I am. I'd been getting more and more nervous as the day approaches."

Megan recalled her own panic the closer she'd got to Scotland, but for different reasons. Tiffany was assured of Tyler's love, and fully expected to be blissfully happy in their marriage. Megan still wasn't assured of anything— except that Devlin liked making love to her now.

"That's normal. They even have a name for it, wedding jitters. I'm just as nervous about this damn ball Duchy is giving, but they don't have a name for that."

"Sure they do. Stark raving—"

"Stop." Megan laughed. "I'm not *that* nervous. And you are coming, aren't you, now that you and Tyler have decided to postpone your wedding trip until the spring?"

"Absolutely. I'll be the one organizing the search parties—"

"Cut it out, Tiff." Megan laughed harder. "Sherring Cross isn't *that* big."

"Maybe not, but at least you remember how to laugh. I was beginning to wonder."

Megan sighed. "I'm sorry. I shouldn't have said anything about my problems when your big day is so close."

"Nonsense. And I wouldn't be surprised if you're making problems where none exist. I can't believe he doesn't love you, Meg. Every man you meet—"

"Devlin isn't like them; he's unique himself. His grandmother told me women have been making fools of themselves over him for as long as she can remember, and I don't doubt it, because I've done the same thing. But all he sees when he looks at me is a spoiled brat."

"You just get a little impatient sometimes."

Megan smiled. "Don't try and put a nice face on it when we both know I'm spoiled rotten."

"Well, so what?" Tiffany huffed loyally. "I suppose he just shrugs it off when he doesn't get what he wants?"

Megan stopped, eyes widening. "Now that you mention it, he reacts a bit like I do."

"Aha, and it stands to reason. If anyone's bound to be spoiled, a bloody duke would be. He probably had ten nannies running after him as a child, and a host of other servants to see to his every need. You just had one nanny and a father who dotes on you, so if you ask me, he's probably more spoiled than you are."

"I'll be sure to mention that—if I ever get to fight with him again."

Chapter 42

It was a beautiful wedding, just what Megan had always envisioned for herself—well, hers wouldn't have been quite so grand as Tiffany's, or with so many guests, just friends and family in her small parish church. But she'd been denied that because her damned inner voice and curiosity had gotten together to conspire against her common sense.

She was miserable on the way home from the wedding, when she should have been only happy for her friend. Devlin was quiet, too, probably just as miserable, but for different reasons, and that only made her feel worse. He could have had that grand wedding, should have had it. Instead he'd been forced to elope to Scotland.

I ought to shoot you.

Me or him?

You. Better yet, you're retired. I never want to hear from you again.

Why is it you always get mad and need someone to blame when you feel rotten?

I'm not blaming someone else, I'm blaming you.

Good God, she was losing touch with reality. Her inner voice was *not* a separate individual. But it was right as usual. Megan really did have a difficult time accepting responsibility for her own misery. And maybe it was time she stopped doing that.

She returned to Sherring Cross the next day—alone. Well, not exactly alone, since she had five strapping servants plus her new maid to escort her. Duchy had gone back earlier in the week, confessing that at her age, she couldn't tolerate the bustle of London for very long, and she also had a thousand things to do in preparation for the ball.

Devlin was to have accompanied her. After all, the St. James ball was only another four days away. But he canceled at the last moment. Business, he said, that had to be seen to beforehand so that he could remain in Kent for a week or so after the ball.

In Megan's present mood, she had to wonder if that was true. Business was, after all, a convenient excuse to separate them. And Devlin's quiet mood yesterday after the wedding had continued for the rest of the day, to include his not coming to her room last night. After seeing how happy Tiffany and Tyler were, perhaps he'd realized that their own "half" marriage wasn't enough for him either.

The day of the ball began with a frigid storm that was nice enough to clear up before the guests started arriving. It was also the day Megan had picked to make her own announcement, albeit privately. She just hadn't decided yet whether to sit Devlin down and confess all to him before or after the ball. Either way, she was bound to ruin his day—*if* he showed up. He hadn't so far yet, and Duchy was starting to fret.

Megan kept to her rooms for most of the day. Tiffany found her there in the afternoon, the new bride of five days bubbling over with good cheer.

"Tyler went straight to the stables. He's decided to buy one of the St. James Thoroughbreds, but he's worried others will take advantage of their invite here to do the same, and the duke's entire stock will be sold before the end of the day. Just about everyone who is anyone is coming, you know. I've even heard the rumor that the queen intends to make an appearance. And you wouldn't believe the traffic on the roads and at the inns along the way. If Tyler didn't have acquaintances in the area, we would have arrived in the middle of the night, because I was *not* going to sleep in the coach."

Megan got her reply in quickly, while Tiffany paused for breath. "You should have come yesterday to avoid the crush, like my father did. You know very well you don't have to wait for an invitation to visit here now. In fact, I expect you to come for extended stays whenever you like."

"With the size of your guest list, we were afraid even Sherring Cross was going to run out of rooms. Honestly, Meg, I doubt there's a lord left in London today."

Megan laughed. "You more than anyone would never believe this house capable of running out of rooms. And besides, I had one prepared for your exclusive use before I went to London. Weren't you shown to it?"

"That miniature mausoleum down the hall? Yes, a maid is hanging up my gown even now. And where is yours? I can't wait to see what you decided on for an occasion of this magnitude."

Megan led the way to her dressing room, though she couldn't generate much enthusiasm for the stunning gown that Duchy had had a hand in creating because she'd guessed Megan wasn't accustomed to the kind of extravagance demanded for *this* ball. The result was a lavish though elegant gown of ivory-and-sapphire silk—not pink, as she had teasingly told Devlin—with a fortune in real pearls sewn along the deep bodice and dotting the train and the single wreath of white roses attached to the side of the gathered skirt.

"Good God, you're going to look like a princess," Tiffany exclaimed.

"No, just a duchess."

Tiffany raised a brow at her friend's dejected tone and accurately guessed the cause. "You still haven't told Devlin, have you?"

"Today I will."

"And you're making yourself sick over it," Tiffany concluded, again right on the mark.

Megan smiled weakly. "I guess I am."

"Then postpone it another day. You already have enough to be nervous about on this one."

"Postpone what?" Duchy asked as she sailed into the dressing room.

Megan made an effort to evade the question. "Has Devlin arrived yet?"

"Just, and the dear boy's quite annoyed with me, I don't mind telling you. I suppose I should have sent him a final copy of the guest list."

"Why? Did you invite someone he doesn't particularly like?"

"*That* was inevitable, but not the issue. No, he had to sleep in a stable last night."

"You're joking," Megan said incredulously.

"I told you," Tiffany told Megan.

Duchy just sighed. "He tried three different inns and not a room to be had in any of them. And he considered the hour too late to impose on anyone he knew. If he had left London at an earlier hour, there wouldn't have been a problem—or maybe there would have been. He simply wasn't expecting such a crowd, though I don't know why not. It may have been ten years since we've had a ball here, but he knows very well that the St. Jameses have always entertained in a grand manner—when we get around to it."

Megan was reminded that she hadn't seen the guest list either, final or otherwise. "Just how many people did you invite?"

"About six hundred, but I expect every one of them, plus a few I may have forgotten who will show up to remind me that I forgot them."

There were ten seconds of amazed silence before Tiffany said dryly, "It's a good thing Sherring Cross has two connecting ballrooms."

"I'd wondered at that," Megan replied in a horrified whisper. "Until now."

Duchy pretended not to notice the astonishment she'd caused. She just loved surprises, which was why she hadn't included the reason for the ball in the invitations, nor had she even told her intimate friends yet about Devlin's marriage. Her sister, Margaret, knew, of course, and she'd had to sit on top of her to keep her quiet about it since her arrival, no easy thing to do with that chatterbox.

"Here's another thing I forgot," she said now, handing over the jewel box she carried. "Devlin had to remind me to open the family vault, though I can't imagine why he suggested rubies to go with your gown."

Megan could, but she was laughing and so didn't volunteer that he thought she would be wearing pink. Duchy had too many things yet to do to stay and question her strange humor, though she did suggest, "You might want to take a nap, my dear," before she turned to leave.

But Megan wasn't a total nervous wreck yet, just halfway there, and called after her before she was out of hearing range, "Is the queen really coming?"

"Certainly," floated back through the open door.

"Certainly." Megan groaned.

Chapter 43

"Make that bloody announcement already, Duchy, or you're going to witness the Duke of Wrothston causing a scandal."

Lucinda glanced incredulously at her grandson, then followed his gaze to where Megan was standing, but was barely seen, she had so many young lords surrounding her. "For heaven's sake, Dev, the ball has only just started. And you can get her away from that crowd by simply dancing with her. That *is* permissible, you know."

"That isn't going to do it," he growled, though he started toward Megan to do just that.

Duchy shook her head after him, unaware that he was going to make his own announcement. But she heard it, couldn't help hearing it, actually, as did everyone else, for the sheer volume he deliberately injected.

"Excuse me, gentlemen, but I would like to dance with my *wife*."

And anyone who hadn't heard that was quickly enlightened by his or her neighbor within minutes. Duchy sighed. So much for being the sole bearer of glad tidings. But then she chuckled to herself. If her surprise had to be ruined, she couldn't have asked for a better way. The dear boy was positively green with jealousy, and there wasn't a person there who couldn't see that.

Megan was the one exception. She had no reason to think that Devlin's appalling rudeness, as she saw it, stemmed from jealousy. She was too accustomed to male adoration to think anything was unusual about the excessive attention she'd been receiving from the moment she came downstairs. There were simply a great many men present, hence the large number wanting to meet her.

Even Devlin's pronounced use of the word "wife" didn't suggest jealousy to her. She'd been giving her name as Megan St. James. It wasn't her fault that it was being assumed she was a St. James relative rather than a wife, since she wasn't aware of the assumption.

No, rude was what he was, and she intended to find out why, saying the moment he pulled her into the current waltz, "If you're still put out because you had to sleep in a stable last night, I'll thank you not to take it out on me."

"So don't thank me."

Megan blinked. That sounded so much like her old Devlin that she was smiling without realizing it as she asked, "Brought back memories, did it, of your brief step-down to the servant class?"

Now that he had her in his arms, his jealousy was fast diminishing, soothed further by her smile, if not by her taunt. So he accepted the excuse she was offering for his appalling behavior—appalling now that he was aware of it.

"I had a perfectly good bed in your stable, Megan, fetched down from one of your guest rooms, hardly comparable with a stack of hay."

"A stack of hay?" she said in surprise. "I hadn't realized—" She broke off her sentence before she sounded too sympathetic, recalling that she hadn't finished scolding him yet. "All the same, it wasn't *my* fault, was it?"

"Quite right. I do beg your pardon."

"As you should. But as long as we're on the subject of complaints—"

"We're not—" he tried to cut in.

"Oh, yes, we are," Megan interrupted right back. "You don't see me for four days and you don't even seek me out to say hello when you finally return. That's not very husbandly of you, Devlin."

"If you knew the state of the typical ton marriage, you'd know that's *very* husbandly of me. But in my case, Duchy told me you were napping."

"I wasn't. You should have found out for yourself."

She'd dropped her gaze to mutter that. Devlin bent sideways to see if her expression looked as sulky as her tone, but she turned her head aside. If she only knew that he'd tried a half-dozen times to get away from the guests who had pounced on him the moment he walked in the door—half his jealous anger had stemmed from *not* having a chance to see her before the ball commenced.

"Did you actually miss me, Megan?" he asked carefully now, unsure if he was getting the right impression from her complaint or not.

"Yes, actually, I believe I did."

"Would you, ah, like to slip away with me for a few moments so that I can make amends and greet you properly?"

"Yes, I believe I would."

He did *not* give her a chance to change her mind, immediately dragging her off the dance floor, her hand firmly in his, but her step hardly up to matching his. He didn't notice, too eager to find them a spot of privacy in a veritable sea of people. Duchy, standing near the doors he was determinedly heading for, with Frederick Richardson at her side, definitely noticed.

"Good God, he's going to make a scandal after all," she exclaimed. "Stop him, Freddy. I'm sure you, of all people, can imagine what he's about to do."

"Indeed, and I'd rather not die tonight just to save him from a scandal, if you don't mind."

"He'll thank you once he comes to his senses."

"That, my dear Duchy, will be too late," Freddy replied and, against his better judgment, moved to block Devlin's exit from the room—just in time. "I say, old man, you aren't thinking of making an ass of yourself twice in one evening, are you?"

Devlin stopped, allowing Megan to move up to his side. "For a friend who hasn't been completely forgiven yet, you're pushing it, Richardson," he said in low tones.

Freddy relaxed at that point, even grinned. "I figured as much, but your grandmother was about to faint from the shock, so what could I do?"

Hearing that, Megan snatched her hand back. Having been dragged across the room, she understood perfectly well what the marquis was talking about, and improvised by offering him the hand she'd just retrieved.

"I believe my husband was rather eager to have us meet, Lord Richardson. If I had known it was you he was dragging me over to introduce to, I could have told him we'd already met in Hampshire at the Leighton ball. A pleasure, though, to see you again."

"Well said, Your Grace." Freddy beamed at her, then winked at Devlin. "And not to undo a brilliant rescue, I'll just steal her away for the next dance, if you don't mind."

"I do mind—"

"No, he doesn't," Duchy said as she joined them. "Run along, Freddy, but don't monopolize the duchess too long. She has to mingle with all her guests tonight, not just a select few." But after the marquis had whisked Megan away, she added to Devlin, "Which you, dear boy, apparently forgot," and then in exasperation, "*Have you lost your mind?*"

"Apparently."

"Are you blushing, Dev?"

"*Apparently,*" he groaned. Then he pulled himself together to ask with all the starch and stuffiness she deplored, "Would you care to dance, Your Grace?"

"Go to the devil," she snorted, turning away from him, only to toss back, "And stay away from your wife tonight, unless you can manage to keep your hands to yourself."

It took more than half the evening, dinner, the queen's visit and departure, the *official* announcement of his marriage, and a bottle and a half of champagne before Devlin felt he could safely approach his wife again without making a fool of himself for a third time that night.

But before he reached her, he spotted another female who had somehow managed to keep from his notice all evening—until now. He turned in her direction instead, coming up behind Sabrina Richardson to pull her rudely away from her group of friends and out onto the dance floor. "I told your brother that if I ever saw you again, I would wring your neck. Didn't he warn you?"

Sabrina stared up at him wide-eyed, but not quite frightened. "Yes, but—but I had to come, Devlin, to apologize. I owe you that."

"You owe me a lot more than that," he said coldly. "Why don't we start with the truth?"

"I just wanted to be a duchess, and you're the only duke around who isn't too old or married already."

"Bloody hell."

"Well, you asked for the truth," she said defensively. "I'm sorry it isn't more complicated than that."

"*Was* there a baby?"

"No," she answered, blushing profusely.

"Have you told Freddy that?"

Sabrina nodded. "When he told me you'd married someone else."

"I hope he blistered your hide."

The blush spread from her cheeks to encompass her entire face. "He did."

"Then I just might forgive him. You, on the other hand, I ought to toss out on your ear."

"Don't be a grouch, Devlin. It's worked out well enough in the end, hasn't it? Freddy said you never would have met your wife if it wasn't for us." Devlin hated to own up to the truth of that simple fact, so he didn't, but Sabrina was continuing. "I thought I'd dislike her, but I don't. Freddy's in love with her, you know."

"The devil he is!"

"He said he was."

"The devil he did!" Devlin looked over toward Megan to see if Freddy was in her group of admirers, and damned if he wasn't. "I knew I should have sent my seconds round to him when I first thought of it."

Chapter 44

Logic told Megan that after the official announcement of her marriage, she should have lost most of her admirers. Logic apparently had nothing to do with it, however, for she hadn't lost any, had actually gained some of the more disreputable kind: the lechers and charming though wicked rakes who considered her ripe for seduction now that she was a married woman.

She supposed she had been lucky not to have come across such men before—not counting her husband in disguise as himself. And although she received seventeen outrageous propositions of one kind or another, from amusing to really vulgar, she managed to keep her temper during each one and fend them off without causing a scene.

Aside from that, she was enjoying herself more than she thought she would, and that was because of Devlin's impetuous behavior earlier in the evening. She had no doubt now that he'd been taking her off to make love right in the middle of their ball. It would have caused a scandal of the worst magnitude and was so unlike her husband the duke—but so like Devlin the horse breeder.

Megan grinned to herself each time she thought of it, and she thought of it every time she looked for and found Devlin, and she did that all night long. It didn't even bother her that the same women kept showing up in his own groups as he circulated and mingled with his guests. It didn't bother her when she saw him dancing with other women and heard their girlish giggles as they flirted with him. She happened to know he abhorred giggling women. She also happened to know that it was her he wanted, not them, because she'd caught a number of *those* looks from him that told her so.

All things considered, she was nowhere as nervous as she had been about her confession, which was still on the agenda for tonight. She wasn't expecting Devlin to return her affections, at least not all at once, though that was now a more hopeful long-term expectation. But she didn't think he'd mind all that much now if she loved him.

"I suppose you've been accepting congratulations all evening."

Megan turned toward the lady who had spoken, a lovely blonde with light gray eyes who made Megan feel gauche next to her sophisticated flamboyance. "That does seem to be the order of the day," she replied.

"Then you're due for some condolences instead."

"I beg your pardon?"

The woman laughed, a brittle sound. "You don't know who I am, do you?"

"Should I?"

"Indeed yes. I'm Marianne Aitchison, the woman your husband jilted at the altar only a few months ago."

Megan just stared, dumbfounded, while one of the gentlemen present said, "I say, Countess, you never got to the altar, did you? Recall Wrothston breaking it off before it got as far as that."

"Then do you also recall that he kept me waiting for ten years?" Marianne almost snarled at the man. "Ten *wasted* years."

Megan was too appalled for words. The bitterness coming out of Marianne Aitchison was palpable. Ten years? Good God, Devlin had been engaged to this woman for *ten years*? Why had no one mentioned that to her before, when apparently it was common knowledge?

"You were amazingly lucky, my dear," Marianne remarked to Megan with less heat, but with no less bitterness. "To get him to the altar before his interest wore off. And it will, you know, quickly, abruptly. So don't expect his declarations of love to continue much longer."

What declarations of love? Megan wanted to know, but asked instead, "Why did you have such a long engagement?"

"Because he kept postponing the wedding, again and again, and when I finally refused to be put off any longer, he broke it off completely."

"But why?" Megan couldn't help asking.

"Why else, my dear? He simply didn't want a wife. But he liked being engaged. That kept all the aspiring mamas from targeting him for their sweet young daughters."

Megan felt sick to her stomach. She knew for a fact that Devlin didn't want a wife, at least not her, and obviously not Marianne Aitchison either. And Megan had no trouble seeing it from Marianne's bitter point of view, to wait ten long years to marry a man, receiving no other proposals because she was already engaged, or having to refuse those that she got anyway. And then to be left without a husband to show for her commendable patience.

The countess was no longer a young debutante, but quite positively on the shelf, as the saying went. She probably had no prospects now, no hope of finding another husband at her age, when there were so many eager young hopefuls on the marriage mart every year. Devlin had, in effect, condemned her to being a spinster.

She didn't know what to say to Marianne Aitchison. She understood her bitterness too well, but it would be trite and meaningless to say so. She felt sorry for her, and furious at Devlin for his callousness, and . . .

"Spreading your venom again, dear Marianne?" Freddy said, suddenly appearing at Megan's side.

"Just setting the record straight," the countess replied stiffly, though with a degree of uneasiness.

"Capital idea." The marquis smiled agreeably. "Shall we hear it from another perspective?"

"Stay out of it, Freddy," Devlin said, suddenly appearing at Megan's other side.

"But I feel the need to atone, old man—especially since you think I'm in love with your wife." Devlin had just cornered him to ask that question, snarled it more like, when they had noticed Marianne with Megan. "Which isn't to say I wouldn't have been in love with her in no time a'tall if you hadn't married her."

Devlin merely tossed his friend a look of disgust before taking Megan's arm and leading her away. She allowed it for all of three seconds before she jerked her arm back and hissed, "You, sir, are despicable!"

He didn't pretend not to know what she was up in arms about. "Condemned without trial, am I? But then our Marianne is very good at generating sympathy where none is deserved."

"What you did to that woman—"

"Give over, Megan," he interrupted impatiently. "I did nothing to her except come upon her at a most inconvenient time—by her reckoning—when she happened to be making love with another man."

Megan stopped cold, her eyes flaring wide. "Then you didn't break off with her because she wouldn't let you postpone the wedding again?"

"Again? We were to have wed eight years ago, and in all that time I set the date back only once, when my grandfather died. But I've lost count of the number of times Marianne came up with one excuse or another to postpone it."

"But that means—*she* didn't want to marry you."

"Not at all. I'm sure she had every intention of marrying me—eventually, despite the fact that we bore no love for each other. It was an arranged marriage after all, one of my grandfather's last outdated notions. She was simply having too much fun being a soon-to-be-duchess without the responsibilities of a wife, since engagement to me gave her the same prestige as if she were already my wife."

"And the fact that she had other lovers was no doubt another reason she was in no hurry to get married," Megan concluded.

"Quite possibly."

She didn't know why he wasn't angry with her. She was horrified herself at the appalling lack of faith and loyalty she had just displayed, and on the very eve that she was going to tell him she loved him. He'd certainly believe her now, wouldn't he.

Megan was furious at herself, but more so at Marianne Aitchison, and Marianne made a more convenient target, since Megan took blame only when all other possible culprits had been eliminated.

But first Devlin deserved one small admonishment for not speaking up *before* she had put her foot in it. "Why the devil didn't you defend yourself back there?"

"A good many people might believe her, but anyone who knows me doesn't," he replied.

Worse and worse, implying she should have been in the second category, which she should have been. "I'm sorry," she said wretchedly.

He sighed. "Megan, you *don't* know me well enough yet to defend me out of hand. I've given you enough reasons not to do so blindly, at any rate."

"Not good enough. I believed a complete stranger without even questioning you. And why does she blame you when she's the one—"

She didn't finish, her face exploding with color at the realization that she was describing her own spoiled tendency to pass the buck when it belonged in her own pocket.

Devlin astutely guessed her thoughts from her stricken expression. "Don't be a fool," he chastised sharply. "You're nothing like her. You don't go around condemning me to anyone who will listen. When you place blame unfairly on someone, it goes no further than your target, and I know bloody well you don't mean half the things you say, that it's just your temper run amok."

That wasn't taken too kindly, effectively banishing all traces of self-condemnation and bringing her husband an I'll-remember-that look before she huffed, "I still say you should be defending yourself, and not just to me."

"When the truth would ruin her? As a gentleman, I can't do that."

"No, I suppose you can't," she replied, and before he could stop her or guess her intent, she whipped about and called out quite clearly through the crowd, "Lady Aitchison, you are a liar."

Devlin groaned beside her. A path was cleared instantly, so Marianne could see her accuser as well as hear her. Conversations abruptly stopped in the immediate area, the silence spreading rapidly beyond. A few couples on the dance floor crashed into others, bringing even the dancing to a temporary standstill, which so startled the orchestra that the music clanged to an end.

In the ensuing silence, Duchy's voice could be heard as far away as the other ballroom. "Good God, what now?"

A few twitters followed that, a few coughs, and a great deal of shuffling feet as the crowd moved closer to catch every word.

At that point, it would have made matters infinitely worse for Devlin to clap his hand over Megan's mouth and cart her out of there, as was his first and greatest inclination. Instead he placed a hand on her shoulder and said as softly as he could, "Don't do it."

She looked at him and amazed him by smiling, seeming totally unaware of the commotion she was causing. "You know I don't take insults lightly, Devlin," she said in the most reasonable tone. "And that I am very outspoken in rebuttal—one way or another. And for Lady Aitchison to slander your good name without cause *is* an insult to me. Had I known she was lying to me about you—well, you know my temper. There's no telling what I might have done."

Devlin had the most absurd urge to laugh. Amazingly, it seemed like she was talking only to him, for only his benefit, that she was completely unaware that every ear in the room was avidly listening. But he knew her better than that, and by deliberately—and he didn't doubt it was deliberate—making her warning—which was what it had been—so public, he had to wonder who else had insulted her tonight. He would bloody well find out and deal with that in his own way, but in the meantime, he simply couldn't resist grinning over the drama she was enacting, which wasn't nearly as damaging as he'd thought it would be. 'Course, it wasn't over yet, either.

"I think you've made your point, my dear."

"Not quite," she replied with just enough true anger to warn him that the scene for the assemblage wasn't over and she was going to say her piece anyway. "You might be too much the gentleman to stop her slander, but I'm not."

There were some outright chuckles over *that* statement, but nothing to stop her from facing a very mortified Marianne again and saying, "They say truth will prevail in the end, that it will even come back to haunt you. Would you care to discuss the *real* reason my husband ended his engagement to you, Countess—or were you leaving?"

It took Marianne a moment to realize she was being given an opportunity to escape complete ruination. She didn't answer. She took the out Megan offered and left abruptly, humiliated, labeled a liar, but no more than that.

"Are you finished?" Devlin asked at Megan's back.

She turned to give him a brilliant smile. "Yes, I believe so. What happened to the music?"

Chapter 45

Megan's comment about the music was like a signal for the resumption of conversation, which returned at full volume. And Devlin had only to glance toward the orchestra for a waltz to begin, offbeat at first, but the melody was corrected by the time he drew his wife onto the dance floor.

"I can't tell you how often I've wanted to do what you just did—or something to that effect," he admitted as other couples began twirling past them. "Thank you."

"It was my pleasure."

"I don't doubt it." He grinned. "It's going to drive the ton crazy, you know, wondering what that reason is that you hinted at."

"So?"

"So do you like causing such a furor?"

"No, but you asked me not to ruin her, so I didn't. If you hadn't asked, I would have done more than only embarrass her, Devlin. I hope you realize that."

"Indeed I do, as does everyone else. So don't be surprised if people get tongue-tied around you for a while. They'll be in dread of causing you the least little insult."

"I don't notice you having that problem."

"Nor will you. I thought we had established that I give as good as I get."

"I believe it was your daring that was established. Speaking of which, mine has been lacking of late."

"You can say that after what you just did?"

She shrugged that off. "That was temper, not daring. You see, I've been meaning to tell you something, but I've kept putting it off."

Devlin groaned inwardly, remembering the last time she'd put off telling him something. Emphatically, he said, "I don't want to hear it."

"You don't—?" she sputtered. "Well, you're *going* to. I'm having a baby."

That caught him off guard. "I thought you said it wasn't likely to happen twice in a row."

"I have no idea if that's so. But this is the baby I was having before."

That *really* caught him off guard, and slowed him to a stop on the edge of the dance floor. "Then—you lied?"

"Yes, but it was for a good cause."

"I recall your good cause, Megan," he replied coldly. "And what you're telling me is that you wanted me to get an annulment while you were still carrying my child. You would actually have left me while you *still carried my child.*"

She flinched at the fury in those words, for all their softness. "I wasn't looking at it from that viewpoint. All I knew was that I was making you miserable."

"Don't you mean that the other way around? No, don't answer that. One more word out of you, and the scandal we've been avoiding by the skin of our teeth will occur after all. I need a bloody drink."

He walked away from her. Ordinarily she wouldn't have stood still for that, would have shouted something to bring him back. But she couldn't do that now. A few people were already looking at her and probably wondering at her dumbfounded expression.

Well, she'd certainly handled that brilliantly. She supposed she should have first told him she loved him, then mentioned the baby after. But she hadn't expected him to get *that* angry about the baby.

She moved off to find her father and Tiffany, needing the bolstering they could supply, because the night wasn't over yet. She was still going to tell Devlin the rest of what she had to say, whether he wanted to hear it or not. But she'd let him cool off a bit first.

As it happened, however, she didn't see him again. He didn't even show up for the conclusion and the departure of his guests. At least half were leaving, those who lived in the area or only hours away, and those eager for an early start back to London. The rest would depart at their leisure the next day, with only a few dozen expected to remain as houseguests for a while.

It was nearly dawn before Megan was able to retire herself. She took the chance that Devlin might have done the same, only earlier, and checked his room before going to her own. It was necessary to enter his domain completely since he hadn't left a light burning, and leaving the door cracked open to give her a bit of light to see by actually made matters worse, creating an abundance of shadows.

She found him in his bed after all, a great lump with the covers pulled nearly over his head. She sat down next to him and drew the covers back enough to see that he was sleeping on his stomach, his head turned away from her, his arms circled around his pillow.

His back was bare. She had the urge to crawl under the covers with him and wait until a decent hour to tell him what else she had to say, but that would be putting it off again, and she'd done enough of that.

She shook his shoulder gently. "Devlin?" He mumbled. She shook harder. "Devlin?"

His head reared up, swung around to peer at her through slanted eyes, then dropped back on the pillow in his previous position. "What?"

"Are you awake?"

"No."

That sounded like his usual drollery, so she plunged on. "You didn't give me a chance to tell you the most important part of my confession. I know the other part made you angry, and I'm sorry, but I really did do it for you, you know."

Her nervousness returned at that point, lodging the other words in her throat. Her hand caressed his back for a moment, then moved up to lovingly push the hair back from the side of his face.

Incredibly, and to Duchy's keen disapproval, he hadn't cut it yet, not even for the ball, though he had at least clubbed it back for the evening, giving him a decidedly rakish appearance with his black formal wear.

She rather liked his hair long herself. It took some of the starch out of him—at least until he opened his mouth to speak.

Her mouth opened finally, the words rushing out. "I love you, Ambrose Devlin St. James." She waited breathlessly, but he said nothing, causing a sharpness to enter her voice. "Did you hear me?"

He jerked awake. "What?"

"I said, did you hear me?"

"Yes, yes, now leave me alone, Megan. I drank too much. Need to sleep it off."

She sat back, incredulous. Well, she hadn't been able to imagine what he might say when she finally told him. Now she knew.

Chapter 46

Megan walked out of the house with her small bag of clothes at approximately three o'clock the next afternoon, one hour after she awoke, and it would have been sooner, except she had to eat and pack first. She didn't call for a carriage. She marched down to the stable, but once there, she didn't call for her horse either.

She wasn't actually leaving, after all, though it certainly appeared that way to the servants she passed. No, she was making a statement, a very loud one that Devlin wouldn't be able to miss; nor did he, having been informed about it before she'd even reached the stable.

When she arrived, she ignored the grooms, who were hesitant to ask what she wanted, after getting a look at her expression—and her bag. They still followed her from tack room to tack room as she searched for what she was looking for. But she was finally disappointed that she hadn't noticed before that there wasn't a room with a bed in it similar to the one Devlin had had in her stable. There being so many grooms here, they had their own quarters in a separate building, and of course it was out of the question to go there.

I noticed a nice pile of hay on the way in.

You think I won't make use of it? He did, so I can.

You won't, but I suppose it will serve your purpose. Do you really think this is going to work?

I retired you, remember? So I don't want to hear that I might be making a fool of myself.

She went back to inspect that pile of hay, dropping her bag in a corner, and kicking and tossing armfuls of hay about until she'd fashioned, to her eyes, an adequate bed in the center of it. She was still standing in the middle of her masterpiece when Devlin arrived, announcing his presence by barking at the gawking grooms to vacate the stable—completely.

Megan squared her shoulders, kicked the train of her cream dress out of the way, and turned to face her husband. She expected him to be in a powerful rage. He probably was, but he was wearing his ducal mien, so she couldn't really tell.

She opened her mouth, but he beat her to it. "What the hell do you think you're doing, Megan?"

Her chin went up at its most stubborn angle. "I'm moving into the stable."

He'd noted the bag in the corner, been told about it, but that wasn't what he'd rushed down here expecting to hear. "You're *what?*"

"You heard me. And I'm going to stay here until I have my horse breeder back."

She looked so mutinous, he didn't doubt she meant it. He just couldn't figure out *why* she meant it. But his frightened rage was receding. She wasn't leaving him. Not that he would have let her.

Bewildered for the moment, he said carefully, "Thought you couldn't stand him."

"You thought wrong," she retorted.

Even more carefully, he explained—just in case she didn't know it, "He doesn't exist."

"He does," she insisted. "You're just keeping him buried beneath all that ducal haughtiness. But I'm giving you warning, Your Grace. If I can't have your love, I at least want Devlin Jefferys back, and I'm staying here until I get him."

His breath escaped in a whoosh of surprise. "Are you telling me you *want* me to love you?"

"If that isn't the most stupid question," she replied, losing her temper over his denseness. "Do you think I've been agonizing for weeks about telling you I love you just because I like to agonize? Very well, so you weren't interested. I'll settle for having Devlin Jefferys back."

Getting blasted like that prodded his own temper. "The devil you will! And if you want to talk about agonizing—"

"I don't!"

"Then let's discuss your 'interested.' I would have been *very* interested if you had ever got around to telling me you loved me, so if you intended to, why didn't you?"

"I did."

"You didn't! I bloody well would have remembered hearing *that* if I'd heard it."

"You heard it, you wretch, last night in your bed. Don't try and tell me—"

"Megan," he cut in, striving for some patience, if even a minuscule amount. "I went to bed with a bottle last night, not you."

That gave her pause. "You really don't remember my coming into your room?"

"No. Did you?"

"Yes."

"Then would you mind repeating what it was you told me that I didn't hear?"

Her eyes narrowed suspiciously at his soft tone. "No, I don't think I will."

He swore a blue streak, striding about, kicking up more hay as he did. When he happened to notice his wife, it was to catch her wide-eyed look of feigned amazement. He stopped suddenly and burst out laughing.

"God, I love it when you provoke me, brat. It sets my blood on fire."

Her eyes got a little wider, especially since he'd started removing his jacket as he said it. "Does it?"

"Don't play the innocent. You do it deliberately, don't you?"

"Certainly not—Devlin, what *are* you doing?"

The white lawn shirt came off and was dropped to the floor. "What does it look like?"

She took a step back, though her eyes were caressing every inch of skin he was baring for her. "It's the middle of the day!" she protested.

"So?"

"So you can't mean to—"

"Can't I? I thought you wanted the duke on the shelf."

"I did, but—but—" She ended with a shriek as she went over backwards into the straw, her damn train tripping her up when she'd taken another step back.

"Falling at my feet again?" Devlin grinned. "I like that."

Megan shrieked and tried to get up, but he was there, on top of her, before she could. Then she was rolling about, making every effort to stop his fingers from stripping her own clothes off, along with the rest of his. Finally she was laughing, having failed utterly, and no longer able to contain her delight in getting the old Devlin back.

"We made love in my stable," she said, tantalizingly streaking her nails down his back and buttocks to feel his body arch into hers. "I guess it's only fair we try it in yours."

"Fair has nothing to do with it," he replied, his voice rough in his passion.

She sighed. "I love it when you put the duke on the shelf."

"What else do you love?"

"You," she gasped as his mouth fastened on her nipple and tugged gently. "Do you think you might ever love me back?"

His head rose to give her a dazzling smile. "What makes you think I don't?"

"Do you?"

"I'm thinking about it."

"I hate you!"

"No, you don't. You love me."

"And?"

"I'm still thinking about it."

She grinned, then chuckled. "You're a wretched tease, Devlin St. James. Are you going to make me say it for you?"

"No." He dipped down to graze her lips once, twice, then gave her a soul-stirring kiss before adding, "Knowing you, you'd say it all wrong."

"I'd simply say, I love you."

"But *I'd* say, I love you—brat."

Three weeks later they accompanied Megan's father home, because Devlin claimed to have business in the area, *and* claimed he wasn't about to be parted from Megan for more than a few days, so she had to come along. But he timed it so they arrived on Sunday morning, and when she realized his ducal coach was stopping in front of her parish church, Megan started to cry.

"This wasn't necessary," she said, throwing her arms around her husband's neck and squeezing tight.

"I know."

"You've already given me too much."

"Nothing can compare with what you've given me—your love. And I'm going to spoil you every bit as much as your father ever did. More, I don't doubt."

She leaned back to give him a watery smile that released both dimples and had the same effect on him that her smiles always did. "Can I spoil you as well?"

Devlin groaned. "You already do. Now let's go set your Lady O on her ear."

Someone had told him the tale, obviously. Megan looked out the window to see the stout figure of Ophelia Thackeray and all three of her daughters—and Frederick Richardson—*and* Tiffany and Tyler. Devlin had planned this well—for her.

"I can't do it. It's mean and spiteful, petty—*brattish*." She glanced back at Devlin. "I can see you went to a lot of trouble, but it just doesn't matter anymore. You're all that matters, Dev."

He put his hand to her cheek. "It was Tiffany's idea, my dear, a belated wedding gift."

"Oh." She grinned brilliantly at that point. "In that case, it'd be churlish of me not to do it, wouldn't it?"

The Duke of Wrothston burst out laughing. "Absolutely, brat."